Michael

Theophany

The Life And

Death Of

A Girl Prophet

Erica House

BALTIMORE   AMSTERDAM   SALAMANCA

First printing

ISBN: 0-9659308-5-8

PUBLISHED BY ERICA HOUSE BOOK PUBLISHERS

eribooks@fred.net

Baltimore   Amsterdam   Salamanca

Printed in the United States of America

For Mom.

*Your life and sacrifices
are impressed upon my affections forever.*

1

THE sun setting beyond the Rocky Mountains reminded Sarah of the candles being snuffed out at the closing of Sunday services back home in Ferrisburg, Vermont. First one peak blew out a tiny piece of the sun, then another, and another. Bright skies grew dim, evolving into a giant stained glass vista. The scene piqued memories of early Sunday mornings nestling into her mother's arms, gazing in wonderment at the works of art that filled the window frames of the old colonial church. "Montana, what a wonderfully perfect place to die," she thought, closing her eyes.

Soon night skies would accent the million-plus campfires flickering in the valley below her, and she did not want to be alone. Distressed to a level she had not felt since London, where eighty children had lost their lives and the blame was laid squarely at her feet by her detractors, Sarah's thoughts drifted to those actually responsible for the atrocity. She would not let herself succumb to the dark memories. She forced her eyes open to drink in the last vestiges of her last sunset.

"Joshua, come sit with me, will you?" she called out. "The sun will be gone in a matter of minutes and I don't want to see it go alone. OK?" Sitting on a patch of new green grass, Sarah picked blades from the clean smelling earth and tossed them into the wind. She watched as they drifted on the wind down the slope into the vastness of the valley below her. "The Samoan is down there; I can feel him."

As Joshua approached her, a few remaining marshmallow-like clouds could still be seen. "When I was a little girl I wanted so much to grab a hold of one of them. They look just like cotton candy." Sarah smiled wistfully. "Maybe tomorrow, huh Josh?"

"Yes, sweetheart. Maybe tomorrow."

Joshua moved next to his charge, the young woman he had been with since the very moment of the installation of her spirit into the tiny fetus that was to house her for the next nineteen years. It had been a wonderful journey with this one and he felt pains of sadness knowing that their time together was about to close. He adored her and her impish sense of humor which had dumped them into more than one cauldron of hot stew over the course of their journey. He would also miss her capacity for love, which he attributed to a pre-mortal progression of rare magnitude, even for one such as she. It was beyond

5

anything he had witnessed, with few exceptions. Yes, he was going to miss this little one.

Occasionally as they witnessed the sleep of the sun, he squeezed her hand or nudged her shoulder with his. Each time she returned his gesture with one of her magical smiles. Sarah was a naturally beautiful woman. Tall with long blonde hair and ice-blue eyes, she struck an imposing figure. Her dark complexion disguised her New England heritage. A simple elegance seemed to flow throughout her entire being, creating the valid impression that she was approachable. "She was born to this," Joshua thought as he stole glances of her in the fading light. "She was born to this."

"How are you doing, little one?"

"I'm OK, Josh. I'm tired and I am beginning to feel a little nervous, you know. But then I am nearly a wreck every time we meet with the people, aren't I?" she giggled. "My goodness, look at all the campfires! Chicky must be right. He said there were close to two million people in the valley for tomorrow. It is hard to believe, isn't it?"

"No, actually it is quite easy to believe, Sarah." Joshua smiled at her. Anticipating the question that he knew would ultimately come, it always did, Joshua stood and began walking in circles about his charge. Occasionally, he gently touched the crown of her head with his fingertips and she could feel his strength. Then the back of his hand would brush her hair away from the side of her face and she could feel his love.

"Chicky doesn't know, does he, Josh?"

"No, sweetheart, he doesn't know."

"Well, that's good. If he did, he would no doubt interfere, and we would have to deal with that as well." Joshua could feel her drawing closer to it, to the question. The question that always hurt him to answer notwithstanding his knowledge.

"Josh?"

"Yes, little one?" He always referred to her in that vein when he felt particularly tender towards her. It was as if she was his little three-year-old playmate again.

"I need to ask you now. I need to know before I can rest tonight. Is it OK?"

Joshua moved down the slope from her about five yards and sat on a large boulder. His bright robe seemed to illuminate the entire scene. With his strong dark forearms folded across his knees and his head bowed he spoke to her, but for the first time since she had known him, he could not raise his eyes to meet hers. They were filled to overflowing with tears that now stained his cheeks. "Yes, little one, you may ask me one last question."

6

He looked so sad to her, almost weak, but she knew he could not be that. She had never seen tears in his eyes. In fact, she did not know that he could cry until that moment. "Josh?"

"Yes."

"Will it hurt tomorrow when I die?"

"No, little one. It will not hurt."

2

THE morning sun crept into Sarah's room. Jay had spent nearly the entire night talking with her. He was her best friend. Sarah had just celebrated her thirteenth birthday; she was finally a teenager. And Jay had given her a beautiful gold necklace; gold as the sun's morning rays raining down on the corn fields outside her window. She would spend the day at the mall with her girlfriends, flirting with boys, but she planned to meet Jay afterwards for a swim in the Battenkill near Larmon's farm. It saddened Sarah that he couldn't accompany her to the mall, but that was impossible. Her parents didn't approve of him. Sarah hadn't mentioned his name since she was ten. She didn't dare.

It was Billy Stewart, a neighbor boy, who had gotten her into trouble with her parents and messed up her whole world. She could remember it as if it were just yesterday. They had met in the school cafeteria for lunch like they did every other day. They had been spending a lot of time together that year. Sarah and Billy were best friends. He was a cute boy and Sarah had a crush on him. He was stocky, with black curly hair and big blue eyes. His lips were full and had it not been for his nearly ever-present smile, they would have wrongfully communicated a pouting personality.

It began over peanut butter and jelly sandwiches and lunchroom milk cartons, the kind that never seem to open no matter which end you try.

"Billy, when you were little, did you have an imaginary playmate?"

"Sure, everybody had one."

"What was yours like? Was it a boy or girl?"

"Are you nuts! Boys can't have a girl for an imaginary playmate. That's disgusting! I don't know anybody who would even think such a thing." Shaking his head back and forth, Billy continued, "Sometimes you ask the stupidest questions, Sarah." He smiled at her. And then after a long pause, "What's with all the questions about Louie?"

"Louie, who's Louie?"

"Louie, my friend. That's what I used to call him. We played together in my room all the time till I was five or six. Then he gave way to real friends." He blushed a little at the embarrassment of admitting to a childhood fantasy. He was no longer a child, you know.

"Oh, mine is Jay. Jay is not a girl by the way. He's a boy. Billy, can you keep a secret?"

"Sure."

"Well, if you are sure, meet me behind the building after school. I've got something really important to tell you. I've got to tell somebody about my problem and you're my best friend. Meet you at three o'clock, OK?"

"Uh huh. You aren't in any trouble, are you?"

Sarah didn't answer him. He took her silence for a yes.

It was a warm spring day in Ferrisburg. The kind that tease school children with melting snow and promises of summer vacation. Most all of the snow in the valley had melted, except in Larmon's Grove where the pine trees sheltered it from the sun's warm rays. Mountain snow was always the last to melt around Ferrisburg.

As the clock struck three, Sarah and Billy met behind the old red brick school building. She was waiting for him under the large maple tree that held the tractor tire swing. The sun was still bright in the sky and the valley seemed to have cornered the market on all of the spring flowers in Vermont.

"Hey, Sarah. So what's up?" Billy approached her swinging his backpack as she sat motionless in the swing, staring down at the circles she was making in the fine dust with her toes.

Concentrating on her dilemma, she hadn't heard him coming, so his voice startled her. "Sheesh, Billy! You nearly scared me to death! Come over and sit by me. Did you tell anyone you were meeting me?"

"No, you said it was a secret. Why would I tell anyone?"

"Good. Look, you got to swear to God not to tell anybody what I'm about to tell you, OK? Cause if you do, I'll be in real butter with Mom and Dad. Do you promise?"

"Look. I already told you I wasn't going to tell anybody. Leave God out of this. I don't need no trouble from Him. You know you can trust me. I never told on you before, did I ?

"No, you haven't, but I never did anything for you to tell on me about."

"Come on, Sarah, did you steal something from McCarthy's Five and Dime?"

"No, nothing like that. Wish I had. Look, it's like this. Remember at lunch we were talking about imaginary playmates? And I was asking you if you ever had one and you said you did. Well, Louie... that was his name, right?"

"Yeah?"

"Well, Louie left, didn't he? I mean, you said your friends and other things replaced him, right? He disappeared and never came back, did he?"

"Yeah, of course he never came back, Sarah. What do ya think I'm nuts?" His response stung her.

"No Billy, I don't. And don't you think I am, but Jay hasn't gone away. He's still here. He has been with me ever since I can remember. This summer when my parents and I talked about him, they got really worried about me. They even took me to a special doctor over in Cambridge. Ya know what I mean?"

"Oh shit! You mean a Shrink? Don't tell me they took you over to old Doc Boright? What the hell did you tell them to wind up in his office?"

"Yeah, that's where they took me. . . and stop swearing, Billy. I just told them the truth, that's all, the truth. You're supposed to be able to tell your parents the truth, you know."

"Well, you should know better than that, you're ten years old, you know. What's more stupid than telling your parents the truth about anything that could wind you up in old crackpot Boright's office. Remember when Lonnie DuPane told his mom and dad he was taken out of his bedroom by space aliens? Hell, Boright had him hauled off to a de-programmer or something like that. Lonnie didn't act normal for months after that guy got through with him."

"Are you through? I'm laying out my worst nightmare here and you're rambling on about crazy Lonnie DuPane's space relatives! Now just listen to me, will you?"

"OK."

"When we got into Boright's office and I first told them about Jay, they all smiled at each other and nodded their heads like they understood. Then as the visit went on and I told them more and more, the looks on their faces changed. And when I told them that I speak with Jay every day, they really looked worried. Eventually after an hour or so they asked me leave the room. Mom and Dad spoke with Boright while I waited outside. When I was called back into the room, Dr. Boright gave me a long lecture about imagination and the boy who cried wolf. They told me to forget about Jay. I was becoming a big girl and I didn't need him anymore. They insisted he was just something in my head. I don't like lying to them, Billy, but they are wrong. It's not true. He still comes to me every day.

In fact, he taught me to ride my first bike. There was Dad running along one side of me holding onto the seat, and Jay was on the other side nearly as close. And when Dad let go, Jay took hold running right alongside of me, whispering encouragement in my ear. Daddy bragged how I learned to ride a bike faster than anyone in the family. But it wasn't me, it was Jay. I rode with him at my side until I had it down on my own.

And when he is around my class at school, I think faster and remember better. Don't get me wrong, I'm not cheating and he doesn't help me, at least I don't think he does. I just seem to learn faster when he is around.

And he's such a good person. He's never mean. He never does or says anything that is cruel. And no matter how bad anyone acts, he always points out the good in them to me. I like him, Billy, and I don't want him to leave. But I don't like lying to my parents about him. I don't know what to do. And you know what, Billy? I'm scared. Sometimes I think maybe they are right, maybe there is something wrong with me. I don't know what to think. All I know is I don't want to go back and see that Boright. I know Mom and Dad mean well and even make sense. I'm not stupid, this is not supposed to be happening at my age. I'm ten now and I'm not supposed to have him anymore. Do you think I'm a little crazy, Billy?"

Billy Stewart had listened patiently to Sarah. He scratched his head and waited a long time before trying to answer her question. He wasn't sure what to say, but like all young people he felt obligated to say something, anything, knowing his best friend was in danger of attack from the adults.

"Cool! What does he look like?" Instantly he felt stupid, but he could think of no sound advice to offer her. This was pretty far-fetched and he wasn't prepared, nor did he think he could have prepared, to offer appropriate counsel to Sarah.

"Billy, you're not taking me seriously!" Sarah, feeling the blood rise in her cheeks, had hoped for better advise than Billy's meager offering.

"Yes, yes, I am. I just want to know what he looks like!" Billy accepted her rebuke, but felt he had to redeem himself by offering further involvement. And he really wanted to know more about Jay. What if? What if Jay were real? That *would* be cool!

"OK, I understand and I guess I've already told you so much. But Billy Stewart, I swear to God, if you tell anybody and I mean anybody, I will never speak to you again. Ever! Do you understand?"

Billy thought to himself, "There she goes again bringing God into this. Why doesn't she just leave Him out of it. Pastor Goldzung will have a fit if he finds out about this."

"Jay has been with me since I was a very little girl, like I told you earlier. I don't know why he comes to me, I'm nobody special. When I ask him why, he just smiles and tells me I'm special. I don't remember a time when he wasn't there. I thought for a very long time that he was just a special part of the family. I never realized nobody else could see him except me.

11

My mom even used to set a place for him at the supper table. Everybody talked to him when I did. He even answered them. They didn't really hear him although they pretended to. I guess that's why their answers seemed so stupid. Jay and I would sit at the table and laugh at them. They thought I was laughing with them. Whenever I got a toy, like for my birthday, Jay had to get one too. And they would get him one, but I would open it and take it to my room so we could play together with our new toys. So I guess you could say that they helped to confuse me. When Mom and Dad told me at Dr. Boright's that Jay only existed in my mind, it really hurt me cause then they lied to me. Didn't they? And I was confused, at least I was at first, but I knew better. I had seen him, I had!"

"What's he look like?"

"He's tall and has blonde hair like me, only blonder. He's really funny and makes me laugh. He plays with me and I can talk to him anytime I want to. He comes and goes as he pleases, but he's usually waiting for me every morning when I wake up. Sometimes he sits on my dresser. That's where I find him. And he always wears this beautiful long, white robe. It's soft to touch. And Billy, wait 'til you hear this! Sometimes he's sooo bright, he's hard to look at!" Sarah was waiting for some sign of approval from Billy.

"Maybe he's an Angel!" Billy exclaimed, thinking he had finally contributed something meaningful to the conversation. He wasn't about to leave room for interruption of what he considered to be a fairly reasonable theory. "Look, Sarah. Do you know what this means? We got a goldmine here? If you tell adults that you've seen an angel, hell, they'll make you a saint or something like that! And then people will pay money to come see ya and you can sell things out of your house. And people will come from all over the world just to visit you and . . ."

"Shut up, Billy! You idiot. Jay is *not* an angel."

Billy was crushed that his hypothesis had been shot down so arbitrarily, but he wasn't about to let it die a natural death. No, this was a good explanation and deserved a fight. "Oh yeah? How do you know?"

"Well, he doesn't have wings for one thing. And another, he's never told me he was an angel."

"Have you ever asked him?"

"No." Sarah was once again disappointed with the quality of input she was receiving from Billy Stewart, the second brightest kid in the fifth grade. Maybe telling him about Jay was a mistake. "Do you want to help me, Billy, or are you just going to sit there and make stupid remarks?"

Billy learned then, as a young man, what all men learn at some time in their lives. When that kind of question is asked by the fairer sex, it is best to be still, keep quiet and look dumb.

"He does the most wonderful magic, Billy. He can fly and he can make things appear and disappear. He even shows me things that are far away or that have already happened. Sometimes, Billy, sometimes he shows me stuff that's *going* to happen! It's sort of like a movie in my mind. It's so cool!"

Billy began to get a little nervous. It was one thing to defend a fellow child from the adults, but it was another to be a part of this kind of major storytelling. His thoughts drifted to Lonnie DuPane. Then his mind leapt to an image of the formidable Pastor Goldzung and how he would explain this alliance to Sarah. He began to waver.

"Sarah, if Jay is real, then call him right now. I want to see him."

"I can't. I could never do that. Nobody sees him except me anyway, and I'm not even supposed to tell anybody about him. My parents would be really angry, I think. Besides, Jay told me after my visit with that quack, Boright, that I shouldn't mention anything about him to anyone until he said it was OK. So I can't call him, Billy, I just can't. You have to believe me, you're my very best friend!" she pleaded.

"OK, I believe you, but as soon as it's alright with him, you have to tell me. I have to be the first to see him, promise?"

"Sure Billy, you'll be the first, I promise."

"Good. Now listen, until then keep quiet about him. Don't stir nothin' up and when you need to talk to somebody, call me. I gotta get home now. It's time to do the paper route and Dad wants me to help him with the go cart tonight. Call me later, alright?"

"Alright, I'll see you tomorrow at school. And Billy, thanks for listening to me. I think you are special."

Billy hadn't even left the school yard when he began to have second thoughts about their covenant. He knew what had to be done; he didn't want to, but he knew. He had overheard his mom and Sarah's as they discussed Jay on more than one occasion, he just never knew his name. Sarah seemed as normal as any other kid, but now he thought maybe his mom was right, maybe she was *special*. He was concerned for her. As he stumbled down Burgoyne street toward his house, his fears for Sarah increased. Maybe she was really, really special and if he didn't do something, she might get hurt. Or worse yet, she might hurt herself. And then how would he feel if he could have done something to help her and he didn't?

It was six o'clock that evening when Sarah's mom received a phone call from Billy's mother. Fifteen minutes later she walked into her husband's den and told him that Jay had returned. The next day, without notice, Sarah was driven off to Dr. Boright's office in Cambridge. Sarah was never really angry with Billy. He had acted out of love and concern. Well, maybe for an instant or two she was really angry, but Jay assured her that Billy's motives were pure. "Makes you think about judging people, doesn't it, little one?"

"Yes, Jay," she whispered silently in the back seat of her parents' car as it sped on toward the massive red brick walls of Cambridge Medical Center.

"Hush, little one. Don't mention my name anymore for a while. Just rest, sweetheart."

After a short interview with the doctor Sarah was taken to the Center for evaluation. She remained there for a week of observation. She wasn't crazy. Jay stayed by her bedside the whole time she was there. He sang to her and smiled whenever she asked him why he had chosen her. He responded, "Because we love you. You are a very special little girl."

3

AFTER the last night of her admission to the Cambridge psychiatric unit, Sarah never saw Jay again. The morning she returned home from the hospital she kept to her room, feigning illness; hoping he would show himself soon, but he did not. Nightfall came and for the first time since the beginning of time, at least as far as Sarah was concerned, her beloved companion did not appear as she lay down to sleep. She was desperate, frantic about his absence and there wasn't a soul in the entire universe she could confide in. She had never felt so alone, so abandoned. When she knelt beside her bed to say her prayers, she begged to see him again, if only for one last time. And when those nightly repeated petitions went seemingly unaddressed night after night, she began questioning her own sanity. The horror that haunted Sarah was the very real possibility that her petitions for normalcy had been answered. The possibility that Jay had been carried away on the wings of her own prayers brought unfathomable anguish to the little girl. His absence made Sarah think that she must be very careful what she prayed for in the future.

She hadn't anticipated the repercussions of spending a week in Cambridge's psychiatric unit. News travels fast in a small town where confidentiality is a scarce commodity. Word of her admission skipped through the halls of the hospital onto the highways of her county and into the barber shop, beauty parlor, and school locker rooms of Ferrisburg. After her return, Sarah became the object of curiosity and then rejection from former friends and schoolmates. Even Billy Stewart avoided her. Sarah wasn't sure if it was because he felt guilty for his betrayal or because he had been listening to the other kids and their parents. It was clear, however, that she was on her own, all alone in her small hometown.

For nearly three years Sarah's life became one of almost solitary existence. Her parents tried to pick up the slack and Chicky was the most wonderful brother a girl could have. But for a young woman experiencing the ravaging hormones of puberty and its consequential emotional roller coaster, parents and brother were not the ideal companions. Sarah needed her girlfriends, but none of them would have anything to do with her. They were polite about it, but the message was always the same: thanks, but no thanks. She spent much of her time reading and doing extra school work. Her grades soared and she became an honor student by the time she was sixteen.

The spring and summer of each of those dreadful years only magnified her loneliness. Understandably, she fought the mild depression that ate at her. She often felt like Hester Prynne, thinking their commonness was not only geographic. It was difficult for her to find joy in anything. She never relinquished her nightly petitions for Jay's return. Remarkably, she felt little anger or animosity towards those who branded and abandoned her. She swallowed hard and mentioned them each night, hoping that by some miracle she would be reinstated into their good graces and society. It did not happen, though.

She had no dates, attended no parties, or other school activities. She did not go to Larmon's to skip stones with the rest of the children, although once she stood on the bridge watching, wishing they would invite her to join them. They didn't, they ignored her. She extended invitations to only one birthday party sleep-over, her fourteenth. Ten invitations were sent out, only three returned to her mailbox. No one accepted. It broke her heart.

New dresses seemed unnecessary. Sarah took to wearing simple clothing, consisting of jeans and a sweatshirt most of the time. Her parents tried to encourage her to dress and go to school dances, but she wasn't having any of their suggestions and they decided not to push her. Understandably, they felt considerable guilt as their decision to take Sarah for help might have done more harm than good. Sarah kept her long blonde hair pulled back in a pony tail and clean as always, but she was not at all concerned with the latest hair styles or fashions. It was as if those years were being cut slowly, one by one, from her life.

The most unbearable of all exercises during these three years was a quarterly trip to see Boright. Naturally, he was as cocky as a healer in a tent revival. He bragged to her parents that he would drive the demons from their daughter and, seemingly, he had. But at what price? What he didn't tell them was that he was also just a little too familiar with their daughter during her first physical. Sarah insisted on having his nurse in the room during all future visits. She was incapable of hate or she would have hated him. She thought about telling her parents about his transgression, but for less than a second only. After all, no one would believe her.

It was early in a March morning that Sarah began her awakening from the long three-year ordeal. Countless hours of petition had submitted to no avail. She had grown into young womanhood during the time of isolation. In July she would be celebrating her sixteenth birthday. This one was going to be good. It would be unlike anything ever experienced by modern man.

16

Sarah's bedroom faced north, looking out into the long deep valley that held Ferrisburg. The eastern sunlight was not yet visible that morning when she awoke. Remnants of moonlight cast a blueish glow on the freshly fallen snow in her back yard. As she stood in front of her dresser surveying the valley, dreading yet another day and brushing her hair, she noticed a mark in the snow below her bedroom window. Then, while the sun began to rise over the mountains, definition came to the disturbed snow. Thinking her eyes were betraying her, she flew down the stairs and into the kitchen where she could get a closer look at the inscription. There, unmistakably and clearly, carved into the snow was the tenth letter of the alphabet, a "J".

Sarah's mind raced for an explanation. How could Billy Stewart have been so cruel, so unkind. The kids had put him up to it, that jerk. She had had enough, she was very near her breaking point. That he hardly spoke to her anymore was bad enough, but to pull such a cruel trick was beyond her comprehension. And then, as she trudged disheartedly back up the stairs to her room, it hit her and she raced down the hall. When she looked out the window she caught her breath. No footsteps! *There were no footsteps in the snow*, nothing except the letter "J". Her heart raced as she contemplated the possibilities.

On each successive morning Sarah flew out of bed to her window to see that yet another letter had appeared in the snow; a letter whose presence only she noticed. The kitchen window had frosted over by new storms and blowing winds. This precluded an easy view of the back yard for the rest of the family. In spite of the typical New England weather, the letters appeared daily and remained untouched by wind or snow drift. The event repeated itself for six successive mornings beginning with the letter J and ending with the letter A. Each single letter added to and ultimately solved the puzzle for Sarah. Her prayers had been answered:

J.O.S.H.U.A.

At first she was puzzled, but it didn't take long for the young girl to make the connection. As a toddler she had had difficulty pronouncing a one-syllable name like Charles. How could she be expected to master a three-syllable one like Joshua? Jay had been Joshua all along! In losing him she had found him.

The name in the snow was completed on March 21. But it was followed by another message. This time it was a date and place: April 6, Larmon's Grove. The date held no particular significance to Sarah, but the place did. She and Jay, or Joshua, had been there frequently. Identified by a huge white barn, the residents of the area knew the place well. Larmon and his family were pillars of the community. They were blue-bloods, colonial stock. Nearly every adult

17

who ever lived in Ferrisburg had used the swimming hole on Larmon's farm and its long tree rope to cool off on a hot summer day. Joshua loved sitting on the bank talking to Sarah while she swam. He never went into the water himself.

Behind Larmon's barn and across a small meadow was Stark's Knob, one of the many ancient mountains that held Ferrisburg safe from the world. It was covered by millions of birch and pine trees. At the foot of the mountain, one hundred yards into the forest, a natural clearing existed. It was known as Larmon's Grove. And Sarah knew on that seventh morning if she was ever going to see Joshua again she would have to be at that grove the morning of April 6.

She knew better than to tell anyone about the message. She wasn't ever going spend another second in Cambridge Memorial. She realized one other thing that morning: she would never, never deny Joshua's existence the way she had that last day in the hospital. The day they had let her go home. That had been a terrible mistake.

4

ON the morning of April 6, Sarah lay in her bed and watched the clock. Like a kettle of water waiting to boil, it moved excruciatingly slow. She was dressed and ready to leave for the grove at three in the morning. The last few months had lit a spark in Sarah, which was noticed by her parents and brother. Perhaps, they thought, it was over. Maybe it was finally time to get on with their lives. They were wrong, it was just beginning. Their lives would never be the same. They, nor anyone alive, had ever seen anything like what the next few months were going to bring them.

It was a beautiful morning, warm. The sun's rays shining through the trees created the impression that God Himself was raining sunshine on her for the first time in many days. Sarah walked the quiet dirt road to Larmon's full of peace and calm. She seemed more keenly aware of little things around her, the grasshoppers, the smell of the fresh grass, the dew on rose petals. Her step was light once again and she kicked stones, noticing that her senses seemed more acute than they had been in a long time. They were as keen as they used to be when Jay was around. She reminded herself that she must stop calling him that since she was now positive that Jay was indeed Joshua. Yes, she was sure he was near. She could sense him.

Soon she was at the top of a rise in the dirt road that afforded her a view of the Larmon farm with all of its little buildings. White barns with green roofs, kept as neat as a picture postcard. The Larmons were good people, in fact, they were the only townspeople who were still friendly with Sarah.

When Sarah finally reached the path at the bottom of Stark's Knob, she began to experience a feeling of foreboding. She was frightened to the point of almost turning back, but she proceeded down the pathway. She heard the voice about halfway into the forest. "You are not wanted here, bitch! Come any further and I will have your putrid little heart for breakfast." It terrified her. She turned, her eyes straining to see where the voice had come from. Her breath escaped her as the deep loathsome voice continued to mock her. "Have you come here looking for Joshua? He's shit. I could crush him like an ant. He will not save you if that's what you think. Listen, you little bag of dung, I'll send that stupid brother of yours one of my special friends. You will never see his little ass again. Get out, go while you can, or be destroyed."

All of her faculties told her to run. She tried to call out to Joshua, but her voice stuck solidly halfway up her throat. Darkness enveloped her. A moist, foul-smelling heat sucked into her lungs as she tried to gasp for clean air. She collapsed on the ground, groping around for some semblance of light. It was as dark as midnight. She lay on the ground weak and terrified for what seemed to be an eternity. The voice continued to mock and threaten her. The language was crude, vulgar, and penetrating. When she felt she could endure no longer, she called upon every ounce of strength left in her to raise herself from the wet forest floor up to her feet. Her first movements were tentative like a newborn doe. Branches of underbrush slapped her arms and face as she began moving aimlessly through the darkness away from the voice. Each breath she drew was like sucking for air through a collapsed straw. She pressed on in the seemingly endless darkness, running as fast as her strength would carry her. She was about to die, she was sure of it. Running at full speed through the forest, Sarah's leg hit a fallen sapling and she crashed falling forward out of the thicket to a pine needle carpet. Lying there she felt what little strength remaining leave her and, with it, her will to live. At the very last moment, that time between consciousness and black, she felt Joshua's presence. And it touched her more forcibly than ever before.

An overwhelming calmness quickly replaced fear. Strength gradually returned to her arms and legs. Defiantly she challenged the voice. "Take me if you wish, take me if you can, but I am not leaving. I will not leave this place." With that announcement, she struggled to her feet. She was still weak , but could think of nothing else but to try to make it to the grove. The small cuts on her face, arms, and legs stung as she began a wild run back to the trail and down the last one hundred yards of the path to Larmon's Grove. Twenty feet from the end of the trail the sinister voice returned in a mocking tone. "Have your way today, *little one*, but I will take you in the end." The eerie laughter was more sinister and terrifying than anything she had ever heard. She ran faster and stumbled into the circle of pine trees. Her heart was pounding as clean air began to enter her lungs. She lay on the ground clutching pine needles, her eyes closed tightly, fearful of what she might find if Josh was not there waiting for her.

"Sarah, you are safe, little one. There is no reason to be afraid. He cannot hurt you now. Open your eyes and say hello to me. I want to hear your voice once again." She could hardly believe her ears, it was Jay. . . Joshua! She turned slowly around to face the direction of his voice. Her eyes squinted open, shy from the light, seeking her familiar companion. And there she found him, standing above the pine needle floor, her childhood playmate, Joshua. He was enveloped in a light so white and brilliant that she could barely make out his features, but it was him alright. Obeying a young girl's instinct, she struggled to her feet and started toward him. But before she took her second step he spoke again. "Do not touch me. Not yet. But do let me hear you say my name." He smiled tenderly.

"Jay? Jay, it is you, isn't it?"

"Yes, it is I, little one. You have grown into a beautiful young woman. We know it has been difficult for you these last few years. No matter, except that you understand that these trials have been for your benefit. They have all been part of the tutorial. You will shortly realize what great value they have been to you."

She couldn't take her eyes off him. He was more majestic, more beautiful than she ever remembered seeing him, and his voice . . . his voice sounded as if it came from directly from heaven.

"Listen to me now, Sarah. Stand before me and listen to my message very carefully. Do not interrupt me, little one. I am Joshua, messenger and shepherd. I am your brother. I have been with you always, even when you thought you were alone. I knew you before you came to this earth and received a physical body. I am here to present to you a wonderful opportunity for all of mankind. But you must understand that you have free agency in all things. There are no requirements that you accept the plan that I will present to you. There is another should you reject it and decide not to accompany me. You will not be thought less of. I am Joshua, messenger and shepherd."

"Of course Joshua, I'll do anything. Just name it!"

"Be still, little one." And with that pronouncement Joshua repeated everything he had just said a second and then a third time.

After a short pause he began again. "For many years, misery has visited this earth as a result of ignorance. Should you accept our invitation, you and I will reveal to its inhabitants the one and only Creator of the universe and all that is known to mankind. As a result of this magnificent re-acquaintance we expect more good than evil to prevail on the earth for a long season. It will be a flood, if you will, a spiritual flood unlike any seen for a very long time. A last chance for this world before its final maturity. We will accomplish this together, you and I.

You must understand that in many quarters this revelation will not be accepted; it will be angrily and violently rejected. Your life and the lives of your loved ones will be endangered. We will have sentinels to assist us, to protect you and your family. But they will only be able to help for so long, and then you and your family will have no more than the protection that the good of this earth can provide. We will do all that we can to shield you from the evil that will oppose us. But you must understand that it will be formidable.

Sarah, unlike the past, I will now be visible to all. They will see me at your side always. They will not be permitted to hear my voice. I will speak only to you. I will answer your questions about anything at any time. You will answer theirs when appropriate. We will travel the earth together, sowing seeds of hope and peace. The Creator will work wonders and good through us, Sarah. I am Joshua, messenger and shepherd." As before Joshua held his right arm squared and repeated all that he had just given to Sarah two more times before he proceeded.

"On a date fixed in time, yet hidden from you because of wisdom in Him who has sent me, we will reveal the one and only true Creator. This revelation will come directly from Him to you and will be shown to you at an appropriate mark in our journey. A time when you are capable of understanding all that will attend that revelation.

You will be blessed mightily, little one. All the wonders of the ancients will lie at your feet and your name will be held for good or evil throughout all the world. Elements of the rich and powerful will conspire against you. There are even those of the spirit world who will be a threat to you. I believe you have already met one of them." At this point a smile of comfort became visible on his face.

"Fear not, little one. You will be protected, for a length of season. Now rise up. Go and sit under the large pine tree and ponder these things." With his message delivered, Joshua drifted away from her and faded from sight. The instant he was gone, doubt stung Sarah. Had this really happened? Was she mad? She shook her head as if to clear the cob webs. Maybe old quack Boright was right!

As she moved toward the tree she noticed that her legs felt like rubber. Her head was light and a slight trembling had taken hold of her hands. She leaned back against the cool bark and wiped her forehead which, in spite of the early hour and the cool shady grove, was covered with sweat. As soon as she touched the ground beneath the tree, Joshua reappeared above her and repeated the same message he had shared with her only moments before. And when he finished the message, it was repeated in its entirety once again. It concluded with additional instructions and the musical authoritative pronouncement, "I am Joshua, shepherd."

Sarah was under the impression that she had been in the grove for a very short period of time when in fact two days had passed, and the low light she assumed was still the morning sun was in fact the setting sun of the second day. What Sarah also did not realize was that at that very moment a massive police search was being conducted by the local and state authorities. It doesn't take too much time to call out the dogs when a former mental patient is missing. Especially when her daddy is employed by National Security Agency.

Nobody in Ferrisburg had any idea who Kent Ferunder really worked for, not even his wife fully understood the sensitivity of his position until the day Sarah disappeared. When Kent made the phone call to the secure number provided for *code black* situations, he never expected the response that took place. Thirty minutes later, he received a phone call from the director of the CIA. A special elite force would be entering Ferrisburg in twenty minutes. If he needed anything further, all he had to do was just call. "And how is Susan holding up?"

Susan Ferunder was frantic; her only daughter was missing after all they had been through, and she was blaming herself. She called Boright around 3:00 p.m. when it was evident to everyone that Sarah was missing. His voice was less than comforting in tone. He expressed serious concern that Sarah might have done harm to herself, given the *perceived social ostracism* she felt. Kent hadn't even contemplated that possibility, but once the seed had been planted, it was all he could think of. His anxiety level soared to the same height as Susan's.

The only calm one in the house was Chicky. He assumed and maintained the role of comforter and spent a good portion of the afternoon taking care of his parents' wishes and greeting visitors. The unique thing about small town residents is their ability to rally around each other when they think a threat from the outside is present. Some of the same people who kept their children from playing with Sarah were now combing the fields looking for her. Neighbor women came calling with food. Men huddled in small groups upon returning from the fields. They stood in circles where their whispered conjecture floated toward open windows, increasing Susan Ferunder's anxiety level even more.

Local residents were all abuzz with the efficiency of the *government men*. Never in the history of the state could such a response be recalled. Vehicles were being searched all over the state at roadblocks. Some businessmen and women, concerned that such an effort would discourage the tourists, were unhappy. These were the first to be run through NSA computers though they never knew it. Everyone came out spanking clean, except Mr. John Miller, the town pharmacist. He had been a sixties activist with an outstanding federal warrant for criminal damage to property. He would be left undisturbed until the girl was found. Then the federal marshals would ruin his day.

The small Mobil station that doubled as a greyhound bus stop was under close scrutiny. Every business establishment and residence in the small village received visits from more than one of the several law enforcement agencies looking for Sarah Ferunder. And every one of them had received at least one visit from the *government men*. Many in town thought this was an awful lot of manpower for a young girl who had been gone only two days and, after all, she was sixteen. But the townspeople didn't know that Kent Ferunder was a high-ranking official with an agency more powerful than the CIA ever thought of being. When it came to intelligence, the CIA was NSA's little brother. This wasn't just anybody's little girl.

When Sarah began her exit from the grove, the transformation had already begun. Joshua had promised her a very special birthday. She was to return on the morning of the 24th of July and he would be there to deliver a present beyond her wildest imagination. Her spirits were soaring as a result of the events that took place and the personage she met in the grove. She felt so good that she was certain her heart was going to burst right through her chest. It really wasn't until she moved towards the edge of the forest that she realized that time had somehow escaped her. The sun was setting. It was a beautiful warm sun dipping below the western slopes. How she enjoyed sunsets.

Sgt. Johnny Petralia and officer Douglas Barney were patrolling the backroads looking for Sarah; they were both local boys. Most of the day had been spent with other officers, but now that the sun was heading over the mountains, they felt they could accomplish more in the squad car together. They were driving down Burgoyne Road on the way to the Larmon farm when it happened. They both had been there at different times during the day with different partners. John had almost taken a swim in the cold Battenkill, but there were no footprints in the soft soil. He ruled out any jumpers from the bank. He couldn't believe Sarah would do such a thing anyway. He had known her since she was a little girl; she wasn't a quitter.

Douglas Barney was new to the force and had only been active for a little more than a year. Although he played football with John, he was his junior by three years. At age twenty-three, he had reached a formidable physical maturity. Built stocky and low to the ground, he had barely passed the minimum height requirement for the force. His black rimmed glasses accented his dark eyes. Douglas had a very disarming smile, conducive to police work. It hid a formidable opponent, as would testify four dumb street thugs from Lake Placid, New York, who tried to rob Miller's Drugs and Soda. It was a brief

24

tussle, with two of the four unfortunates spending quality time in Cambridge Memorial's orthopedic unit. No shots were fired and all Doug had to show for his heroism were a few cuts and bruises. He was a fine young man and John was very glad to have him on the small town force.

As the squad crested the dirt road by Larmon's, Doug was the first to spot Sarah. She had just begun to emerge from the thick grove of pines that covered Stark's Knob. They couldn't have been more than one hundred feet from her. "Oh Jesus, John, stop the car! Look. There she is. That's Sarah Ferunder; I'd know that walk anywhere. Jumpin toad frogs. Tell me I ain't seein' what I think I am. Shit!"

Johnny Petralia was more dumbfounded at the sight than his partner. The distraction almost took fifty percent of the town's squad cars into the side of one of Larmon's biggest barns. John was a big man at 6'5" and 245 pounds. He was all muscle. In the small town of Ferrisburg he was the town's only police Sgt. and reported directly to the chief of police, his father. Tony Petralia was in his early fifties and clearly grooming his boy to be the next chief of police. But nothing dad could have taught Johnny prepared him for what his eyes now saw. It was a full twenty-five seconds after he saved the squad from the barbed wire fence and the near-miss with Larmon's big white barn before he was able to compose himself.

Sarah had no idea as she made her way through the tall grass outside the trees that a bright white aura surrounded her entire body. She was busy gazing at the sky where stars now started to rise in the east. And she was listening to night birds on the wing searching for the million crickets now adding their voices to the symphony. Sarah also did not realize that thigh- high grass was caressing her ankles. It was clear to both Douglas and Johnny as they sat a mere thirty yards from her that her feet were a clean three feet off the ground. She didn't seem to notice them at first. As she moved closer to the edge of the grass where the DOT tractors had mowed for the first time this year, she descended to the ground. Then she took her eyes from nature and noticed the squad car.

Moving toward car she smiled. "Hey guys, whatcha doin' way out here?"

"Sarah, is that you? Are you OK?" Douglas called out the passenger side.

"Sure it is, Douglas, I'm OK. Why do you ask?"

"Well, half the state is looking for you, silly. You been missing for two whole days. Your parents are all worked up and the town looks like the national guard has just landed. Where the hell have you been, young lady?"

"Been upon Stark's Knob hiking and watching the furry creatures. What do ya think, Big Foot got me?" She giggled. "Looks like I'm in trouble again, huh? I was having such a nice time, I just lost track of it. Are they really mad?" Sarah thought that Doug's description of the search was just hyperbole. It wasn't at all.

"No Sarah, they're not mad, just worried as hell. Come on, why don't you get in the car and we'll give you a ride home."

"Nah, Doug, thanks anyway. I'd rather walk home. I'm not really in the mood for a ride, if you don't mind. And I'm sure you don't." She smiled again. It was very peculiar, but Sarah began to get messages in her mind. Like sentences coming from Johnny. She could tell he was really frightened of her for some reason. She just couldn't figure out why such a big man would be so scared of her. "Look, why don't you guys just get on the horn and tell them you located me and that I will be home in about fifteen minutes."

John Petralia just sat there numb with his mouth open while Douglas and Sarah had their conversation. Sarah finally walked over to the squad and leaned on his window sill. She laid her soft left hand on his large tanned forearm.

"And what are you so nervous about, Sergeant Johnny Petralia, heartthrob of every young girl in Cambridge County? Cat got your tongue? Heck, big guy, you look like you just saw a ghost!" She winked at him. With that pronouncement, Sarah smiled at Douglas and began her journey toward her home and a beautiful mountain pasture in Montana.

The only thing Johnny Petralia could do the rest of the evening was stare at his left forearm. He had sustained a long deep wound from a screwdriver just two days earlier while working on the village squad car. The laceration healed the instant Sarah touched his arm.

5

LONG after Sarah entered her home and was safe in the arms of her parents, John Petralia and Douglas Barney sat in the squad car, staring at her front door. They didn't speak to each other for nearly twenty minutes.

After she left the side of the squad car at Larmon's, they followed closely behind her all the way into town. They called Chief Petralia who notified search command that she had been found, was in good health, and was on the way home. By the time she reached the outskirts of town, her physical appearance was as normal as any other young person from the quiet little village.

Her explanation to her parents and the authorities was simple. She had gotten lost on the journey to Stark's summit. She finally made it to the top early that morning, but it took some time to get her bearings once she reached it. She began her descent right away which was a mistake. She had to stop frequently for rest, and halfway into her descent she decided she could go on no longer without some sleep. On a soft bed of pine needles she fell asleep for four hours or she would have been home sooner. She was very apologetic. The scratches made by the tree branches the day before lent credibility to her story and her parents were so happy to have her home safe and sound that they never suspected she might not be telling the whole truth. Sarah didn't want to fib to her parents, but she justified it by reasoning that the practicality of the situation dictated it. She couldn't very well meet Joshua on July 24 if she were being held captive by Count Boright!

As soon as the *government men* heard that Sarah had been located and that she was not the victim of a kidnapping, they disappeared into thin air. Nobody asked any questions and nobody got any answers. It was as if they had never been at the scene.

After their silent vigil in front of Sarah's home, John finally put the squad into gear and drove back to the police station. Neither Doug or Johnny had had much sleep in the last forty-eight hours. But then, most of the townspeople hadn't.

In spite of their sleepless history, they both looked as though they had just polished off a case of Jolt Cola when they walked through the front door of the station.

"You two look like hell!" volunteered Tony Petralia. He was a small wiry man, his olive brown skin reflecting second generation Italian heritage. He and John were inseparable friends who, unlike many father-son teams, worked very well together. "What you guys need is a good cup of Momma's coffee. I got some right here. I'm so proud of you little snakes. Found Sarah and showed up the foreigners, whoever the hell they were. Goofy looking group, huh? I'm as glad to have their suspicious looking asses out of my town as I am that we found little Sarah.

Look, you two reptiles finish this coffee while I clean up a little paperwork and take care of some supplies. Then we'll mosey over to Annie's Diner and have some supper. Momma has been at the Ferunder's all day preparing food and drinks for the rescue workers. If I bring you two pups home for supper, she'll shoot me. I'll be right with ya." With that Tony disappeared in the direction of a supply room located in the rear of the station. He always called the boys names. It was his way of expressing his fondness for them. The young men joked every morning about what species they would be that day.

Doug and John said very little to anyone since the moment Sarah left the side of the car and began her two mile journey to her home. They kept their eyes glued on her the whole time. Doug remembered calling the chief to let the search team know that she was with them, but remembered little else. They both recalled watching her as she walked in front of them, never once turning around to acknowledge their presence. Now as they each settled into brown, cracked leather chairs behind their respective beat-up desks, the questions that were churning their brains to mush, surfaced.

"OK, you tell me, big shot. What the hell went on out there tonight?" Doug didn't look at John as he asked the question. Incredulously, it was if they had done something or seen something wrong.

"I'm not sure. I don't have the foggiest idea what we saw and I don't know what we are supposed to do with what we saw," John answered.

Doug sat squeezing his left thumb and forefinger on the bridge of his nose up under his thick black frame glasses. It was as though he was trying to clear his vision, unsure of what he had seen. What was real and what was the product of tired, strained, sleep deprived eyes? "What in God's name did we see, John? It's just not possible. What do ya think?"

John was still inspecting the spot on his arm where a one and a half inch laceration had been only hours earlier. "I only know three things for sure, Doug. I don't know what we saw. I'm not sure what happened and I don't have a clue what to do about it." With that he held out his left forearm bent at the elbow and pointed to it. "Any idea how this healed so perfectly in the twenty seconds she was leaning on it? I don't, Junior." He referred to Doug as Junior whenever he wanted to tease him about his underclassman status.

"Think about what?" The chief walked back into the room and plopped down in a new leather chair behind his desk.

John looked to Doug for encouragement. There was none. Doug just shrugged his shoulders and shook his head back and forth. If John was going to do what Doug thought he was going to do, he wanted to see the older man's reaction before he jumped in. John and his dad had no secrets and he wasn't about to start now. So at the finish of a long drawn breath John began his report.

Tony sat listening attentively to his son's description of the events of the day. Occasionally he would glance over at Douglas, who out of a sense of loyalty to John and the excitement of the moment, had taken his feet off his desk, sat bolt upright in the chair and nodded in agreement with the facts as they each remembered them.

"Look for yourself, Dad. You saw that cut last night when I stopped by your house to borrow bandages for it. Hell, you and I talked while Mom poured hydrogen peroxide on it. The laceration is gone. It healed the moment she laid her hand on my arm. I could feel it healing. Look close, there isn't even a scar where the wound was, Dad." Tony took his son's outstretched arm in his hand and looked at it for some time. He even asked to see John's other arm to make sure he wasn't mistaken. When he had finished his inspection, he pushed his hat back on his head and let out a long slow quiet whistle.

"Johnny, mind if your old dad asks you a question or two of ya?"

"No, go ahead."

"I'm gonna be retiring here in just a few years, you know that, don't you, son?"

"Sure, but what the hell does that have to do with this?"

"You young guys think you're so smart. How come you got no patience? Just hold on and I'll tell you what one has got to do with the other. When I leave, your mom and I want to go back to the old country for a year or so. We want to travel around a little bit. I suppose you know that I been hoping that you might have interest in taking over here. And that you might give the young pup," nodding toward Doug, "the same opportunity that I gave you. The townspeople respect you both. You do want the job, don't you, son?"

"Yes Dad, but I don't see any connection between what you're talking about and what Doug and I experienced tonight."

"Well shut up, son, and I'll tell ya," he smiled. He loved having fun at the expense of the young ones. "I guess I don't have any quick answers or explanations. If I have learned one thing in my fifty-six years it's that some things are best left for the Lord to sort out. Some things just aren't meant to be understood. Just accepted." He was writing something on a small piece of yellow paper.

"I do have some advice, though. You know this is an elected post, don't you, boy? And if I were to poll the town today you would be a shoo-in for the job. But once you run around town talking about a flying girl who made your owie all better, I wouldn't give a plug nickel that you could keep your current job. My advice is to keep your mouth shut, son, if you know what's best."

John could hardly believe his ears. His father had never given him such ill advice! "Well, Dad, I've seen and heard a number of strange things tonight and I understand where you're coming from, but I saw what I saw and that young lady is not as nuts as many folks around here have been saying she is. And if it comes down to my losing my job for telling the truth, then these good people will have to do without my services." This was the first time that John had ever been disappointed in his father's counsel.

Doug could feel tension in the air, and it needed to be softened. "Chief, I think what John is trying to say here is that the people might not like the message, but they have to respect and trust the messenger. They have to have complete confidence that we are honest. I know what we have told you tonight is the damnedest thing to believe, but it did happen. That little girl is special somehow. If nip comes to tuck, I gotta stand up alongside Johnny and tell what we saw." He was shaking like a leaf, but he knew he had done the right thing.

Chief Petralia leaned back in his chair for a moment, his hat still pushed back on his head. He looked both of the young officers square in the eye. It was a hard look which ended only when a wide smile broke it off. He reached across the desk and handed the small piece of yellow paper to John. Written across the face of it was Tony's real advice, "Tell them the girl is special. Always tell the truth, son." Without looking up from the paper John passed it on to Doug. He sat still in his chair, thinking how much he loved that old man. Doug smiled broadly when he saw the message.

"Good thing you young pups came out with the right answer or I'd have fired both your asses no matter one's kin and the other nearly is. Now let's go across the road to Annie's Diner, order the special, and thank God for mysteries."

Because Sarah's parents were so happy to have her safely home, they failed to ask the obvious questions. If they had, they might have had some clue that all was not what it appeared to be. Questions like, how is it Sarah got lost on a trip she had made countless times with her friends? Why wasn't she hungry or thirsty after two days without food and drink? And why had the scratches that covered her legs, arms and face disappeared in less than two days? Or even simply, if she had made it to the top of Stark's Knob, why hadn't she started a fire in the Ranger's cabin? Certainly she was smart enough to know that the smoke would have alerted searchers.

These were questions that Dr. Boright carried around in his beady little brain, but he was going to wait until their next session to bring them up. He did not know there would be no more sessions. The next time he saw Sarah, he would be the patient.

The only one in the family to look at Sarah with a new set of eyes was Chicky. He noticed something different about his little sister. He wasn't sure what it was, but he liked it. Her parents just hadn't noticed, though her father should have with all his training.

Sarah lay on her soft warm bed the night she returned home, contemplating the events of the previous two days and how absolutely wonderful she felt. Her entire being was bursting with emotions of compassion and forgiveness, love and energy. She felt badly that she had fibbed about her adventure, but she had no choice for the time being. She would set it right soon. She was more content and confident than at any time in her life. And when her mind raced forward to July 24, her pulse raced with it. What was it going to be like? Was she worthy of this? Was she mad? There was still room for doubt to creep in occasionally. Very little room, and getting smaller all the time.

The following days marched on slowly for her, but were not without fascinating landmarks of development that reshaped her life and, more importantly, her perspective of it. The first was her ability to hear the thoughts of others when she wanted to and to feel their emotions as deeply as she cared to. She was a good student and she was very careful with this new gift. She did not want to violate private thoughts. Her ability to communicate on a somewhat primitive level with small animals surprised her. It began with a tiny gray squirrel in her back yard. At her unconscious thought that she would like to pet it, the little bundle of fur dropped its food cache and headed for her lap. Sarah momentarily felt the instincts of the animal, its concern for its own safety, and then comfort. It was a few moments before she realized that she was feeling the animal's feelings as it obeyed her wish.

A few days later the healing of a small sparrow who had accidently flown into the bay window in the front of the house aroused even higher anticipation in Sarah. She knew that Johnny's wound had healed, but she hadn't actually seen it. It was covered with a bandage. She did hear his thoughts when he realized what she had done. The sparrow took only a brush of her finger. And she watched the broken wing heal. The little bird sprung from her hand and was halfway across the yard before she could close her gaped jaw.

In 1985 the Chicago Bears had won the Super Bowl and the hearts of a million fans. They crushed the New England Patriots by a score of 45 to 10. That special season was inspired by a most unlikely gang of personalities who won the admiration of adults and children all over the world. Sarah Ferunder had become a Bears fan, too, much to the dismay of Chicky. She never let him live down the thorough trouncing the Patriots had received back in the 80s. So each time the Bears met the Patriots, Sarah pulled up a front row seat in the living room.

On July 25, one day after Sarah's birthday, the Chicago Bears would be hosting the New England Patriots in the first pre-season ABC Monday Night Football game of the year. Sarah had never been to Chicago, but she was going, and it promised to be a night the world would never forget.

On the 23rd of July, Sarah spent the evening with her folks, enjoying a steak dinner grilled in the back yard. She thanked her family for the lovely gifts. CD's from Chicky, a beautiful necklace from Mom and Dad, and another bottle of pretty pink nail polish. But the best of all was a copy of the keys to each of the three family cars. She was Sixteen! And next week she would have her license. Even with all that had taken place in her young life she didn't realize how little use she would have for it.

The following morning after a light breakfast Sarah announced that she was going swimming with friends at Larmon's. Afterwards they were going into town for ice cream from the Dairy Queen and a show at Berman's Theater. She would be home by supper time and once again thanked everyone for making her special day so special. Sarah's parents were so happy that she seemed to be back in the swing of things again. Sarah was off to keep her appointment with Joshua.

This time the trip to the grove was peaceful. The birds seemed to be in observance of some holiday. They were still. It was quiet. No crickets sang, no frogs hopped, no butterflies fluttered around the meadow. It was as still as anything she had ever seen. But the stillness brought with it a sense of calm reverence, a sense that something important was about to happen and she was excited about the day. She had been waiting for it longer than anyone could

32

possibly imagine. She had been waiting longer than just the time she'd spent on earth.

She walked slowly down the path, savoring each step, looking at each plant through new eyes, touching the trees touching boulders. She was sixteen, but she was older than all of them. When she finally entered the perfectly shaped small grove, she knew that she had been born for this moment. A small pillar of light fell on her, much like a spotlight would on an actress. The light became more intense and grew until it filled the entire circle of the grove. And then from the light came an unfamiliar voice. It was terrible, no, wonderful, and powerful and strong. It was a male voice and when it spoke the few words it did, her entire being was filled with a sense of love beyond earthly description.

"Sarah, here is Joshua. Messenger and shepherd. Listen to him, little one. Sarah, here is Joshua. Shepherd and brother. Listen to him, child."

She felt her knees go weak, but determined to remain standing.

"Welcome Sarah, it is good to see you again. I am told that you have been a good student and have learned well since we last saw each other. I am so proud of you. Are you happy to be here with me again?"

Her ability to speak seemed to have escaped her for a moment. "Yes, I am. I feel a little strange right now, though. I really am happy to be here, Joshua. I have missed you and I am so looking forward to meeting the people with you."

"I know you are, Sarah. That is good. I know you have been taught many wonderful things since we last met. You have had a chance to ponder these things in your heart and feel good about them?"

"Yes, Joshua, I have."

"Well, then if doubt has been slain and you are ready, we should proceed. Are you ready, Sarah? Are you ready to start your journey with me?" She still could not see him through the glare of the light that filled the grove.

"Yes, Joshua, I am ready."

"Sarah, come closer and kneel before me, please. Bow your head and close your eyes until I ask you to open them and rise."

Sarah sunk submissively to her knees and closed her eyes. When she did so, she felt the warm comfort of four hands on her head. The peace that filled her soul was delicious beyond what words could express. The warm comfort seemed to spread from the hands down her body to the tips of her toes. It was as if someone had poured freshly melted butter on her head and it had begun to run over her. Unintelligible words began to flow from Joshua. It was a language the likes of which she had never heard before. While she could not make out the meaning of individual words, she could feel the essence of them. The soliloquy began with a pleading character to it which progressed into one of thanksgiving, then one of supplication and, last, one of obedience. She didn't know how she knew these things, but she was certain of them.

When Joshua's words came to an end, she heard his voice in her own language. "Rise up, Sarah, and look on your old friend Joshua. Come give me a hug and tell me you love me once again." He smiled at her as she rose from the ground and flung herself into his strong, friendly embrace. Tears of happiness flowed down her cheeks as she told him how she had missed him and how lonely she had been without him. Tears of a thousand days of frustration fell down to the ground. When she was finished, she was as limp as a wet towel. He led her to the same tree that she sat under in April. He handed her a cup to drink from and she sipped a sweet liquid she had never tasted before.

As he stood before her this time she noticed the beautiful white robe he was wearing. It was trimmed along the hem in blue and gold. He wore nothing on his feet and a folded white hood sat down off of his shoulders in the back. A small beaded rope of curious workmanship, like nothing she had ever seen before, fit around his waist and gathered up the robe to him. Nothing physically had changed about him. He was the same tall blonde handsome playmate she remembered from her early years. She seemed to detect an energy, however, that she had not remembered present before.

Sensing her assessment of him, Joshua laughed. "One of these robes will be waiting for you when you return to your room today, little one. I will call for you tomorrow evening at ten o'clock. We will only be away for a short time. But tomorrow is very, very important. Wear the robe when I come for you. Your parents and brother will be fine. By the time we return they will be aware of all that has taken place, even from the very beginning when you were just a little toddler. We will spend time with them when our journey has ended and we have returned. Now, if you have no questions, it is time for you to return home and enjoy your birthday with your family."

"Well, I do have one question I need to ask before tomorrow. What shall I call you?"

"Who am I?"

"What?"

"I said, who am I?"

"You're Josh."

"Then that's what you shall call me," he smiled.

Sarah's laugh broke the serene quiet of the grove and the ice. The events of the last two months had intimidated her and she had forgotten to remember that Josh was her brother, so to speak. When he asked the question concerning his identity, he also placed the answer in her mind. "This is going to be fun," she thought. Sarah was still just a sixteen-year-old girl.

The next night Sarah used the Bears football game to occupy herself and her parents. She kept one eye on the clock, though, and when the middle of the second quarter came it was time to go upstairs and dress. Before she went upstairs she made her parents promise to watch the game so they could tell her who won in the morning. She was tired from all the day's activities.

She locked her door and replaced her dress with the white robe she found lying on her bed the night before. The instant she placed it on her body she felt different. There was a sense of duty about her. As soon as she combed her long flowing hair, she thought of Joshua, and when she looked into the mirror he was standing behind her across the room.

"Hello, little one. Are you ready to leave?" She was startled by his entrance and could only smile in response to his question. "We are going someplace special. It's sort of a birthday present. Maybe you could call it a re-birthday present." He laughed at his pun. It took her a moment and then she joined in his laughter. He could not be heard by others. She must remember that.

"Come take my hand. You will feel a bit strange the first time, but do not be afraid, I am with you. No harm can come to you, remember that. We will return shortly and do not worry about your parents as they will have company soon." Sarah crossed the room and placed her hand in his. She felt as if electricity were going to shoot out of her fingertips. Her heart was pounding a million miles a minute, she thought. He looked down at her and with a glance calmed any fear that she had. It was time to go. She felt a short rush of wind, the smell of a large body of water and a slight nausea. There was a sense of motion for a second or two, and then they were still. When she opened her eyes, she could not believe what she saw.

"Do not be concerned, Sarah. They have not spotted us yet. It will take them a few minutes and even then they will not believe what they are seeing. That is one of the things you and I will correct in these next few years. They have forgotten how to believe." He smiled at her. Sarah was, for one of the very few times in her young life, without words.

It took no longer than Josh had told Sarah it would. The camera man on the northside roof of Soldier Field in Chicago was the first to spot them as they stood three hundred feet in the air above the south end of the stadium. When he put the camera on them and barked into the producer's headset located in a

35

white trailer outside the west entrance to the stadium, his words somehow got all jumbled up. He was dumbfounded.

"Just shut the hell up and calm down, damn it. I can't understand a damn thing you're saying. How am I going to make any sense out of this with you babbling on like a baboon? Number seventy-two, get a shot of the south roof. Barbara, get a hold of the stadium people and find out what the hell the halftime show is here. By the way, where the hell are we?" he grinned. "I've been on the road so much, I'm not sure what city I'm in. And Barb, if you messed up and something is going on that Al and the gang should have mentioned, I'm gonna have your ass over a hot grill before we go off the air."

Barb was a competent associate producer and she hadn't been moved to the network's prime fall product by missing important civic events. "Roone, the only thing that is going on tonight is presentations to children from a local hospital. They don't know what we are all excited about. Should I give them a feed on seventy-two?"

"No, that's it. They are doing something special for the kids. Tell that jackass on number sixty-three he can go clean his pants now. There's nothing going on here except one low-keyed halftime show with a bunch of handicapped kids. And tell him if he ever does that to me again I'm gonna fire him. And then tell him I'm a blowhard and I love him. Let's wait and see if we should tape this thing for a lead-in from the halftime interviews."

The veteran producer stared at his young protégée. He didn't care how bright she was supposed to be, what potential she might have or how nice she looked in those jeans and tight sweater, if she screwed this up he was going to jump all over her cute little ass. Millions of Americans were watching his production even if it was only a pre-season game. She had better not be wrong.

It was nothing Barbara had overlooked. Her boss was about to capture the scoop of a million years on tape. Some lead-in.

6

A FULL moon reflected up from the still waters of Lake Michigan. The lake, dotted with hundreds of sailing masts moored across from the stadium, did not betray the chaos about to take place in the ABC production trailer.

"Barb, get a close-up on those kids until I get off this call to New York, will ya?" The producer placed his hand over the mouthpiece and turned to another technician. "Hey Larry, have we got anything on Peter Pan and Tinker Bell yet? What the hell is holding those damn Park District geniuses up? Dammit, they either know what the hell is going on in their own damn ball park or they don't."

"No, Roone, neither the Bears front office nor the Park District people claim to know what the hell this is all about. The police department and security is keeping a close eye on the situation."

"*The situation*? Just what the hell is *the situation*? I'd give my ex an extra alimony check this month if some SOB could just tell me what *the situation* is!" He looked accusingly at his new assistant, Barbara Scalia.

Barbara was starting to feel the pressure too, she had never screwed up a pre-production assignment and she was convinced she hadn't this time. She was tired and she wasn't in the mood for accusations no matter who the author was. "Look Roone, I missed nothing. These people don't know what the hell is going on here themselves and if they don't know, I sure as hell can't. Can I? So, if you got a problem spit it out or get the hell off my ass." He liked her.

"Nah, I got no problem, Barb. My only problem is I got a short temper and a big mouth. Help me out on this, will ya?" His smile conveyed sincerity. She knew that she would enjoy working with him. He was impossible to stay mad at, and he was cute.

"OK, Roone. Look, this is some kind of a surprise for the kids. I'm not sure who didn't tell who about it, but what the hell else could it be. Whoever is behind it did a pretty damn good job, didn't they? Look at them, looks real as hell, doesn't it?"

"Yeah, my ass is real too, Barb, but I don't want to spring it on ten innocents sitting in wheelchairs. And I especially don't want to put it on the air for sixty-seven thousand house fans and a viewing audience of twenty or thirty million. Shit, the thought of those kind of numbers is making me sick. Look, I gotta regroup here. So we don't know what's going on. If it's for the kids, it's gotta be good PR. Yes, good stuff, all American football game, crippled kids and ABC. Why the hell didn't I think of that before? I've got forty-five seconds of commercial left before we go up to Larry, Curly and Moe." Roone didn't particularly like the announcers. They had less talent and made three times his salary.

"Give me the headset. Al, Frank, Dan, listen up. Something's cooking at the south end of the stadium. We haven't got a handle on it yet and I doubt we will before we cut back from commercial. You may have to wing it if things start to pop. We'll be with ya as soon as we get something out of the local idiots. We think it's tied to the kids. If it is, run with it and for cripes sakes make sure you mention the call letters every five minutes or so. Don't forget. Call letters every five minutes or the suits will have all of our asses in the frying pan when we get back to New York."

Elevated three hundred feet above and fifty feet south of the stadium Sarah stood next to Joshua, trying to believe the sight before her eyes. A warm breeze off the lake was the only thing at the time that convinced her she was not dreaming. She kept looking towards it as if it would say something to her. A million lights from the city and their twins reflecting off the lake winked at her. The stadium below them looked like a enormous ring with an emerald jewel center.

The scene was distracting; she nearly lost track of her whereabouts. She had a vise-like grip on Joshua's left hand. His voice broke the silence and the spell.

"It's pretty, isn't it?"

"Oh yes, it's beautiful, Josh."

"It's time, little one. Are you ready?"

"Yes. I'm as ready as I will ever be. Let's go see the children." She looked at him and smiled. With those words she left behind her childhood. She was about to become so much more.

"Just keep hold of my hand and walk with me. Once we touch the ground I will follow your lead. You'll know what to do, follow your heart. Whatever you want to happen will. You understand that, don't you, Sarah?"

"Yes."

He squeezed her hand. "I hope you enjoy your birthday present. Have a good time, sweetheart."

As Sarah followed Joshua's lead, they began moving in a northerly direction toward the stadium. They proceeded forward simultaneously and began their decent. When they reached the rim of the stadium, they were only two hundred feet above the crowd. That's when camera man number sixty-three spotted them and went nuts into Roone's headset once again.

38

"My name is Lizbeth."

"Well, Lizbeth, tell Sarah why you are here tonight."

"I was at the hospital and they said I could come."

"And tell me why you are at the hospital, OK?"

"My hips keep commin out. So I had a coperation on my left hip and I'm gonna have another one on my right one once I go home and rest up." Lizbeth had spent the majority of her young life in her wheelchair. She didn't know much life without it. Whenever she attempted ambulation, one of her hips would painfully dislocate. The bilateral muscles and tendons affixed to each joint were too weak to hold the bones in place. After hanging inverted at forty-five degrees for two weeks in a Bradford frame, a contraption used in Canadian traction, her tendons just might be stretched far enough, with corrective surgery, to hold the hip joints together. But the child would grow and the process would have to start all over again.

"You know what, Beth? Can I call you Beth? I just love that name. I don't think you want to have any more *coperations*, do you? So you won't, is that OK with you, sweetheart?"

"Yes ma'am." She nodded her head, bright eyes never questioning, never asking how or why. In that instant Elizabeth Brown became a perfectly healthy child.

"Now, how would you like to help me? I want you to take my hand so we can walk over there and see your buddy." She pointed to the a little boy next in line. Sarah looked up at the parents who were now nodding their approval to little Beth. With that encouragement and Sarah's hands, Beth came out of her wheelchair and placed her beautiful little feet solidly on the ground for the first time in her life. Taking Sarah's hand once again they moved toward little Jerry Thompson. The crowd felt electric, half believing what they were seeing, half not.

When Lizbeth broke from Sarah and ran to Jerry, giving him a bear hug and a kiss on the cheek, a roar went up from the fans as if the winning touchdown had just been scored.

Sarah, Beth, and Jerry visited the next wheelchair and the next and the next, each time enlisting a child as they made their way down the line to the last little boy. His name was David Stein. The picture reminded Joshua of a mother duck with her little ducklings, and he smiled at the procession.

David had suffered anoxic insult at birth which resulted in partial cerebral palsy. He was fortunate since his mental faculties were intact, but he was unable to walk, feed himself or breathe very easily on his own. He could speak with difficulty. When Sarah and her little tribe approached him, he had tears in his eyes.

"God in Heaven, this is great stuff. Sixty-three, you got the best angle on this, make sure you get a close-up on this kid! Frank, you guys better talk it up, damn it. Sounds like we got a bunch of mimes in the booth. I want the guys with the boom mics on the field behind the parents. Get up closer to her if you can. Barb, sweetheart, we are going to be famous people in the morning. God, I love this game!! Jimmy, get a shot of the north end zone crowd. Except for the kids they got the closest look at these people, whoever the hell they are. And pretty boys, if you don't stop Moe from sucking on that damn flask and confusing what network he works for, he will be back doing commentary on boxing for CBS in the damn morning."

"Well, David," the boom mics picked up the conversation midstream, "why don't you want to come out of the chair for me?"

"Never been out of the chair, and Bobby isn't here," came a simple answer from the little boy.

"Oh I see, you're frightened about coming out and your friend Bobby from your hospital room isn't here to be with you, is that right?"

"Uh huh."

Halftime was well over by now. Seeing events unfold from the locker room televisions, players had streamed from their dressing rooms to the north end zone. Some were kneeling, some were standing with arms resting on teammates shoulders, jerseys were off, as were helmets. A few could be seen with bowed heads and moving lips. All were quiet, some had tears running down their cheeks.

"David, if I promise to come see Bobby tomorrow, will you come and play with us?"

"Yes." A big smile broke out across his face and bright eyes lit up.

"Well then, big boy, you see those guys at the end of the field there? Why don't you run down there and get a jersey for Bobby and I'll see him wearing it when I come to visit him?"

"K." David was a boy of few words. Sarah hugged him and when she came up to her feet, David followed and buried his little face in her robe.

"Now," she said, turning to the other children, "I want you all to meet my friend. Then he and I have to leave for a little while." Mother duck pulled the little ones toward Joshua. He drifted slowly to the grass and gathered them with his arms close to him. The crowd applauded politely, almost quietly.

"Sarah, introduce us. Tell them how much I love them. Then tell them it is time for us to leave, but before we do so I want to see them race to the players." He smiled again, walking among them, touching each on their head. He lifted each one and kissed them on the cheek. Sarah introduced Joshua as her special friend and conveyed his message to them.

Parents were in varying states of emotional shock. There were many tears of relief and incredulity. Years of pain, worry, suffering with and for their children were being wiped away before their very eyes and they had no words to explain what was happening. They had no emotions left to bare and wanted to say something that would express adequate gratitude. There was nothing that could be said. Sarah and Josh heard their thoughts and turned to face them. With a simple nod Joshua and Sarah acknowledged them. Thank you was not their due, it belonged to another.

On cue from Sarah, the children dashed madly toward the weeping giants in the end zone. Large men fell to their knees to welcome little feet who had never run before. Many of the men had new appreciation for the gifts their creator had bestowed upon them.

When the children reached the men, Josh took Sarah's hand in his and squeezed it tight. "It is time for us to leave now. Did you have a nice birthday present, Sarah?" He nudged her in a playful manner.

"Well, I was hoping for roller blades, Josh, but if this is the best you can do. . .!!" He laughed loudly at her fun.

They did not exit as they entered the stadium. In a millisecond they were gone, leaving behind them a stadium of people witness to the beginning of a time of new possibilities. The second half of the game was never played. This was the first time in the history of the league that a game had been canceled for such a reason. And nobody really knew what the reason was. But neither the fans nor the players wanted a football game after what they had just witnessed.

Roone sat on a three-wheeled stool in the trailer, having turned coordination of the coverage over to the lame-ass officious news boys. He was numb. He was just fine, in control, while the show was running, but now he felt like a wet dish rag. If he had his wits about him now, he should be previewing tapes to make sure he had everything, and coordinating feed to New York. But he just sat staring at number sixty-three's shot of the children who were now joined by stunned parents, press, and security personnel as they frolicked with the biggest kids in the stadium, the players.

Barb was handling the feed to the news boys. She was a real pro. It took no time for word to get out. ABC was sending feed to every major news and cable network in the world. Media people were going nuts with the Chicago story. Over twenty million people had been tuned in to that game. Before the crowd even hit the exits, every sort of expert one could put their finger on was being roused out of bed. Men and women, religious, psychologist, psychiatrist, physician, security expert, expert in mass hysteria all had phones ringing off the hook. What the hell happened, what did this all mean?

There were no auto accidents leaving the parking lots that night. No arguments on the way to the cars. In record time the stadium lot was as quiet as the lake. The moon was high in the sky now and seemed to be pleased with the events of the evening. The entire lakefront bathed in a beautiful red hue.

ABC and Barb got the jump. Roone was a professional and, while tired and drained, he was astute enough to get Barb over to Children's before the news boys beat him to the punch. Barb had a live feed through the local affiliate, Channel Seven, directly to the Vice President of Public Relations for Children's Memorial Hospital of Chicago. After a brief statement, denying any foreknowledge of the events that took place in Soldier Field, Mary Robbins consented to a brief interview. She declined to confirm the identify of any patient since that would be a breach of confidentiality. She could neither confirm or deny that any of the children had been brought back to the hospital for observation. And she certainly refused to dignify allegations proposed by another news source that the hospital knowingly participated in what could only be described as a detestable publicity stunt.

Deep in the belly of the Federal Building, located at Jackson Boulevard and La Salle Street in downtown Chicago, the children, doctors, parents and CIA agents knew that what had taken place was anything but a cheap publicity stunt.

And in Ferrisburg, Vermont, in a small home on Pond Street, Kent and Susan Ferunder had some very special visitors.

7

KENT FERUNDER had started out that Monday like any other work week. His insurance office on the main street of downtown Ferrisburg was a front for the NSA. His secretary had been imported to the area ten years earlier. She worked for the Ferrisburg First Federal Bank for two years to establish a cover until Kent hired her away under an appropriate pretext. Every morning she would make a pot of coffee and place it next to a plate full of pastries in the small office reception area. And every day at 4:00 p.m. she would throw everything away except what she, Kent, or the very occasional customer would pick up.

Ferunder's Insurance wrote less business than any insurance agency in the state. Kent's books were done by agency accountants, and what little business he had was processed through a legitimate brokerage set up by the agency in Hartford, Connecticut. His wife didn't know the extent of his involvement with the intelligence community. The fact of the matter was that he was one of the country's best cryptologists. As a member of SIGINT, the foreign signals intelligence mission, he was part of an effective high tech organization, collecting foreign signals or communications of interest to the national security of the United States. Of course no one knew which signals were of interest unless all of the communication on the information highways was listened to. So Kent's job was to listen to as many of them emanating from the Middle East as possible. He and some friends once calculated that each message to reach the desk of the President of the United States was backed by thirty-five thousand that were of no importance at all.

Since people object strenuously to others reading their mail, and governments generally object even more strongly, codes were used to confuse the eavesdroppers. Kent Ferunder and his buddies were employed to bust the codes. Direction of the Agency was supplied by top government channels, so it was not unusual for Kent to have direct access to the President's immediate advisers. Add this to the fact that the agency Kent worked for operated under the control of the Secretary of Defense, who by special Presidential directive acts as an executive agent for the government of the U.S., and it was easy to understand the activity level that took place in Ferrisburg when Kent Ferunder discovered a missing daughter.

Kent had worked many years in numerous covert operations, but when his family started to grow he decided upon a slower paced venue. Not wanting to lose such a valuable asset, the agency proposed the front from which Kent could operate. His traveling days for the agency would come to a halt. It had all worked out very well. Up until the Monday night football game, that is.

Kent and Susan had been taping the game for Sarah. When halftime arrived, they, like most of America, headed for the kitchen. Kent was in charge of popcorn and Susan was making black cows. It was only a few minutes into the treat collaboration that Kent received a phone call from his neighbor Larry Ott. Larry owned several computer outlets around Vermont and northern New York. Kent and Larry had become best of friends and were often found drifting down the Battenkill with rods and reels in hand.

"Kent, are you guys watching the game?"

"Sure, stupid. Who isn't?"

"No, I mean are you watching it right now?"

"I'm in charge of popcorn, Susan is making drinks. What's the matter, that rice burner you bought this weekend not working?" Kent wasn't prejudiced, he just couldn't resist teasing Larry about his new Sony thirty-five inch television. Larry was a technogeek. He had to buy anything and everything that had more than twenty buttons and thirty functions. His home looked like a Radio Shack on speed.

"No, I'm not BS-ing you, Kent. Get in there right away."

At that point the phone went dead. Each of the men thought the other had ended the conversation. Neither had.

Kent and Susan entered the living room just as Roone was giving the pretty boys their second pep talk. They could clearly see what was the obviously impossible on the screen in front of them. Seconds passed and Kent bolted from the living room up the stairs and down the hall to the right toward Sarah's bedroom. Susan was quick on his heels. Just as they reached Sarah's room, Chicky returned from his girlfriend's home totally unaware of what was taking place.

Chick had been helping Patricia's father rewire a used boat he just purchased. When Kent and Susan confirmed an empty undisturbed room, they returned downstairs where they found Chicky, eyes as big as poker chips fixed on the television screen. He was swaying back and forth, muttering an expletive that expressed his astonishment quite succinctly. His father moved to his side and whispered, "Amen."

Susan was the first to notice the presence of the two men in her home. She couldn't see them, but she felt them. She could feel their eyes on her, but strangely no uneasiness accompanied that knowledge. When she turned around to verify her feeling, she gasped. It was loud enough to draw Kent's attention. Chicky followed the eyes of his mother and father up the staircase. Standing at the top were two men dressed in white robes. They each outstretched an arm. An invitation was clearly being extended.

One man looked to be African, the other Oriental. Once seen they turned and headed in the direction of Sarah's room.

Kent held Susan back, pushing her to the arms of their nineteen- year-old son Chicky. Walking down the hall to his study, Kent took a key quickly from his wallet and opened the bottom left door of his desk. No one was allowed into the desk, ever. In the family this was the eleventh commandment and no one ever thought of breaking it. Kent pulled a nine millimeter Glock semiautomatic revolver from the desk. If somebody had made the mistake of slipping into his home, they would be discouraged from ever doing it again. Kent was an expert marksman and had been in situations where the Glock was used with terminal force. This was another secret no one in his family knew about until now.

Returning to the bottom of the staircase he told Susan to wait downstairs and call the police. For a reason she could not understand she did not do as he asked. And if she had she would have discovered the dead phone lines anyway. Susan and Chicky followed Kent up the stairs. As they approached Sarah's room they noticed the door ajar. From the top of the stairs they could see light inside the room. It was a typical teenager's room, messy. Kent was the first to enter. He turned to his right and lowered the gun from the ready position to his side. His face was awash with bright white light as he stood with an expression of disbelief on his face. Chicky and Susan followed him into the room. Their eyes seemed to betray them as they came to rest on the two beautifully robed men standing at the head of Sarah's bed, one on each side. They reassured Kent they meant no harm. He placed the weapon down on a dresser just inside the door. Susan's vocal cords were paralyzed and Chicky was speechless for the first time in his young life.

The Oriental spoke first. "I am Sun Ce. This is Andani. We mean no harm and knew of no way to approach you without causing some alarm. We ask your forgiveness if we have frightened you. We have been near Sarah since the day of her birth and will remain with her until her mortal probation has concluded. We will allow no harm to come to Sarah. She will be here with you shortly to speak with you, as soon as the children are well."

With that he smiled and waited in anticipation of the questions that were bound to come. When none came, most probably because of the shock of what was being unveiled to the family, Andani stepped forward.

"Your daughter is indeed a special spirit who has been chosen to bring a reawakening to the earth. My companion is from the great land of China. Sun Ce was a magnificent warrior in his time. I was a Chief among Chiefs in my country during my mortal probation. We are sentinels now and have been given your daughter as our charge. We love her as you do. We will take good care of Sarah. You needn't be concerned for her well-being ever again." And then he read Chicky's mind and laughed. It startled the family out of the state of dumbfounded silence.

"No Chicky, we are not aliens, your sister has not been abducted and we don't intend on taking you anywhere either. Please feel free to ask Sun Ce or me any questions you have."

"OK, what have you done to Sarah? What the hell is she doing on TV? If anybody hurts her, I'm gonna get them."

"Spoken like a true warrior," Sun Ce responded. "We have done nothing to Sarah but to educate her. You will learn more from her. She will be here shortly and you will see that she is well." With this answer to Chicky's question he turned towards Sarah's mother.

"Do not fear for your child. She will be here within the hour and will calm all your anxiety. I promise you the things that we have said are true. Won't you please go downstairs and wait for her. It won't be long now before she is here. She is with our senior companion Joshua at this very moment and they are nearly finished with their evening's sojourn. If there are no questions. . ." Incredibly, neither Kent or Susan Ferunder could muster words. They were experiencing something that could not be happening. Only Chicky demonstrated the ability to communicate with the sentinels. As the family walked down the stairs toward the living room, leaving the sentinels behind, they still weren't sure they had experienced what they had.

Reaching the bottom of the stairs they suddenly came to their senses. It was as if they had been in an intellectual fog. Heads clearing, they moved quickly to the television in the living room. It appeared that the events on the field at halftime were over. A camera shot provided by number sixty-three provided a view of the children still running around in the end zone with the athletes from both teams while the crowd applauded wildly. A commentator was heard to say, "The only thing that we can indeed say for sure is that our cameras do not record mass hysteria or hallucinations as some reported experts have already ventured on other networks." The pretty boys could be seen with ties undone, shirt collars opened and a dazed look on their faces.

Recalling that they had been recording the game for Sarah, her parents couldn't rewind the tape fast enough so that they could see in its totality what the nation had witnessed earlier that evening. Before still unbelieving eyes the tape revealed Sarah's participation in a modern day event of historic proportions. Kent kept rewinding the tape whenever a close-up of Sarah came on the screen. He had to keep convincing himself that it was his daughter. Chicky's demeanor was completely different than that of his parents. He seemed to have recovered completely and as the tape rolled forward, it met with his own special cheers of approval. "Neat, cool, rad!" Chicky was still a teenager.

Susan's eyes were filled with tears. She cried with joy for the children as any mother would and as millions had that evening. She cried for her daughter who was a vision of loveliness and seemed to exemplify all that was good in the world. And she cried because she finally realized, in the middle of the tape recording, that the last three very painful years suffered by her daughter were the result of a very big mistake. The tears tasted especially salty when that realization set down upon her.

When Sarah walked down the stairs in her jeans and a Chicago Bears sweatshirt, it was close to 11:00 p.m. eastern time. She was tired and thirsty. When she had arrived back in her room just moments earlier, there were a pair of roller blades on her pillow with a note attached, "Love, Josh, Andani & Sun Ce."

Her parents were watching the evening news. Ted Koppel was hosting a special *Nightline* with numerous experts speculating about what had occurred and about the identity of the participants. The theories were as numerous as the guests. When one of the experts offered the theory that we had had our first visit from extraterrestrials, Chicky roared with laughter. He was joined by Kent and Susan and for the first moment in the evening the ice was broken. Sarah stood on the stair steps behind them and smiled.

Frequent camera shots of the scene of the *Chicago Children's Miracles*, the now deserted Soldier Field, served as background for the carrot-topped anchor. Someone had scattered flowers all around the empty wheelchairs that had been left behind. The ground crews were working everywhere except the area where the children had been seated. That had been cordoned off with yellow crime scene ribbon.

Roone had recovered. He had purchased the wheelchairs with a hefty six-figure contribution to Children's Hospital. Flowers, empty wheelchairs and

ABC. How the hell could the suits in New York not love this stuff. God, he loved this game. While a lowly tech went in search of flowers, it fell to Barb to go out and place them just right so it would make for a great shot. The whole time she scattered the three dozen mixed flowers around the wheelchairs she cussed Roone. "The bastard knows I have allergies."

As Sarah watched the television over their shoulders from the third stair, neither her parents nor Chicky sensed her presence. She hadn't wanted them to yet. She felt an overwhelming sense of love for each of them. She felt a little sad that their lives would never be the same now. But soon her thoughts returned to those children and she smiled wildly, almost laughing.

She started down the stairs and couldn't help thinking as she kept one eye on the television news anchor, "If they think tonight was special, just wait until tomorrow."

"Hello guys, watch'a watching?"

8

TUESDAY morning, grand rounds were being conducted at Children's Memorial Hospital of Chicago, and every nook and cranny was buzzing with talk of the children. Any unit who had one of the children as a patient, any nurse, doctor, technician or housekeeper who had any personal knowledge of one of the children became an instant celebrity. The entire hospital and its staff was the center of worldwide attention.

Located just north of downtown Chicago, the hospital was surrounded by prominent yuppie neighborhoods where the streets were busy with traffic and parking was irritatingly scarce. The neighborhood was old, but most of the brownstones were recently restored to their former glory by the young professionals who could afford the outrageously high cost of such a venture. Its population density boasted it as one of *the* places to live in Chicago. The traffic and parking problems normally plaguing the residents of the area quadrupled today with the influx of media vehicles and curiosity seekers. Police traffic control officers arrived well before early morning rush hour which began at 6:00 a.m. Tempers flared as residents, trying to escape the area for work destinations, fought media caravans and the curious who were trying to enter.

Vendors had hit the streets as soon as the vans dropped them off five blocks away. They were selling a variety of pirated materials. T-shirts with pictures of the Chicago Bears and the children were being sold at nearly every intersection. The slogan surrounding the picture read, "I Attended The *Chicago Children's Miracle*." There were miniature wheelchairs with a similar labeling. Balloons with the hospital image on them were being sold to school children and their parents as they waited for buses. Capitalism was alive and well on the early morning streets of Chicago.

There wasn't an area of the city that wasn't affected by the previous night's event. White ribbons decorated trees, churches were open and *full*, someone quipped, "the second Chicago Miracle!" And horns started blowing, the result of a Christian radio station's suggestion. No one seemed to mind. And now the roof was about to blow off the top of Children's Memorial Hospital of Chicago.

The mayor of Chicago appeared at an early morning press conference where he read a prepared statement and consented to answering a few questions.

52

"The people of the city of Chicago, along with many millions of people across our great country, were witness last evening to an event of considerable significance. We do not have the answers to many questions being posed to us today. We wish we did. What we can say, however, is that all ten children who attended the game last night to receive recognition for their bravery under trying physical challenges have been examined by the finest physicians available as of this morning. Each and every one of them has miraculously received completely perfect bills of health. While we do not understand how this gift was bestowed upon them, we can only be grateful that we have been witness to this miracle.

This morning, we encourage all of our citizens, indeed all people, to consider the events that have taken place in our great city. Perhaps it would be appropriate for each of us to reflect upon our own personal beliefs and values. It is a day, an opportunity, for the city to come together as one in thanksgiving and praise. Good morning has a new meaning here in Chicago today. It is a good morning, a very good morning to be here in Chicago. May God bless you all and thank you."

The mayor was a good family man who had watched, as had many of his fellow Chicagoans, the magic of the previous evening. He was genuinely touched by what he saw. He didn't know at the time he was delivering his statement that something was taking place twenty-four blocks north of his office that would make the Soldier Field experience look like kids play.

At Chicago Children's, Dr. Lawrence Holland was standing at the nurses station on the eighth floor cardiac intensive care unit, reviewing nursing assessment notes, when he heard Sarah's voice. It was early yet, 6:45 a.m. Most of the nurses were in the small unit conference room, exchanging shift report information relating to each of the little patients assigned to the unit. When Dr. Holland looked up from the chart, he fully expected to see a long lost friend because nobody at Children's called him Larry. While he was an excellent surgeon, he had the bedside manner of a pit bull. The patients didn't like him, parents didn't like him, even most of his colleagues didn't like him, but he was the best pediatric cardiovascular surgeon the hospital had, one of the very best in the world. The nurses respected him, but hated working with him because of his gruff, abrasive personality. He was all clinic, no emotion, at least none that ever showed. A strange combination for a pediatric physician.

His colleagues, the nursing staff, and other employees did not know that Dr. Holland had not always been a pit bull. The second year of practice as a general surgeon in a small city in northern Utah had destroyed a good man. That morning he was the on call surgeon for the emergency room. It was a nice summer day and he had been at the country club preparing to play a short nine when his beeper rang. A young child had been struck by an auto while riding his bike. The child was en route and, according to the medics, he was going to need a *chest cracker* pronto!

Holland arrived at the trauma center with all due speed. Rushing into the surgical suite, he found the patient already prepped by a first assistant. The little boy had been hit by a drunken driver and dragged nearly twenty-five feet before being expelled by the car. He was an unrecognizable mess. Dr. Holland worked furiously to control the internal bleeding, but as he put it to the assistant, "I just don't know how to plug the holes and bail the boat at the same time. This poor kid is bleeding everywhere."

The child expired on the table, never really having had a chance. Dr. Holland was devastated whenever he lost a patient, but he especially hated to lose a pediatric patient. It wasn't until he began removing his gloves that the surgical drape came down and he recognized the birthmark on the child's chin. He felt his legs turn to jelly as he screamed and threw himself on the child, begging him not to die. It was his own son, Charlie.

Holland fell into a state of depression, divorced his wife a year later and finally immersed himself in work, shutting out the rest of the world. He never completely recovered from that day. He began hating God while sitting on a laundry cart in the supply room adjacent to the surgical suite where his son's blood was being mopped off the floor.

Dr. Holland looked down the long hall toward the voice that had called out his name. In between Sarah and Joshua stood a blonde haired little boy. He was as real as the floor Holland was standing on, but the doctor blinked several times to make sure his eyes weren't playing tricks on him. The little boy had the most wonderful smile, a familiar one. It couldn't be, could it?

"Hello Daddy." It was his voice! He would recognize it anywhere, anytime, even after twenty years. He knew Charlie's voice when he heard it. The chart and pen fell from his hands as he began moving slowly, cautiously toward the little boy. And then as he got closer, he broke out into a dead run towards him.

"I came so you could see that I'm OK, Daddy. I miss you sometimes, though, and I want you to be happy, Daddy. Grandpa and Grandma said it would be fine if I came." Holland dropped to his knees, swooping the boy into his arms, hugging him madly, sobbing and laughing at the same time. Tears cascaded down his cheeks onto the little boy's neck. "It's alright, Daddy, I'm just fine, really," he said, hugging his father back as tightly as his little arms permitted. And then Sarah's hand rested on Holland's shoulder, and in a soft and gentle voice she invited them into a unoccupied room. "Let's go in here."

Holland followed, holding onto Charlie and smelling his smooth soft skin. His mind was clearing now. This was the girl and her companion. He had seen them on the news last night and said a silent prayer. He sat down on the bed, holding his little boy, sometimes holding him at a distance to make sure it was really him and that he hadn't fooled himself with another child.

Finally he looked with amazement at Joshua and asked, "How?"

Joshua did not answer the question, but turned to Sarah, indicating that she was the one to ask and would be the one to answer. So Holland looked at her. His eyes pleaded with her, but before he could utter the question again, she spoke. "It doesn't matter how, Doctor. What does matter is why. Maybe you should ponder that question. Charlie is fine, see? Don't be angry any longer, Father did not take him from you. He was not lost because of your abilities or lack of them. An eternal physical law was complied with, that's all. It was an unfortunate accident. And now you see for yourself that Charlie is well and happy and with family. He will only be permitted to stay for a short time here. So why don't you two visit while we stand outside the room."

Sarah and Josh moved toward the door. When she reached for the door knob, she turned again to Holland and said, "Oh, by the way, Doctor, you should know that Charlie will be waiting for you as a little boy. And when you and his mother join him, he will be yours to raise just as if you were never separated. You have the ability to belong to each other through all the eternities. Just as you did before you even came to this earth. Now, you may say the goodbye you have desperately wished for all these years and prayed for last night." She smiled and closed the door.

Twenty minutes later a red-eyed and smiling Dr. Lawrence Holland emerged from the small patient room. He looked at Sarah and Joshua. "How in the world can I ever say thank you? I don't know who you are or why I have been allowed to experience this, why me...?" His voice trailed off.

"Why not you? You are as worthy as anyone." There was a long silence as the doctor who had saved so many children's lives seemed to struggle with Sarah's response.

"And if you want to know how you can say thank you, how about a hug for starters?" She winked at him. Holland grabbed Sarah in a bear hug and lifted her off the ground. There were tears in his eyes. He put her down and looked at Joshua. Holding out a hand to him, offering the personage a handshake, Doctor Holland wasn't sure about the protocol. Joshua moved to the doctor, ignoring the hand, and embraced him. Joshua communicated his thoughts to Sarah.

"We love you, Lawrence. Have peace now and do not hesitate to share what has happened here this day. Only remember one thing. Sarah and I did not do this. It was a gift from your Father."

When Holland turned around, he saw thirteen nurses emerging from the conference room. They noticed him and the visitors at the same time. Clip boards, cups, pencils, and charts hit the floor, dropped by women who couldn't believe their eyes. They didn't know which of the two personages was more fascinating to watch. Only one of the nurses had enough presence about her to react in any way other than complete shock. Maria Hernandez was an older woman. She was a good nurse. She was loved by the other nurses because she was an on the job mother to all of them. Many referred to her as mom.

Maria stepped forward, looking directly at Sarah. As the trio approached the immobile group of women, Maria pulled a rosary out of her uniform pocket. It was as standard equipment for Maria as was her stethoscope. When Sarah came within four feet of her, Maria began to genuflect, crossing herself as she did. Sarah caught hold of her wrist just as Maria whispered, "Madonna."

Lifting her to a full standing position, she held her hands and said, "Oh no, mother Hernandez. I am not who you think I am. My name is Sarah. I am from a small town in Vermont called Ferrisburg." Then Sarah's smile broadened. "This fine companion of mine is Joshua, and you may have guessed that, indeed, he is not from Vermont!" The levity caused spontaneous laughter. Even Joshua joined in, though only Sarah could hear him. Holland laughed for the first time in many years. The nervousness of the nurses had been broken and now in her new role she was seen by them as approachable. She had accomplished what she had set out to do and Joshua was proud of the way she had done it.

Looking over the group of nurses, Sarah noticed one in the back of the group who did not seem curious. She was standing with her arms folded and head bowed. She was still embarrassed.

"Ronnie, how are you? I am so happy to see you again." Making her way through the crowd of nurses, "Please, may I give you a hug?" Ronnie Lipinski wanted to shrink from the spotlight, but Sarah was beside her instantly. She took Ronnie by the hand and walked her away from the rest of the people gathered in the hallway.

"You look so pretty today! Do you always wear your hair like that? I wish I could do something with mine, but it's so fine and refuses to take a perm, you know?" Ronnie could have been flattened by a feather! Here was this girl, this angel, this god, this beautiful creature talking to her about hair styles like they were old girlfriends. Sarah knew her heart. It was good. She also knew her thoughts.

"Ronnie, don't be afraid, we are sisters, you and I. And I am no more special than you or any of the others here. You must believe that. And when you see what we are going to do here today, you will not feel the hurt you have in the past. None of these little ones are ever lost. I promise you."

Squeezing her arm, she leaned over and whispered two things that sent shock waves up Ronnie's spine. "You slept very well last night. And when James called for your daily order of drugs you told him to go to. . .well, you told him no!" She smiled. "You did say that, didn't you?"

"Yes, last night was the first time in eight months that I have been able to function without them."

"Ronnie, we have been asked to do something here today that I think you are really going to enjoy. Do you want to know what it is?"

Stunned, but smiling, Ronnie answered with a simple, "Yes, very much so, yes." Sarah whispered in her ear.

"Surely you must be joking!"

"No, I'm not! Let's rejoin your friends now." Sarah walked with Ronnie back to the nurses surrounding Dr. Holland and Joshua. Holland was relating all that had taken place with Charlie while the nurses were in shift report. Joshua was watching Sarah work her magic.

She was a miracle in and of herself in Joshua's eyes. She was as natural as any he had seen. No, she was more natural. She might be one of His most wondrous miracles. Joshua thought as he watched and listened to her, "She *was* born to this."

Sarah looked in his direction and smiled. She wondered what it was about Ronnie that made her feel sad. Joshua did not answer the question.

Sarah surprised the nurses when she scooted up onto the nursing station desk, swinging her feet back and forth as if she were taking a coffee break with girlfriends. "Now that we have met you all and have fallen completely in love with each and everyone of you, we have something we would like to share with you." Joshua knew what Sarah was up to and it was working so well. The astonishment encountered from the fans the previous evening would not do here and Sarah was doing a fine job of taking the worship and adoration out of them before it began. They wanted the assistance of the nurses once they were underway.

"Sarah, tell our good friends about the wonderful things *your* Father is going to do here today." Sarah turned and looked surprised at Joshua. He had never used that verbiage in that context before. "Yes, I know, Sarah. He is

57

much more comfortable being called Father. I should have told you before now." He smiled. "He believes the other titles are too removed from His true relationship to his children. And since they are, for the most part, titles given Him by mankind, they exhibit some lack of understanding. I agree, don't you?" He stunned her. She was nearly speechless; he had never taught her anything of that nature other than in the most formal of settings and tones. It appeared that this was going to be a remarkable day in more ways than she had expected. She was excited.

Suddenly, Sarah was overcome with feelings of love for a Creator who would think enough of His children to want to be known as their Father. It seemed to fit Him the best of all the titles that referred to Him.

It was time to begin. "Ladies, we are going to walk through your unit this morning and touch every little heart beating on this floor." She smiled. "And as we do, they will be completely cured of any disease that has touched them. They will all live long, healthy, natural lives without further illness beyond that which is normal and expected for them. If you will, we need you to help us by watching the children when we have left each room. They will be full of energy, you know. And for some it will be the first time in their young lives that they have such strength!" The nurses looked at one another with incredulous smiles. Nurses have hearts of gold. Some grasped others' hands and tears were seen on some of their faces. Unlike most, their motives were pure.

"We are going to start at room 800." Sarah decided that now would be a good time to share the rest of the itinerary. Joshua knew that what was about to happen would have dire repercussions, but he hid this knowledge from Sarah. She had a lot of time to learn and some things are best learned by experience. Good and evil, all experience is tutorial in nature and without one, the other can't be truly appreciated for the fullness of the lesson.

Sarah continued, "And then we are going to go to each floor and each department in this hospital and empty the building." And that was exactly what they did with the thirteen nurses and Dr. Larry Holland in tow. As they cleared a unit, even entire floors, they enlisted others to look after children. As the rooms emptied, hallways became playgrounds. Counting the ancillary departments, the emergency room and everything a patient could be treated or seen in or on, over three hundred and fifty children were completely healed in less than two hours and twenty-five minutes.

Larry Holland was seen giving horsey back rides on his hands and knees to a group of children in the main lobby. One nurse was overheard by Sarah to say in a joking tone, "Hell Cathy, that's probably the damnedest miracle I've seen today."

"It wasn't disrespectful," Sarah thought with a smile. "It was funny. Even Father has a sense of humor. Maybe that's an understanding we have lost. Perhaps I can help them remember that."

Sarah, Joshua, and their entourage of nurses, medical staff members, housekeepers, dietary workers, volunteers, and of course the children and their parents were more than a quarter of the way through the hospital before somebody thought to call the suits in administration. They were more nonplused than the rest of the staff. There was no manual in the hospital that told them what to do if they healed everyone. They couldn't very well throw anybody out and didn't know what else to do. So they stood in departments all over the hospital, in the main lobby and hallways, watching their hospital overrun by healthy children of all ages. One vice president was heard to lament, "The place is in the control of inmates."

Toddlers and sixty-year-old physicians were dancing with parents, children, nurses, and each other. It was unlike anything any of them had ever hoped to see in all their days.

The mission was so complete that the suits, who remained in a bureaucratic daze, didn't realize that patients in ambulances, automobiles, on buses, trains, in strollers, and helicopters, and every other imaginary way of transportation, on the way to the hospital, were now also healthy. Sarah and Joshua stood in the main lobby of the hospital near a beautiful fish tank, watching the children play with the adults. Holland, having finished his tour as a horse, now had a child on each knee looking at a picture book with them. The original thirteen nurses were scattered throughout the hospital.

"It is time to go, little one."

"I know, but I wish we didn't have to."

"Yes, I feel the same way at times like this, but you will feel quite weak in a little while and we need to get you home. You have a big day tomorrow and you need your rest. Let's go out and meet Miss Orlando before we leave, shall we?"

Everyone in the lobby had one eye on the two strangers who were seemingly responsible for this joyful pandemonium. As they slid out the front door, an unsuspecting member of the press was standing at the bottom of the traffic ramp leading up to the main entrance of the hospital. The press, who had been kept at a necessary distance from Children's, hadn't yet a clue about the story taking place inside. Nor did they know that the events taking place just yards away would, in comparison, dull last evening's events at Soldier Field.

Pat Orlando from the *Sun Times* had gotten past police ropes with a nurse's coat and a hospital ID badge borrowed from an old college roommate. When she looked up the ramp and saw Sarah and Joshua watching her, she nearly fainted. This was the kind of story a young reporter dreamed of. Joshua beckoned to her with his hand. She began the journey up the ramp with a stumble, then recovered her balance and bolted the rest of the way up, screeching to a halt a few feet from Joshua. Fresh out of breath, she searched for words, but sound wouldn't come. Only thoughts of ineptness bounced around in her mind. "What good is a reporter who can't open her mouth enough to get a question out at a time like this?"

Joshua looked at Sarah and asked her to finish so they could leave. Sarah looked at the young woman with kind eyes and settled Pat's nerves.

"Hello Patricia. You probably know who we are. My friend Joshua thought you could use a scoop! Tomorrow at six o'clock Joshua and I will be in a field just outside the small town of Ferrisburg, Vermont. The place is known as Larmon's Farm. Won't you please come?" Ms. Orlando nodded in the affirmative, she still couldn't talk.

"And, Pat," looking toward a hoard of reporters now running toward them, "please don't invite your colleagues." Sarah smiled. The companions were gone before they could hear the only question Pat Orlando managed to squeak out of her nearly paralyzed throat. "Eastern time?"

9

JACK BOAR sat at the head of the long board room table as his colleagues and employers moved about the room with great animation. The atmosphere was one of elation. They couldn't be blamed for the euphoria that permeated every nook and cranny of the hospital. However, Jack noticed two men in the room who weren't smiling, Kevin Guest, the vice president of finance and Rev. Gerald Dragasick, the director of pastoral care. They had been out of the building when all hell broke loose that morning. They hadn't heard of the events unfolding at the hospital until they started a luncheon sponsored by the Illinois Center for Health Care Systems.

When Kevin and Reverend Dragasick entered the conference center, their peers swarmed around them. They especially wanted to speak with Jerry. "As if we had something to do with that bullshit last night," growled Dragasick. They were both presenters that day, Kevin speaking about Health Maintenance Organizations and Jerry addressing the inherent conflicts of interest and ethical issues of those health delivery systems. They were right in the middle of lunch when Kevin received Jack's call.

"No, don't break off the commitment. You and Jerry go ahead with your presentations, but get your ass over here for a four o'clock special board. There will be several members who do not understand the long range implications here. You need to be thinking of a financial disaster plan or we are both going to be out of work in a few weeks."

Kevin clued Jerry in when he returned to the table. Rev. Dragasick knew there was something wrong when he saw the expression on Kevin's face as he made his way back to the dais. Kevin was a little more than pale. "What's up, Kev?"

"You better grab your ass, Jerry. She has been in the hospital. Jack just called. We don't have a single patient in the entire damn place. And believe this or not, we don't have one in route. And even if we did, the whole place looks like anarchy on damn Sesame Street."

Dragasick leaned in close to Kevin and spoke to him in low tones. They had been good friends since childhood, both of them growing up in the western suburb of Downers Grove. "I'll tell you what, Kev, that little bitch isn't fooling me for one second. She may be pulling the wool over a whole mess of starry-eyed, spiritually challenged assholes, but I've had the draw on this since the shit

61

hit the fan last night. And I am never wrong when it comes to these things. And this little stunt proves my point. This is not, and I repeat, not, the way God works, dammit. This is pure satanical bullshit.

She and that devil she has with her may put Children's out of business, but she sure as shit isn't going to put me out of business. How did the two little bastards get in the door? One of the first things we should do is fire every son of a bitch in the pastoral care department who was there and didn't stop it! Heavenly messengers, my ass. Just look what they've done to us. Remember this Kevin, 'Beware of false prophets, who come to you in sheep's clothing, but inwardly are ravenous wolves.' Matthew 7:15. You can bet your ass, Kev, these two devils are the beginning of something sinister. Don't let yourself get caught up in this circus."

Reverend Dragasick's foul mood had not worn off by the time Jack Boar had decided to call the board meeting to order later that day. "Ladies and gentlemen, I think that most of those who are going to be in attendance at this special board meeting today have arrived. We should get on with the business at hand. Can we all get our coffee or other refreshments and take our seats so we can start?" Boar had been in more than one pediatric tertiary care system since completing his master's in health care administration from Xavier College in Ohio. He had bounced around the country a bit, but he was young, bright, compassionate, and an ass kicker. He was all quality and all bottom line at the same time. His favorite quote came from a Pauline epistle, "I am all things to all men". His adaptability was one of his most valuable assets, and he would need all of his special abilities if he were going to save this hospital. It was in critical condition with a prognosis worse than any patient he had ever seen.

"Minutes from the previous meeting of the board have been waived so we can move on to the only issue on the agenda. That issue, ladies and gentlemen, is the possibility of saving this institution after the events that took place in the hospital today. While we are happy, even delighted for those children involved, our responsibilities go far beyond them. What of those that will need to come next month, next year, two years from now? Will we be here to care for them? That is our dilemma as I see it.

We have approximately one hundred and twenty days of operating cash on hand. Normally, that is more than sufficient to assist us through any significant disaster of a financial nature. We would also have sufficient means of recovery from the risk transference programs of the hospital. However, there is no insurance to provide coverage for the situation that we currently face. There obviously has been nothing of its kind in the history of health care that any of us know about."

Board members began to rustle, and questioning glances could be seen emanating from the very members Boar was concerned about. They would need education. "You and I are the governing board of this institution. It is our job to see that appropriate management is in place to ensure the long term viability of Children's. No doubt you understand the responsibility we have and feel the same way I do about our home here. I meant no disrespect to the wonders of what took place here today. I don't know how or why this happened..." looking down the table at Rev. Dragasick, whose head was lowered and shaking subtly to and fro, "...nor do I pretend to understand who is responsible for these wonders. That's Jerry's job, and I have no intention of meddling in that arena. Let's leave the ecclesiastic issues to him." Boar smiled, Jerry did not. He continued drumming his fingers on the table.

"My management team will be holding a strategy meeting right after this board has concluded. We have knocked around some preliminary ideas and I have asked some council members to present them to you informally this afternoon. I know you will forgive the usual fluff, we have been very busy around here today. Joan, why don't you bring the board up to date on your staffing suggestions?" Joan Amier, vice president of operations and nursing services, took the floor.

"Thank you, Jack. Well, good afternoon everyone. My problem is the easiest. This evening we will be contacting all eight hundred members of the nursing staff, all nurse aids, technical workers, ancillary allied health professionals and three hundred and fifty doctors to tell them the hospital will not be open for business until further notice. We will encourage those employees who have vacation time to begin mandatory vacation utilization. Those who don't have vacation accrual may utilize sick time accrual. The rest will be laid off until further notice. We will try to arrange outplacement services for many of our staff. A skeleton administration staff will be maintained to effect the shutdown. It is fairly simple, cut and dried. We have no patients, we have no revenues coming in. We can't afford to pay people to do nothing. We don't even have referrals. Patients waiting to be transferred and en route to the hospital were also effected by the events of this morning. If anyone has any questions, I will be more than happy to try to answer them for you."

Jennifer Portland from the Chicago *Tribune* had been asked to be a board member by Jack Boar. Jack's mom raised no dummy. It was very advantageous to have the editor of a big city newspaper with millions of readers on the board. She didn't know much about anything but the rag business, but she had been very kind to the hospital since her appointment to a board that paid her forty-five thousand dollars a year for six meetings.

"Joan, dearie." She called everyone dearie. "Why can't we just have our staff admit more patients? Won't that take care of our problem in the long term?"

"Good question, Jen," Joan lied. It was a moronic question. "We have a real catch twenty-two situation here. The doctors can't admit because we don't have enough on-hand cash to fully staff an empty hospital. And we can't staff the hospital because we have no patients!" Jennifer stared at Joan as if she knew exactly what Joan had said, but she didn't have a clue.

"Thank you, dear, this does seem to be one hell of a mess, doesn't it?"

Jerry Dragasick was sitting right next to her. His mom hadn't raised a fool either. He passed her a note. 'Jen, how about dinner and a cocktail after the meeting?' She looked at it for a millisecond and nodded an acceptance. She liked Jerry. He was a good-looking man.

"Kevin, how about a short five minutes or so. Give us a rundown on the direction you will be discussing with the management team after we adjourn?"

Kevin was happy for the children that were the object of something he didn't understand, but he wasn't nearly as adversely passionate about it as his childhood friend was. He just wanted the hospital to be there for the thousands and thousands of future children who would need them. The girl and her friend wouldn't be there for them. He wasn't sure about the details of recovery, but on the way to the hospital he had an uncanny bit of inspiration designed to effect the cash they needed to open the doors.

"Thanks, Jack. I won't take long because, frankly, the management team needs to get their heads together as soon as possible. Thank God we have a mess of volunteers to make the shutdown and reopening as smooth as possible. For the board's information, I have met with Jack for the last hour or so. We *are* going to reopen this hospital. It is not going to be easy and a number of faces will not be with us for a while. But we are going to do our damnedest to pull it off. And if we can't do it, you can be darn sure nobody can.

What we are going to need is cash. Cold hard cash and plenty of it. There are only a few ways to generate the kind of funds we need. Patients, patients, and endowments. We are going to have to call on every individual, corporation, local and federal government branch, and parent of every child who has ever been treated in this facility. Ron Rabine, our VP of fund development, has a regiment of people already working on it as we speak, thus his absence. Ron's personally on his way to Hollywood to see old friends who are connected with our telethon efforts, formally called, if you will excuse the expression, The Children's Miracle Network!"

The room exploded with laughter. Ron hadn't meant to be humorous, it was just there. "I think that's an oversimplification of the plan as best I can articulate it. We also have assets we can liquify if we must, but that could only be characterized as covering funeral expenses. People, Joan hit the nail on the head. Our reserves will be depleted in about two to four months. With the lay-offs we might be able to stretch it a little but we also have outstanding debts that must be paid. Without enormous endowments we are doomed for sure. We are going to need everyone of you and the extremely valuable resources each of you brings to the table."

The room was quiet, grimly quiet. Each of the members looked at others in disbelief. How could have the joy of the morning turned so black, so fast? Clearly it had. Jack Boar took the floor to address the board one last time.

"Well, I think we have done the first thing we are charged with doing and that is making sure the board is aware of any situation that represents a threat to the welfare of the hospital. We have a lot of work to do. I suggest we call our families and tell them we are going to be late, very late. Let's get started."

A determined Jack Boar pushed himself away from the table and rose out of his chair. There wasn't a person in the room who didn't think he could pull this off. Not one, except Jack Boar.

The members strolled out of the deserted lobby into the main drive of the hospital. It looked like one of those roadside altars you see in Buddhist countries. Flowers and candles covered the cement everywhere you looked. Reverend Jerry had Jennifer by the arm as they walked south toward the parking garage which had been taken over by media. The bastards had purchased or leased segments of the multi-leveled garage across the street from the hospital to set up their cameras. *Hard Copy, American Journal, 60 Minutes, 20/20, Dateline,* the airwave trash rags had taken over Jerry's hospital parking lot, or at least they were holding it captive in the glare of their umbrella-backed lighting equipment. Held captive by people Jerry disliked the most, phoney people with phoney tans, teeth, and breasts. They disgusted him.

Sarah was home well before the board meeting. Her parents waited on a tired, hungry girl as Joshua stood watching over her. She felt good about the events of the morning. Mom and Dad were excitedly asking questions. Chicky sat at the kitchen table, saying profound words like, *Sheeeeit.* He forgot Josh's presence every once in a while and his father would remind him with a stern look. He had been warned up to the limit, but Kent felt the circumstances were so unusual, so incredible that even he had used a few of those expletives himself. He cut Chicky a little extra slack.

Yes, Sarah thought, it had been a wonderful day. The looks on the faces of all those parents and nurses. It has been a wonderful day. And wasn't that Charlie such a cute little guy? She smiled to herself. She learned much from Joshua this day and there was so much more to learn. But the first new thing Sarah would learn in the morning would be taught by the Chicago *Tribune*.

10

WEDNESDAY morning Sarah was rudely greeted by early morning television news that picked up on the desperate financial plight of Children's Memorial Hospital in Chicago. The slant was inspired by the spin of the Chicago *Tribune*'s front page headlines: *Devil or Angel?*. The front page story lauded the healings that had taken place, but questioned the wisdom behind the shortsighted event. "Is this a manifestation of God or is it a deception of the lower world, or neither? If from a superior being, could the current long range implications be of no concern? Was this a cruel hoax of some kind perpetrated with some kind of mass hysteria?" And of course there were the usual alien theories that had thousands of otherwise reasonably intelligent people heading off to every mountain, dale, and lake with more than two syllables in its name. The story was less than kind to Sarah and Joshua as it addressed the financial devastation now being suffered by the hospital. It delved into the larger question of treatment for patients who would now be without a facility to treat them, should the hospital fail. And its imminent demise was just what was being proposed by one *anonymous member* of the board of directors.

"You can bet your sweet ass and that beautiful mole on it, my dear, that our hospital is in one hell of a financial bind. And if *we* don't do something about it, I'm gonna be giving sermons in some one cow town in Wisconsin and your pretty little butt will be out a forty-five thousand dollars a year stipend. We won't need you as a board member if there is no hospital. Think about it. Pass me my drink and a cigarette, will you, sweetheart?"

Sarah was rattled when she realized the seemingly disastrous situation she and Joshua had left behind them. She called for him the instant she tore herself away from the first news story. She was sitting in the living room with her parents while her father tried to make sense of the whole thing. How could the media diminish what was obviously so good? He had to concede to some of the issues raised, though. There were a crapload of people out there without jobs, a hospital in one hell of a financial mess, and what were future patients going to do?

"Good morning, Sarah. You slept well?" Joshua was beside her the instant she thought of him.

"Josh, what's going on? They're mad at us. After all that we did, they are angry with us. I thought what we were doing was good. It was good, good for the children, and good for the people. Wasn't it, Josh?"

"What do you think, little one? Was it good or no?"

Sarah thought for a while before answering. Joshua usually asked her to tell her parents what he was communicating to her. He could have easily let them listen to his thoughts, but he wanted them to get used to addressing Sarah. It was the appropriate thing to do.

"It was the right thing to do, Josh."

"Why was it the right thing to do, Sarah?"

"It was right because Father asked us to do it. And He never asks anyone to do anything that is wrong. So I don't know the answer to the hospital's problem, but what we did was right. I felt it then and I feel it now. And somehow the hospital will make it through this, won't they?"

"Yes, Sarah, it's a little thing called faith. Most have lost it in this generation. The people who run the hospital have so immersed themselves in the economics of the situation there that they have taken no time to answer the question the paper raises. "Wouldn't a providential hand recognize the long range implications?" The answer is so obvious. They lack a commodity so much more necessary than currency, Sarah. They lack faith. As you know, we are here to restore it. Yes, they will have some struggles along the way, but they will make it."

Joshua was proud of her answer. The financial crisis at Children's would last no more than one month. They were about to receive an endowment of two hundred and thirty million dollars from an anonymous real estate developer and a major insurance company. The real estate professional had been a patient in Children's nearly thirty years earlier. The insurance company spin doctors wanted the publicity, but what really made them step forward was the actuarial projections of cost to the company if tertiary care was not adequate in the Chicago market place. The spin doctors would get the headlines they wanted, except where it counted the most.

At six o'clock that evening Sarah and Joshua met with a numbed Patricia Orlando who was accompanied by a staff photographer. When she was approached by the press outside of Children's shortly after Sarah and Joshua had vanished, she nearly told them the truth of the conversation that had taken place. When her senior editor saw her being interviewed on the special edition of the five o'clock news he could have kissed her. It took her almost an hour to get away from her colleagues and into a cab where she could return to the paper. A phone call from the cab to disclose the scoop secured a private charter, the photographer, and an unlimited expense account. She couldn't help but laugh to herself. "Why do we have to be meeting in Vermont, couldn't they have picked Paris?"

During the subsequent interview that took place, Sarah disclosed everything that she and Joshua were about. Pat was told the story encompassing the young years of Sarah's life up to the instant before they entered the stadium on Monday night. She told Pat everything except Dr. Boright's unusual and unacceptable way of conducting a physical. When the interview was concluded, Pat Orlando was on the brink of being one of the most famous young journalists in history.

"Goodbye, Patricia, we will look forward to reading your story. If you need me for any reason, call my parents. And be sure you don't give out that phone number. Not even to your editors." She smiled at Patricia, leaned forward and kissed her on the cheek. The camera man stood by trying to remain in the background, a simple recorder of events as he had been trained to be. Never interfere with the event, just record it. Sarah turned to him. "Come here, Sam."

He balked at first, but slowly laid down his camera equipment and came close to her. She reached out her arms and embraced him. As he drew near, she whispered in his ear. "This is too important to just be a witness, Sam. Your brother Tim is just fine. He said to say hello and to stop eating so much pizza!" She planted a small kiss on his cheek, then held him at arm's length so she could see into his eyes. Yes, he was a good man. The brother, Tim, was lost in Viet Nam. A wonderful older brother. And Sam loved him dearly. Sam also loved Home Run Inn Pizza more than any food on earth.

He smiled back at her, leaned forward and whispered, "Thank you, Sarah, God bless you. Thank you." There were tears in the big man's eyes.

Sarah turned to Joshua and said, "We have to leave now. I want to go to Cambridge Hospital to see Doctor Boright, he's dying."

Four weeks later, in an exclusive resort less than two hours northwest of London, an unusual assortment of men and women began to assemble. Eleanor Webster McDonald had been appointed Chair of the ad-hoc commission codenamed "Bountiful". She hailed from Boston, and was a cousin to the President of the United States and a bright woman. Webster was her maiden name, which she had adamantly refused to give up upon marriage. And yes, she was a direct descendant of *the* Websters, as in Daniel and Dictionary and Delia. She was a Harvard educated physician by training, but hadn't practiced medicine in years. She was employed by the Department of Defense as the senior research scientist, specializing in biological warfare. She was one ruthless, calculating bitch according to her subordinates, and the most wonderful woman God ever put on this earth according to her superiors. Of course they couldn't suck up enough to her because of her relation to the President. She was only thirty-five years old and enjoying her vicarious power.

When the NSA documents on the events in Chicago reached the President's office, he called on her. She was one of the brightest, most level-headed people he knew. He had wanted her to be Surgeon General, but they both knew she could not stand the test of a congressional grilling, considering her background and present occupation. She had an analytical mind and he could trust her.

A few miles away in Manchester, England, Sir John Crowther, current Minister of Finance for Great Britain, former Falklands war pilot/hero, royal blood lines, member of the Union League Commission, and the most corrupt son of a bitch that ever set foot in Parliament, was sipping brandy in a pub and enjoying local company. He was a gentlemen's gentleman, most highly thought of by his peers, who he managed to buffalo for over a decade now. His father and mother were "on the other side" and Johnny had poured through their vast holdings like honey on a hot rock. He spent more than he made and thus fell victim to *Corrumpere Pecunia* and was thus mockingly known among his closest family members as Prince Venalis. Part of Sir John's dark side was his weakness for loose women and the kinky sex clubs of Amsterdam where he spent much free time and tons of money.

As Sir John entered his limousine, Vice Admiral Jorge Roberto Vasquez arrived in Glasgow. He would be picked up by private helicopter and taken to The Samling at Dovenest where he would join the rest of Bountiful. The Vice Admiral represented the interest of South American countries. He was a longtime political insider of the President of Argentina. Vice Admiral Vasquez was appointed to his position and while he was the fourth highest ranking naval officer in his country, he had been to sea only twice. Both times he had encountered violent sea sickness and was unable to leave his quarters. The official word was that the Vice Admiral had suffered a mild heart attack, but word quickly spread through the ship when the attending medical officer failed to conceal his order for Dramamine along with the cardiac medicines which were ultimately dumped down the toilet.

The Vice Admiral did have special talents and connections, though. Most of his friends and business associates were heavily involved with supplying the world its recreational drugs. These men and women also had vast resources at their disposal. At the moment they were very concerned about the future of their business. When the men who lost Ronnie Lipinski as a client reported the etiology of her sudden cure to their street bosses, it did not take long for the word to travel from the north side hospital parking lot to Buenos Aires. The news stunned the drug lords.

Located on beautiful lake Windermere, The Samling was considered one of the most beautiful, discreet meeting places in the world. It was small by some standards, but used by a wide variety of the world's most influential business people for corporate retreats. Unlike any government location, there would be no press to invade the commission's privacy, and they needed absolute secrecy. Sitting on sixty-seven acres of meadows and woodlands, it had been easy to set security forces around the premises. The entire place had been swept for listening devices prior to any arrivals and was scheduled by NSA agents for debugging every sixteen hours.

There were twelve comfortable guest rooms with every accommodation a business man or woman could desire. Twelve conference room chairs looked through a large glass window out onto Lake Windermere. The view was breathtaking. The Samling sported the most sophisticated electronic and video-conferencing equipment in all Europe. And the owners were paid triple the going rate to find other accommodations for previously booked guests and to fit Bountiful into their schedule. Government fire inspectors also helped The Samling's management make the correct decision.

All of the twelve participants who had been selected for the commission traveled around the world with a variety of assumed names and passports before heading to The Samling. As Crowther and Vasquez left for The Samling from their separate destinations, Hone Heke, a two hundred sixty pound Samoan, sat quietly in the bar of the Thai Pan Pacific Hotel in Bangkok waiting for a phone call. He bore the name of a legendary Samoan Chief as if it were his own. His real name had been lost in a hundred shuffles and scams. Both the Mossad and the CIA had used him on more than one occasion. His specialty was assassination. Explosives were his love and preference.

By noon the following day the last of the Bountiful members were assembled in the conference room of The Samling. The only item on the agenda and the sole reason for the creation of the commission was Sarah Ferunder and her companion. Gathered around the table were some of Sarah's soon-to-be worst enemies. People with multiple interests representing multiple interests. Economies, military, industry, organized crime, drug cartels, entertainment/fashion, all were represented to one degree or another. All agreed that whoever this girl and her companion were, wherever she came from and whatever her ultimate purpose was, it was evident that what had happened to the hospital in Chicago was just a microcosm of the hell that would break loose,

71

globally, if she were not stopped. And the reason this group had assembled was to see to it that she was.

Each President of the United States of America is sworn to preserve and protect the Constitution of his country. However, his duties reach beyond the normal external military threats to the sanctity of the Union. The President, by virtue of his powers, exerts a decisive influence on the economic life of the United States and thus the world. The economy can be influenced through a single stroke of his pen. His duty to protect the country extends to those forces that would throw his nation into economic chaos just as plainly as any military threat.

When the NSA/CIA reports on the events that took place in Chicago reached the President's desk, he immediately called a cabinet meeting. The results of that meeting were now unfolding in the small wooded resort in England. While the commission was headed by the President's cousin, she would never implicate him nor would any of the members pose any threat to their respective superiors. They had all been targeted for assassination at the successful completion of their mission. The plotters insured that bodies would vanish altogether. A commission member's time was as limited as that of the little girl from Vermont.

The odd assortment of men and women sitting around the luxurious conference room table eyeballed one another with a mixture of curiosity and distrust. Just as Eleanor McDonald decided to call the meeting to order, she noticed a short black Mercedes limousine moving quietly around the lake and up the front drive. The vehicle went unnoticed by the others in the room. "He's here, thank God," she thought. The instant the limo pulled to a halt outside the main door, security men surrounded it. A handsome man dressed in black, wearing a large brimmed hat that covered most of his face, moved confidently into the building. He was escorted to a luxurious suite reserved only for the use of heads of state.

Settling into a large leather chair, he tossed his hat onto a nearby couch and allowed himself the luxury of a glass of wine. Only two people on the commission would ever know the Stranger. None of the others would ever meet him. Once Eleanor was advised that the Stranger was in house, she called the meeting to order.

"Gentlemen, good morning. Thank you all for coming. My superiors sincerely appreciate your attendance and the cooperation of the interests you represent. Each and every one of you bring a unique perspective to this table vis a vis the problem that we have before us. We all know why we are here. We have an enormous, even awful, burden placed upon our shoulders. While each of us may be coming at this issue from different points of view, we share a common concern and, I presume, a common goal.

We have a collective responsibility to preserve the stability of the world's economy, culture, class and power structures just as they have been for hundreds, and in some cases, thousands of years. For some of you it will mean the preservation of entire societies that are now being threatened by something we don't quite understand. The mere fact that we do not understand the threat does not mean that we should not meet it head-on and eliminate it." Looking down the table at Sir Johnny, she acknowledged his desire to speak.

"Mrs. McDonald."

"Eleanor please, John. We are going be spending considerable time together so I think those of us who are comfortable with first names should use them."

Sir John Crowther sat straight in his chair and looked around the table at the collection of misfits the Prime Minister had forced him to associate with. He cleared his throat.

" As I was about to say, Mrs. McDonald." He wasn't going to let this miserable colonist bitch open this room of thugs to informality with a member of the British royalty. He thought, "Americans, no bloody manners any of them. They enjoy eating food with the same fingers they pick their noses!" They disgusted him.

"I think it is important to direct our concerns to the main issue here and that is as follows. If what happened to that little infirmary in Chicago repeats itself on a global scale, everyone in this room will be dealing with anarchy in a little less than three months time, according to my people. The only thing this group has to decide is how we eliminate the woman. Without her I feel fairly confident that her companion will also vanish. There needs to be little discussion about other alternate courses of action as far as I am concerned."

"Well, John." Eleanor McDonald ignored his demand for formality. She thought to herself, "We kicked your asses once, you damn limey, and I will personally kick your crooked bony ass all the way back to Amsterdam before I let you take control of any meeting I'm running."

"I appreciate your input, but this is a commission of twelve especially selected individuals, all of whom have come a long way and should be heard. It may be very well that your position is the correct one, but *we* will decide that as a group. I want to emphasize how important it is that we achieve consensus on any plan of action we decide upon. We must be in this together to succeed and survive as a group.

One other thing. There must be no possibility that word of this group's existence or its mission ever gets out. There will be zero tolerance of leaks here." Eleanor gazed around the table slowly, looking each member squarely in the eye before her eyes settled once again on Crowther. She looked at him with slowly narrowing eyes. "So if some whore in Amsterdam starts a vicious rumor she heard from one of her drunken patrons, his testicles will be hanging from the Tower of London before the sun sets that day." She cut him. Crowther sat still and bled quietly, like a school boy who had just been caught with his hands under his desk in a health education class.

"Now let's see what we know about this little girl and her friend and what we don't." Her secretary began passing shiny black folders with the word "Bountiful" around the table. It contained dossiers on everyone Sarah and Joshua had been in contact with since the Monday night Children's Miracle. There were dossiers on her parents and brother.

"After we have had time for dinner, I would like to reconvene the meeting and discuss your ideas. I would invite the group to discuss regional, individual and personal concerns to the extent we all feel comfortable with one another." There wasn't anyone in the room that felt comfortable with the other. They all had their own dossiers on each other. Vasquez detested Crowther. He smiled at the thought of a man who would have to pay for female companionship. "No wonder," he thought, "that we Argentineans hate these lily white bastards the way we do. They can't even seduce a woman with class. They are undeserving of respect."

Down the hall the Stranger looked on with his own dossiers in his lap. His people supplied them. And they were more comprehensive than any Bountiful or its sponsors could think of producing. As the dark figure sat in the quiet room, a newspaper article folded neatly and placed in his lap stared up at him. The Chicago *Sun Times* article written by Patricia Orlando was a pure joy to most who read it. To the man in the dark room it meant war. This little girl had to die and he was there to make sure the commission reached no other possible alternative. And when they had executed their plan, he was going to make sure they were handsomely rewarded, three hundred and sixty million dollars, American, split twelve ways. They would all have the traitor's share.

Three thousand one hundred and sixty-two miles away, Sarah and Joshua sat under a tree, listening to young African children sing. It was a month into Bountiful's commission. The scenery and the children were beautiful, but the meeting taking place at The Samling and the things that were being proposed concerned Sarah. Joshua knew she feared for her family and the people around her, but there was little he could do other than to comfort and reassure her at this point.

"Sarah, don't be afraid. Andani and Sun Ce are watching the follies near London. Neither you or your family is any danger. The one we are to wait for is far away from England. And we will not have to deal with him for quite some time. Enjoy the children and then we will be on our way to Accra."

"I want to see the animals before we go." Her countenance brightened.

"Yes, little one." Josh smiled. He loved watching her with the children. She was such a natural. She never ceased to amaze him. "Ask the children to come with us. We will show them just how tame the lion can be," Joshua said.

"Yes, that's a great idea!" Sarah took a young Moshi-Dagamban girl by the hand and led her with the other tribal children out of the shade of the tree into the dry heat of nearby Ghanaian grasslands.

When Sarah and Joshua first appeared, the elders looked on as the women shrank back from the people who came from the sky. Sarah's golden hair and long white robe was majestical in itself to these beautiful people, but Joshua's presence held them in total awe. The village children ran out to meet them the instant they heard Sarah's invitation. Surrounded by the children she reached out her hands to touch them; those who were afflicted with the minor diseases of the village were made well. There were no serious illnesses present among the little ones, and she was happy for that.

The little village seemed to reflect what Ghana represented on a larger scale. It was a nation that, compared to many of its neighbors, was doing relatively well. It had a troubled past, one of horrid slavery, revolution and struggle. But the young country was growing and there were many noble spirits here. Many who loved mother earth. And yet by worldly standards the country was poor. Only one in nearly four people owned a radio and only one in seventy-six owned a television. There were thirty-two thousand kilometers of road in the country of which only six thousand kilometers were paved. And only two airports boasted a permanent surface. But the people of Ghana gave nothing away when it came to nobility of spirit. Sarah had chosen this country to illustrate to the rest of the world the nature of true riches.

After singing and playing with the children Sarah began a walk into the open grassland with them. The adults followed closely behind. Interestingly, they were not as much afraid of Sarah and Joshua as they were respectful. They had refreshing thoughts, Joshua noted. They had asked for nothing.

Sarah and her brood walked half a mile into the tropical heat. She noticed that it did not seem to bother her as much as she thought it might, being from New England. It was one hundred and ten degrees in the sun. Sarah guided the children to a lone tree and sat down. When they sat near her, she asked them to sing for her. When they could not agree on a song, one of the village women stepped forward, smiling at Sarah. Moving cautiously around Joshua, she spoke softly to the children. Moments later Sarah sat in the shade of the tree, listening to the sound of the sweet children. She would always remember their eyes and their smiles, she thought. "How little they have of material comforts, yet how happy they are."

When they were through singing, the teacher returned to her place beside her husband. Sarah rose and held, in turn, each of the twenty little ones in an embrace for a moment. She turned to Joshua.

He nodded to each of the children and moved toward them. The tree under which they sat began to bear fruit. Bright red fruit not unlike apples, but Sarah had never seen anything like them. They were not apples, that was all she knew. She was as amazed as the children and the villagers were. Joshua moved closer to the tree and picked one of the large red fruit from its lowest branch. When he had it in his grasp, he turned and walked toward the adults. Some of them began to retreat a little, some began to kneel in submission. Sarah had to assure them he would not harm them. When Joshua came to the Chief of the tribe and his wife, he broke the fruit in two and gave a half to each of them. They smiled and accepted the fruit, although Sarah could tell neither of them really wanted to be the first to try it. Yet they did not want to insult the God who was among them.

"Sarah, tell them we are not gods. Tell them who sent us to them and why we are here. Perhaps if you have some of the fruit it will alleviate their fears. And Sarah, if you are a particularly good girl on this trip and don't get us into trouble like you did in Chicago, maybe I will teach you how to make such delicious fruit grow from a barren tree." A broad smile swept across his face. He enjoyed being with the simple people of this beautiful tribe.

"OK, smarty," she whispered to him. "I'll have some of the fruit, but the next time you do this to me, I'm calling Andani and Sun Ce. By the way, this is close to Andani's home, isn't it?"

Sarah took a fruit from the tree and approached the teacher. Dividing the beautiful red fruit in two, she offered one half to the beautiful tall black woman and bit into the other half. It was sweet. Sweeter and more unusual than anything she had ever eaten. Its consistency was like that of a large strawberry. It was as if someone took a million tropical fruits and mixed them altogether. She was amazed by its refreshing qualities and good taste. When she took a bite from the fruit and smiled, the teacher followed. And when she had done so, the Chief and his wife did the same.

Joshua turned and pointed to the tree, inviting the rest of the village to partake. They moved quietly toward the tree and each picked fruit from the branches. Having done so, they passed the first fruits to their children. Sarah understood this simple gesture as one not of cowardice, but of respect. It was done to show that they trusted Sarah and Joshua with the well-being of the children. And when the children began to eat, Sarah knelt and began to cry. The beauty of the place, the children and the people were overwhelming her. The first fruits ate of the first fruit.

The sun was still high in the hot blue Ghanaian sky, when the small group finished eating. Sarah stood and addressed the Chief. "My brother, this tree shall always bear fruit for your people. From now until the end of time our Father of the heavens will provide fruit where there was none before, so that you might know that He is. And that He loves you and your people. When you come to this tree for nourishment, you will remember Him and take both physical and spiritual nourishment. Teach your children and grandchildren of the day when He sent two of his servants to bring word to you of His love for all of His children. Invite your neighbors to see the tree and its fruit. Share it when moved upon to do so. The fruit must never be exchanged for goods or money. If it is, the tree will die and great dishonor will be brought to your people. Now I have something to show your little ones, do not be afraid. No harm will come to them."

Sarah turned and walked beyond the tree out into the plain. She raised her arms and stood facing in the direction of the great Lake Volta for a short period of time. Much to the alarm of the people, a lioness and her young, something rarely seen during the heat of day, rose out of the distant grass and moved on a trot towards her. And then to the north a herd of zebra began wandering in a southerly direction toward them. Sarah moved out further to meet the animals. More species appeared, elephants, vultures, hyenas; it looked like a jail break from the Brooklyn Zoo. From a distance the villagers watched in awe as the golden haired girl moved among the animals, bending to kiss this one and pet that one as she spoke to them.

The animals lay next to one another, seemingly indifferent to their respective place on the food chain. Several moments passed when Sarah called for the children of the village. The children responded as any group of children would, with glee. But they knew better, these little ones. On any other day these animals would either be dinner or the children would be dinner. But this day was different than any day that had visited their village in two thousand years. They ran to Sarah and the animals with outstretched arms and innocence, the way children are made to.

Joshua stood under the tree, admiring the scene. This was a good world. After thirty minutes he spoke to her.

"Sarah, we must go to Accra tonight. It will be busy there and tomorrow we are to go north to the forest lands. It is time to say goodbye to your friends."

Hearing him from afar in her mind, she looked at him and waved. "I don't want to go yet."

Joshua knew he was going to have his hands full with her. She had only been with him for a month and was already showing signs of independence. He smiled when he looked out at the majestical scene. He loved her. He wished she wouldn't have to experience the sadness of the following morning, but some things he was not to interfere with, and this was to be one of them.

"Stop being silly, little one, it is time to bid farewell to the children and your new friends."

"Alright, I'm coming." Sarah gathered the children to her and with a swoop of her arms the animals dispersed as if they had just awoke from a strange dream and found themselves sleeping on the dinner table. The obvious concern with which they scattered brought cries of joy and laughter from the children and the tribesmen, and women felt the joy in the hearts of the little ones.

Sarah walked toward Joshua. He moved out to meet her. She could see the villagers and their children embracing over his shoulder. Then they left for Accra.

Sarah lay her head down on the pillow in the small little hotel and first realized the toll the heat had taken on her. She was exhausted and thirsty. Just as she was about to drift off to sleep, she heard a familiar voice.

"Sarah, it is I, Andani. I have brought you water and fruit. Eat and drink before you rest so that you will have strength in the morning."

"Oh thank you, sweet Andani. Your home land is so beautiful. We met wonderful people today and played with the children and animals, and Josh made fruit grow on a tree and..."

"Shhhh, be quiet, little one, and get some sleep now. You can tell me all about it in the morning before you go to Bolgatanga. Now sleep and Sun Ce will be here with us in just a few moments. You have had a big day for such a little one." The room went quietly, peacefully dark, giving way to dreams of magical giraffe and yellow alligators.

11

IT was unbearably hot by the time Sarah finished washing in the wooden bowl of water the next morning. Knowing that she and Joshua were to take conventional transportation to Bolgatanga in the north, she dressed in jeans and a t-shirt in the small room. Actually, Josh wanted to go to the northern city instantly so that the time spent with the people there could be maximized. Sarah preferred walking part way and taking a bus the remainder of the journey so that she could see more of the countryside and the rural people. The decision was hers.

In the plaza below her sparsely furnished room a crowd had gathered. Many had walked miles to get a glimpse of the "lady angel". Some began walking the moment Andani spoke on the wind to the great chiefs and medicine men of the tribes of Ghana. When she finished a breakfast bowl of fruit provided by the hotel, she went to the window and opened the shutters. A sea of brown and black faces looked up and greeted her. Children, perched on the shoulders of mothers and fathers so they could see the girl from the sky, waved and shouted to her. Sarah heard individual names in her mind as her eyes moved on them. She called to them in their native tongues with greetings from relatives who had passed away long ago.

This was an unusual land and an unusual people. Sarah knew that Heavenly Father was pleased with them and wanted them to know Him better. Most of the people, if not all their leaders, had been obedient to the law which He had given them. Now the time had come for more law, much more. And Sarah was the messenger selected to deliver it. Early on in her experience she occasionally questioned why she had been selected, but now she knew that the time for that question had passed. She began to wax strong in confidence.

After the initial impact of her appearance at the window, the noise gave way to a low curious murmur. Sarah leaned over the sill, seeking out a bent old woman. She spotted her among the crowd. Leaning on a staff of curious workmanship, swallowed up by the throng of people, she could hardly raise her head for the osteoporosis that had nearly doubled over her spine. Sarah asked if she might come down and visit with her. The matriarch beckoned with a withered hand for Sarah to come to her.

The owner of the small neat hotel housing Sarah respected wishes for privacy and kept the hall outside her modest room and the lobby clear of people.

79

She learned that, as much as she loved being with the people, she needed rest. Often a visit with them drained her. Joshua told her that she would acclimate somewhat to this weakness. But for now she had to make a conscious effort to pace herself. She never mastered the art of moderation when it came to sharing herself, though.

She descended a narrow wooden creaky staircase to the lobby which was a small but neat welcoming room for new guests. Overhead fans, barely turning in the early morning sun, pretended to stir the hot musty air and bring cool thoughts to guests. It was already one hundred degrees and only eight o'clock in the morning. There were beautiful green plants in each of the corners of the small lobby and a clean but well-worn scarlet couch against one wall. Two-year-old magazines graced a faded coffee table placed in front of the couch. Clean white painted walls held photographs of the owner's family, an old map of Accra and pencil drawings of familiar village scenes. An old American Express card sign, peeled half off the main entrance door, was the only evidence of westernization in this hotel, that and the Coca Cola machine, of course. Lying on the floor of the lobby was a handwoven tapestry being used as a welcome carpet. It was the real jewel of the hotel, yet it was faded and worn with time.

The front desk was small, and the giant Ghanaian standing wearily behind it made it appear even smaller than it actually was. His name was Mohammed Azuma. A descendant, it was rumored, of a once great African chief. Few who had heard the family fable believed it, however.

The tapestry that covered much of the small lobby caught Sarah's attention. She had been too tired to notice it the day before. It had been made many years ago by the old woman sitting in wait for Sarah. Nearly fifty years of dust and soil, ground in by foot traffic, faded dyes that painted pictures of the wild animals, the grasslands and scenes of Accra. It must have been a beautiful piece before age, climate and human traffic wore it down to a glimmer of its former self. She looked up from the carpet to see the giant staring at it also. The old woman had been commissioned by his grandfather many years ago. He watched Sarah cautiously.

"I don't blame them. If this hadn't happened to me, I would be gawking right along with them," she thought to herself.

Sarah's eyes rose from the carpet and met his. She smiled at him, catching small faces over his shoulder peering through the doorway and windows. She began her trek across the carpet to the desk. She smiled to herself and secretly thought, "Fruit on a tree? . . . Piece of cake, Josh."

80

As Sarah stepped onto the carpet and made her way toward the desk, each step, each touch of her foot, brought restoration to the tapestry. Color and form began taking place where faded dye was only seconds before. *Oohs* and *ahhhhs* could be heard from the small portion of the crowd who could see. Azuma's eyes, now big as half dollars, remained glued to the miracle on the floor. It was a small thing, but it had been in his family forever, or so it seemed. By the time Sarah had completed her short journey to the front desk, the carpet looked as if it had just been created. Tears slowly ran from Azuma's eyes onto chiseled ebony cheeks. They were lost in the perspiration brought on by the morning's heat.

Standing at attention, he did his best to compose himself. "Good morning, Miss, I hope that you rested well. I picked the fruit for your breakfast basket myself this morning. Is there anything else I can do for you, Miss? Would you like some coffee?"

"Oh no, thank you," Sarah said. Azuma was very nervous that he might say something inappropriate and offend her.

"I rested so well. Your hotel is just lovely. And the fruit was the very best fruit I have ever had in my life." He beamed with pride. "And I hope my staying with you has not caused your business harm." She smiled, knowing he had never seen such crowds around his hotel in all his life, and that he owned the only soft drink and ice cream stand in this part of the city.

"Oh no, Miss! It has been a very large honor for me to have you stay at the hotel here with my family."

"Would you prefer I speak to you in Ghanaian?" she asked. "I can, you know."

"Oh, it is unnecessary, besides, you give me the opportunity to practice my poor English." He secretly wished that his ancestors could see him speaking with the angel from the sky. They would be so proud of him. Sarah heard his good-hearted thoughts. She felt a very close bond with this wonderful man.

"I want to meet all of your family tonight. I have a special gift for you. Please invite your friends as well; we will eat with them when I return from Bolgatanga if it pleases you?"

"Oh yes, Miss, very much so. Thank you."

"Now I must go out and see the people for a little while. But before I do I want to touch your face for a moment. May I? Is that permissible?"

"Yes Miss, you may." His nervousness escalated another notch as he bowed his large frame down to her so his face could be easily reached. Sarah couldn't help but smile that such a big man would be so nervous around her. She was still just a little girl from Vermont. She reached out her right hand and placed it on the bearded left cheek of the big man. She moved it up to his temple, which was warm and moist with perspiration. Noticing the difference between their flesh tones, she delighted in the beauty the two contrasting colors produced alongside one another. "This is what makes us special, Mohammed. It's so perfect, so absolutely beautiful. Why has the world missed this beauty? Our *differences* are what makes us beautiful but, unfortunately, at times, also so vicious."

She looked into his eyes. He was indeed a giant of a man, but in her presence he was just a little boy. She reached her left hand to his right cheek, holding him for a moment, smiling into kind eyes. "May I bring a friend to your supper table tonight?"

"Oh yes, Miss, you bring whomever you wish." He thought how exciting it would be to have Joshua in his home. But it wasn't Joshua who would stun the giant and his family.

"It wasn't an accident that I chose your home, Mr. Azuma," she thought.

Soon she withdrew her delicate hands, but as she removed them, she tenderly wiped tears from both sides of his face with her thumbs. His head lowered once again out of respect for Sarah, and for his ancestors. She took both of his mammoth hands in hers. "Now he will not have the heart attack that would have ended his mortal probation this afternoon," she whispered to unseen friends.

She turned and moved toward the doorway.

"Thank you, Miss, for fixing my carpet," he smiled at her.

"Was the least I could do!" she smiled back at him as she continued on toward the doorway. Joshua, Andani and Sun Ce watched from a distance and smiled.

When she reached the door, she turned back to him and stuck out her hand. "Come and join me with the people." She beckoned to Mohammed who had now composed himself. He followed her until she reached the door where the crowd parted before them.

She moved into the throng of people, touching this one and that, speaking French, Mole-Dagbani, Dagaare, Frafra, and Gurenne, tribal languages indigenous to the region. The people were polite and the children excited. As she pressed on, she came upon the elderly matriarch bent with age, but not broken in spirit. Her face was wrinkled and weathered like leather, but it retained its beautifully brown earth color. She was a slight woman, but she had a quality of strength about her. Her clothes were clean, but well-worn and faded with the sun. What had been bright reds, yellows, and greens were now more quiet shades, but she did not care about faded colors. She had more important things on her mind. Her hair was a soft, curly grey with remnants of the black that whispered of her beauty when she was a young girl. Her eyes were tired. Brown eyes with a twinkle in them that mocked age. To that spark of life that had carried her through young womanhood, wisdom had been added. All in all Sarah thought she looked as if she were an extension of mother earth herself. She was magnificently beautiful.

Sarah was drawn to this spirit. She made a path directly toward her as she had promised from the window. The crowd opened as she moved in the old woman's direction. Sarah's eyes remained fixed on her. When she reached her, the matriarch sat down upon the ground, placing her head beneath Sarah's. Another act of respect and trust.

"May I sit by you, sister?" Sarah's first words in Dagbani inspired a near toothless smile from the elderly woman.

"Yes. That would please me so, little one." Patting the ground at her side, "Please, do sit with me." It pleased Sarah to hear the phrase that only Joshua and the sentinels used. She sat in the dust, facing the old woman.

"I swear, little one, the sun is starting to wear this old woman down an hour earlier each day now. Unlike these babies..." She looked at the faces crowding around the two women. "I am not afraid to ask the question nor to hear the answer, should you be so kind as to share it with me. In fact, I welcome what they, in their youthful ignorance, fear." She chuckled.

Sarah knew her question and the answer well before the woman asked. She knew it even before she left the hotel. She would give the woman a chance to speak, to ask the question, to exercise her faith. And a chance to have the respect that would come as a result of having had this conversation with Sarah.

"I am an old woman and, as you can see, I am well enough for an old woman. But that is not good enough for me. I am young in heart and spirit. And my mind is sharp like a new spear, but this old cage restrains my spirit, holds me back. I have many children and they have many children. The cycle is complete and I wish so much to join my ancestors, and my husband. I want to walk the plains among them without hindrance. I cannot walk so far without this old cane, you know? I miss my friends and have none left here. You and I both know my ancestors are not far from us," she whispered. "So what news have you for this old woman, Sarah?"

Sarah took hold of the woman's hands and held onto them. They were rough, calloused with labors of the fields, cracked and scarred, but there was a soft gentleness about them that held Sarah's interest. She traced the lines with her eyes, wondering what journeys had caused them, what loves they had caressed, who they had comforted, how many meals they had lovingly prepared.

83

She was unaware as one of the old woman's hands made its way to the side of her face. Gentle fingers brushed hair away from her cheek where it had stuck, moist from the heat. Two sisters born a million miles apart, sitting in the dust under the savagely hot Ghanaian sun sharing eternity together. Many in attendance understood the lesson behind the scene.

"It is working," Joshua thought as he watched the two women and scanned the crowd with approving eyes. "It is working."

Sarah sat for a few more moments, enjoying the woman's touch while she listened to the singsong voice of Africa in the air. Listening to a grandmotherly song, softly she leaned her head forward and rested it on the shoulder and chest of the woman she came to comfort. The crowd gave them room. Tears streamed down the faces of men and women as they realized the essence of this vision. All the museums in the world never held a piece of work as precious or beautiful to gaze upon as this sight. A young white girl from faraway America nestled into the arms of a loving ebony sister.

They sat together for nearly twenty minutes, the woman continuing to hold Sarah as they exchanged smiles and tears. And when it was time to move on, Sarah raised to her knees in front of the matriarch. "Woman, rest this night and close your eyes upon your great homeland, Africa. Your sojourn has been long and you have earned the love of many children and neighbors. It is time to rest. You will walk with your ancestors before the morning sun rises." Sarah kissed her forehead. She and the old woman rose together, embraced and then the bent figure moved into the crowd, feeling her way with a bent cane, a peaceful smile on her face. Just before she moved outside of earshot, she turned to Sarah.

"I will be near you in Kalispell, child. Don't you worry now."

Sarah smiled at her and turned to move among the people, when she heard the voice of an announcer coming from the speakers of a small radio sitting on the table of the soft drink stand owned by the manager. She cried out in anguish as the news violated her ears. She turned toward the hotel, looking for Joshua. An unearthly silence spread over the crowd when Sarah cried out. Joshua appeared in her window of the hotel just fifty feet from her. He held out his arms and beckoned to her. She rose to meet him, a puzzled horrified look on her face. Andani and Sun Ce were in the room with Joshua. She knew from the look on their faces that she would not get the news that she wanted. She prayed that what she had heard was a mistake, but it wasn't.

A hundred miles away in the middle of the night, as the local chief of the Moshi-Dagamba slept close to his wife and children, mercenaries had crept silently out of the African mahogany forest, moving slowly toward his hut.

They carried in their arms the best weapons of destruction money could buy. The first mortar shell hit the village as Sarah lay quietly asleep in her hotel room. The shells fell like tropical rain on the tiny village. Huts were blown to pieces as metal shards ravaged small soft bodies and their parents. Every soul in the village visited by Sarah and Joshua the previous afternoon was slaughtered with the exception of one child.

The lives of the villagers had been taken in exchange for a simple commodity: wood. African mahogany, to be exact. The village chief had filed a complaint with the local magistrate, asking that lumber smuggling in the area be curtailed. His petition was ignored by the authorities, and by very important men sitting around a board room in New York City.

The little girl who had held Sarah's hand on the walk to the "Tree of God's Fruit" sat near the bodies of her little sister and brother, weeping. Her left hand had been severed, but the heat from the round had seared the vessels and bleeding was remarkably controlled. There weren't enough pieces of her parents left for her to realize they had been in the small hut with her. Her mind slowly became occupied by the smell of charred bodies and the sounds of the lions at the perimeter of the village who would soon come calling as was nature's way.

Joshua held Sarah in his arms where she found shelter, but no comfort. She sobbed uncontrollably and begged him to undo the unthinkable crime that had been committed. He did not respond. He just held her in his arms and rocked her while he stared out the window at the dispersing crowd, and at a lovely old woman bent with age, as she made her way toward her home with the bent cane of African mahogany.

Andani stood by with tears in his eyes. He had witnessed many atrocities among the peoples of the African continent in the last four hundred years. Sun Ce controlled a warrior's rage that such a cowardly thing would be done to innocents. He understood the villagers were fine, it was the agony that such a deed left behind that angered him. The devastation for the survivors insulted his sense of mercy. The deprivation of a natural life and death for those who had been slaughtered incensed him. But he had been *translated* and knew to put the rage behind him.

Sun Ce loved Joshua, as did Andani. They had been together for hundreds of years now. He understood the majesty of Joshua's spirit. Even as the tragedy of this day was unfolding, Joshua was formulating a tutorial to pass on to the little one. He had no thoughts of revenge in him, instead he lamented the degeneration of the human spirit that allowed men to participate in such a crime. His heart ached for them. But he also knew that the murderers were in for a confrontation the likes of which they could not imagine. And Sarah was going to provide it.

She stayed in his arms for a long time before Joshua answered her question, why? He wanted her to have her opportunity for grief. This would be the beginning of one of Sarah's most important growth opportunities, one of her more significant tutorials. He was needed to see how she would handle it. She would do fine, he was sure. "Sarah, come sit on the bed for a moment, sweetheart, and listen to Andani. This is his home, his people."

Andani spoke to her softly. The tones of compassion and love were nearly unbearable for her. "It is also difficult for me, little one, so do not be ashamed of your tears, they separate us from all other species here on this earth. No other animal sheds them, did you know that? Yes, they are able to mourn, but none has the ability to shed a single tear. It is a gift from Father.

It is difficult for a former king to see his posterity spill the blood of brothers and sisters. Many of those slaughtered in the village were my own blood, but so were many of those who murdered them. So I ask you, little one, for whom should I feel more concern: the murdered or the murderers? My heart seems equally divided among them. Yet I know that in the eternal scheme of things the offended are much better off than the offenders. And that is my dilemma. One group lost to earthly life and the other to eternal life.

And for what are the offenders lost? Wood! The lumber companies have plundered this land prior to the birth of the grandparents of these murderers. They steal the African mahogany from the forest, buying or eliminating those who oppose them. They rape our land of our trees and our people of their souls. Which is the greater crime? The pitting of brother against brother, or the theft of spirit? When you mourn, little one, mourn for all, including the men whose souls were bought with wood. And as difficult as it is, mourn for the men who bought those souls."

Two large tears which had welled up in the King's eyes spilled over and fell like great waterfalls down his cheeks. Sarah's head bowed and leaned against Joshua's chest. Tears streamed down her face.

Joshua's eyes remained fixed on the land beyond the window, waiting for Sarah to tell him what she wanted done about this. He waited patiently for two hours, knowing he would do whatever she asked. After time had passed, Sarah gained composure and spoke to her companion.

"Joshua, I want Andani and Sun Ce to go to the village right away. I want them to clear everyone out of it. Nobody is to reenter the village until you and I get there. I want to see it. I want Sun Ce to deliver a message for me. I want him to speak to the leader responsible for these murders. I want to speak with

86

him and the rest of the murderers when we get there. And I want Sun Ce to tell them this, 'There is no place to hide from me.' Tell them that. Do you understand me, Sun Ce?" The tears that rolled down her face were inspired now more by anger than grief.

"Yes, little one, we will go and deliver the message as you wish."

Inwardly Joshua thought, "She was born to this."

That very afternoon Joshua and Sarah walked side by side in full white robes toward the small village. Each step of the way, additional people joined in behind them. The army wasn't showing itself, fearing that they might be mistaken for the mercenaries. Sarah knew that the village was safe from disturbance. It had been cleared and no one would be permitted to reenter. When Andani and Sun Ce appeared at the village, they did so with power and authority. Those who were in the village fled as if the devil himself had just appeared and none dared to approach. Witnessing the arrival of the two sentinels, a multitude gathered on the outskirts of the village.

The murderers hid in the jungle from which they had been vomited the night before. They dared not move after Sun Ce delivered Sarah's message. They sat as if frozen to the steamy jungle floor. They feared for their lives and questioned whether the price had been worth the risk. There was no genuine remorse among these men. Their only regret was one associated with getting caught. As she walked dusty dirt roads on the way back to the village, Sarah took note of the lack of conscience.

She walked barefoot for five days in the searing heat of the equator. Her feet were not made for such abuse, but all efforts at persuasion from Joshua or the people met with a cold stare. They became bloodied and blistered. She would only permit that they be wrapped in a rough cloth, brought to her in a small village by a little girl. She wept as the girl washed and wrapped her swollen feet. The tears were not born of pain, they were inspired by love.

Watching the scene, Joshua thought, "She's growing up. She's taking charge like we knew she would." She spoke in every village along the way offering comfort, healed the sick, calmed those in need and provided food where necessary. By the time she reached the outskirts of the village on the fifth day, tens of thousands of people had gathered.

Andani could be seen by the crowd standing in the air on one side of the village, a flaming sword held threateningly above his head with two hands. Sun Ce mirrored his image on the other side of the village. They had stood motionless like that for five days now. No one dared to violate the perimeter that had been established by the two sentinels.

When Sarah was still five miles from the village, word spread that she was coming. The entourage that followed her came to a halt when she sat down under a shade tree with Joshua to rest. Pointing to the green forest nearby, she spoke to him for the first time that day. "Joshua, I want to be alone with you for a few minutes if you don't mind." They were gone in a burst of light. It was disconcerting to the people who had walked with them. When they returned, Joshua had confirmation that Sarah was growing into everything expected of her. They started once again for the village where bodies lay rotting in the hot Ghanaian sun. The stench was repulsive. When they drew within sight of the village, Sarah asked Joshua to bring the murderers out of the jungle. And then Sarah began her lone walk past The Tree of God's Fruit.

The tree appeared as barren as a tree that had died a thousand years ago. Not a leaf remained on it, nor was there any fruit. The fruit had been thrown to the ground by the percussions of the bombs and lay rotting like the villagers. The stench swelled in the noses of the multitude, causing great offense, but they did not move. Had it not been for the presence of Sarah and those attending to her, these people would not have taken the risk of coming near this *cursed place.*

Sarah, unaffected by the stench emanating from the village, passed by Andani, disappeared from sight, and entered the village. The crowd's attention turned northward towards Joshua. In the distance he could be seen, returning from the forest. Behind him a long line of men dressed in military style clothing marched single file. At first the crowd thought the men were soldiers sent to keep peace and control. But as they neared, it became apparent that these men were those responsible for the massacre. Suddenly there were jeers, shouts, spitting, and threats of death. The men were terrified; this was neither the time or place to expect mercy, and they had no reason to expect it.

A small child was the first to notice something unusual.

"Look, momma, look at the pretty flowers," she smiled, darting towards The Tree of God's Fruit which suddenly began to sprout green leaves, flowers and fruit before the eyes of the multitude that had gathered. In the distance Sarah could be seen coming out of the village. A group of people also followed single file behind her. It was the villagers.

They who had laid dead for five days were alive again. They were dressed in beautiful native clothing, reflecting the colors of the land in which they lived. The workmanship of the material was unlike anything ever seen by those in attendance. They were clean from their wounds, clean as the day they were born. In their arms they carried their little ones past thousands of deliriously stunned people. Mourning relatives broke away from the rest of the crowds and ran wildly to meet them.

Meanwhile, under the cover of a lone shade tree, two dozen men in military clothing watched in utter disbelief. Some fell to the ground weeping. None had the strength to face what they knew was to be their punishment. They were about to meet the children they had slaughtered . . . slaughtered for twenty-five dollars per man.

In the midst of this most incredible of all scenes ever witnessed by the modern world, the flash of a muzzle from the tree line went undetected. It was directed at Sarah.

12

THE weapon's report turned the heads of those closest to it. The cross hairs of the scope steadily lay between Sarah's breasts, deadly aim taken on her heart, a second shot planned. The first hot lead projectile spiraled toward her, its red hot hollow point waiting to explode once it penetrated soft white skin. The would-be assassin was still holding his breath in anticipation of the second shot when the fire hit him and the tree he was hiding in. The spontaneous combustion was so white hot that those who had turned in the direction of the gunfire shielded their eyes and reflexed away from its brilliance. The round intended for Sarah never made it more than ten feet from the end of the barrel before it melted. Sun Ce had been watching the shooter since he left the airport in Atlanta the previous day. His mission to assassinate Sarah never stood a prayer of success.

The shooter's failure, his doom, was noted by another in the crowd and what he observed made his blood run cold. Where there once stood a mature tree concealing a human being, a small pile of smoldering ash remained as the only testament that either had ever existed.

"Let him go," Joshua spoke to his two companions as they watched the remaining mercenary scurry through the crowd. "He poses no threat and it will be good for those who sent him to know, firsthand, the fate that awaits those who try to harm the little one."

Sarah did not hear the shot, but when the tree burst into flames, her eyes flashed in the direction of Sun Ce. Instantly she knew what had just occurred. It stunned her.

Her concern over the attempt on her life fled on wings of faith as she learned firsthand of the eternal concept that *there must be opposition in all things.*

The villagers remembered nothing about the attack on their village or the destruction of their bodies. Sarah watched as they moved among each other, examining hands, holding faces, kissing their children. Occasionally one of the resurrected would glance toward Sarah to let her know that her mission among them was a success, that they understood what she had brought to them. Many of their countrymen reached out and touched them with an indescribable sense of awe and wonderment. On the Ghanaian plains, old tribal rivalries died that day, slain by faith, hopefully never to be resurrected again.

Sarah felt compassion now for the men who murdered the villagers. As she moved toward them, she couldn't wipe away the thought that they had murdered their own souls as well. It saddened her to the point of tears, yet some of the tears were born of a lingering anger. Sins had been committed against these men, also. She understood that now, but she could do nothing for them or the men in New York City. Both groups were lost, lost for eternity. It was another irrevocable Celestial law.

Bountiful members sat around the expensive mahogany table, listening to the mercenary's eyewitness account of the disaster in Africa.

He explained away his own cowardly failure to execute his half of the assassination plot. But the thought of pulling the Glock's trigger had never even occurred to him. And he had not waited for a closer view of the nonexistent remains of his companion. He had made his way from the scene as quickly as possible. His heart beat hard like a deep majestic African drum. He feared it could be heard, pounding out a confession. Sweat poured down his forehead onto his face as if vital fluids were running away from his brain. His eyes darted furiously about the massive crowd in a look of fiery desperation. He knew that his adversaries were watching him move. It would just be a matter of time before he too burst into a furious fiery end. Survival, that was all he wanted, that was all that occupied his mind. If he could get out of this mess, he was going to return the retainer and wash his hands off this horseshit assignment. He should have never accepted it. Something told him this assignment was a skipper.

Sun Ce stood three thousand one hundred and sixty-one miles away and listened to the coward's report replete with false bravado. He knew that the mercenary had not gleaned anything from the tutorial. They would meet again, soon. Unfortunately, when they did, Sun Ce thought, the man would be a coward still, a coward close to meeting eternity, "and I will make the introduction." Had the coward even thought of drawing his weapon that day in the Ghanaian jungle, Sun Ce would have turned the man to dust.

Sitting at the head of the board room table, Eleanor McDonald was visibly shaken. A glimmer of perspiration sat like dew on her upper lip. She hadn't slept through an entire night since the debacle in Ghana. She was not only concerned about the failure of the mission, but also the thundering pressure that it had brought down upon Bountiful. She had received a very secret ass-chewing from Mr. Cousin. There wasn't a representative in the room who hadn't been dressed down by their respective superiors. But Eleanor wasn't pale as a result of these demands for immediate success. She was frightened to death of the man sitting down the hall in the master control room, listening to the report with growing anger and disapproval.

Bountiful had actually been in existence for only a matter of weeks. What the hell could be expected from her in that short period of time? When the thought crossed her mind, she distinctly heard his voice. "Do it, Eleanor, get it done now or I will get somebody else to do it."

She couldn't conceal the shiver of fear that claimed her entire body, causing her to drop her cup of coffee. Sir John observed the physical toll taking place on the supposed leader of the group. He smiled at her with disdain.

Crowther mistook her concerns about the secret guest for fear of Sarah and her companions. He felt compelled to step in and rescue this operation from the misfits the Prime Minister had forced him to work with. "Madam Chair, may I have the floor?" he asked.

Eleanor dismissed the mercenary with warnings of secrecy and instructions that he would be escorted to debriefing. She turned to Crowther, mentally conceding it was best to let him get on with his rambling snobbery so Bountiful could consider the next best course of action. She despised the Englishman possibly more than anyone in the room, save the Argentinean.

"Well, bloody damn hell, people." His voice was stern and loud, authoritative in its quality for the very first time since the group had met the despicable man. Rising to his feet and slamming his fist on the table, he woke everyone in the room up. "Just how difficult should it be to get this whole mess over with? We are talking about the elimination of a sixteen-year-old baby and a damn ghost. If we don't quit pussyfooting around this little disturbance, this inconvenience, this little snotnosed little shit, we may all find ourselves splattered at the bottom of Dover's finest."

He looked around the room, fixing on the expressions on every member's face. Incredulously, "Oh, bloody hell! Surely there isn't an idiot in this room who doesn't realize that failure means just that?" There were several at the table, including Eleanor McDonald, who hadn't the slightest clue. The Englishman flopped down into his chair in disgust and took out a cigarette. Smoking was agreed upon by the group as violating the majority's right not to smoke. He looked at the black shirt and white collar across from him as he lit up. "Screw you." He had gained everyone's attention and some degree of respect, except for that of the clergyman he had just insulted.

"What we are talking about here, my dear naive friends, is success, or death. It's that damn simple. And our task, it seems to me, notwithstanding our miserable failure the first time out of the gate, *is fairly damn simple!*"

Crowther's increasing use of the expletive, accompanied by an occasional pounding on the table, was instrumental in keeping the attention of the Bountiful members. His leadership began to show itself, removing doubts many at the table had about him. Looking directly at Eleanor McDonald with obvious dislike, he said, "Oh, don't be so indignant, Eleanor. You always knew what end we were here to accomplish. I believe, my dear lady, that it was one of your own damn playwrights who said, 'Assassination is only an extreme form of censorship.' So people, let's start censoring and quiet this witch. It is time to save our own miserable lives and move on. Thank you for the floor, madam Chair." He spat the words disgustedly in Eleanor's direction and slowly sunk down in his seat. He placed his elbows on the arms of the high back leather chair and touched the fingertips of each hand against one another as he purposely fixed his gaze out the window at Lake Windermere. He had secured respect from his colleagues and was now basking in the prestige of it when McDonald made her fatal mistake.

"Surely, John, you are not insinuating that the very authority that created this commission would be responsible for our..." she could hardly bring herself to articulate the concept, "...our elimination?"

Crowther fired a glance at her. "I thought you knew what the hell you were doing here, Eleanor! Get your head out of your ass, woman. You can't be so stupid as to not be aware of our fate if we fail to successfully execute this assignment. Not one of us is ever going to leave here alive if we don't eliminate that damn child, and do it soon." Eleanor didn't realize it, but he had just assumed the leadership of the commission. "What we need here is something extraordinary, something that will get the job done. Something that will level the playing field."

"Well, John, we tried the quick fix. We ran off to the jungles with conventional weaponry and a half-assed plan. We went along with your insistence that we get this done quickly, but it simply didn't work, did it? We got the whole bloody mess stuck right back down our bloody throats. And I'm not sure intimidating the members of this commission is in the best interest of anyone, or of the success of the assignment, for that matter." Because he refused to look in her direction, she stared at the side of his face, trying earnestly to burn a hole in it.

She pounded the table herself, this time rattling glasses and cups. "I'm speaking on behalf of the President of the Damn United States!" She decided she liked his use of the expletive also. "Nobody, and I mean nobody, in this room is in any danger of harm. We have a job to do and I agree that we should get on with it. But, dear Johnny," she made the name whine, "we are *not* going

93

to go off half-cocked again. There is simply no more room in my gullet for failure or the ass-chewing that attends it. Furthermore, I intend to ignore your histrionics for now, but if your lack of civility continues, I will have your pompous ass removed from Bountiful altogether. Don't make the mistake of thinking I can't do just that." She regretted the threat the instant she had said it.

Softening her assault, "We do not need to be placed under false duress. That's all I mean. The real fan hitting shit is quite good enough for all of us, thank you. And I'm sure as I point these things out to you that I speak for the rest of our colleagues around the table as well." She didn't, except for one.

"Oh, one more item I would perhaps point out to you, dear John..." He hated her informality, especially when she drooled it in front of the rest of the commoners. "In the incredibly stunning possibility that you perhaps did not hear the same report the rest of us pleasured in this morning, we are *not* dealing with just any sixteen-year-old little girl with an apparition for a playmate. And if you could get your overinflated arrogant head out of *your own ass*, you might acknowledge that." Her attempt at regaining respect from the group was valiant, but unsuccessful.

Crowther never let his eyes leave the window or Lake Windermere. It pissed her off to no end and he knew it. By the end of the day she would be history. He looked across the table at the dark-skinned Argentinean and smiled to himself, "You're next, you bastard, you're damn next."

The large suite located fifty-seven feet down the hall from the Samling board room was empty except for the Stranger. It was quiet in the room where a large video monitor recorded the activity being filmed by a camera trained on the participants around the large African mahogany table. He killed the sound of Eleanor's voice with a flip of a switch. He had heard enough.

Light from a few small panel lights located on the massive control board combined with the video monitors to cast a blue tint into the room. The technical amenities provided by this sophisticated suite supplied executives with the ability to contact anyone, anywhere, anytime in the world. The Stranger glanced around the room, taking in technology that had been assembled at great cost. He smiled to himself. "How ridiculously crude."

He was a tall man with a medium build. Modestly long black hair matched coal black eyes. His eyes caught people's attention. If you looked closely at them, you could see light yellow streaks in each iris that gave him an unearthly beauty. Although his age appeared to be in the mid-thirties, his exact age was not known, not even by his closest associates of which there were but a handful. Unlike many of the rich and powerful, he employed men and women

94

who did not talk to anyone about their employer. He was extraordinarily handsome.

He never dated or bedded the same woman more than twice. It was an inviolable rule adopted by him at his conversion. A joke at first and then a policy.

His long slender fingers lent themselves to his classical bent as a pianist. He had studied all of the masters with some of the finest instructors in the world. He thought nothing of strolling to a piano at a crowded party and launching into Mozart or Haydn until he was covered with perspiration and feeling as if he had just bedded every wonderful woman in the place.

His skin was dark, olive Mediterranean dark. His normal body temperature was higher than normal, routinely registering at one hundred and two point three.

The Stranger carried himself with an air of confidence not commonly found in men appearing to be his age. When he entered one of the one hundred and thirty-seven rooms of his estate *Gadianton*, time seemed to stop for his guests of the evening. He was the consummate host, a man's man, a woman's man, a dangerous man. A very dangerous man.

The source of his wealth was the subject of much speculation and debate. It was a great mystery and he did nothing to answer it. The most popular theory was that his parents, of whom he never spoke, issued from the royal blood lines of Europe. Not only did he never mention his parents, siblings or other family, if they existed, he forbade any conversation or questions about them.

First-time guests to Gadianton were given an important and thorough briefing by his staff. They were always advised that family was a taboo subject and painful to their host. The matter was considered terribly inappropriate and not to be raised under any circumstance. No one ever disobeyed the simple request not to introduce genealogy as a conversation piece, except a young female journalist from the Albany *Sun Times*. She apparently left her manners on her dresser next to her press credentials. The subject was quickly changed by a stare from the Stranger that would have struck a more alert offender down in her tracks. Months later the Stranger sent a generous bouquet of flowers to her funeral. She had been in a terrible automobile accident. A road hazard ruptured her gas tank and her small sports car exploded over one of the many cliffs along Interstate 87. He also sent a generous but anonymous check to her elderly parents.

Rumors surrounded the young woman's death and dispute accompanied the road hazard, gas tank theory. The Stranger knew of the rumors that attempted to connect the accident and the indiscretion, but once again chose to do nothing to quell them. He considered the rumors surrounding the accident an ally.

When the Stranger left Gadianton to hold court for the mere mortals who flocked to pay him hommage, he was set upon by all manner of favor seekers. Most times he granted the wishes of those who sought him out and were willing to pay the price of his friendship.

Eleanor had been willing to pay the price. She met him at a White House dinner hosted by President and Mrs. Cousin. The Stranger was one of the few who had been asked to stay at the conclusion of a Perlman concert. Eleanor latched onto the only other overnight guest and was in his bed before the lights were cool in the hall outside his room. There in the Lincoln bedroom she spent the most satisfying night of passion she had ever experienced. In fact, it was the only night of satisfaction she had ever experienced in a man's bed. By the time the morning arrived, the Stranger owned her soul.

As he watched the mini-drama playing in the boardroom before him, his blood began to boil. First he had to listen to the coward's report and then to Eleanor. She was such a disappointment, after all he had done for her. If she couldn't handle Crowther, how could she successfully deal with the assignment in front of her? "She is totally unfit for this," he thought.

The Englishman. Now there was a truly despicable fellow. He might get the job done as it should have been in Ghana. Crowther was the one alright. He was dying of course and would be gone within six months, but he was only needed long enough to get rid of the girl. And then he could turn into multiple tumors and bleed his guts up. No one would care. Aids. That was what was going to kill him. He had no idea he had it yet, but it would soon escalate and he would die a most agonizing death. He was already spitting blood, which amused the Stranger. Crowther attributed his bleeding morning spittle to a chronic sore throat. "Yes," the Stranger thought, "how could I have overlooked this perfectly corrupt little man?"

McDonald left the board room after three hours of bickering, finger pointing and debate over the next operation to be set into motion. She walked beside the Argentinean, hoping desperately to gain an ally. She knew Vasquez hated Crowther even more than she did. "Sounded like a circular damn firing squad in there, didn't it?"

"Yes, Eleanor, my dear friend, it did. I found myself staring across the table at that pockmarked English bastard, wondering if we have the right target in our sights." He smiled.

"I know what you mean, Jorge." She smiled back. "What do you think? Can we get a two for one discount? Let's face it, no one in Argentina will fall down in a fit if the world is one limey short, will they?" She laughed. "Come on, let's get a drink, Admiral, maybe we can have a bite together. We haven't had time to really get to know one another and I would so enjoy that. We can chat and knock some things around. What do you say?"

Looking directly at her breast with no pretense of anything other than what he was thinking, the Argentinean said, "Eleanor, there is nothing I would rather do...," his eyes moved toward hers, "...than you. I mean of course, dine with you." He smiled broadly. She took him by the arm and changed direction toward the dining room.

Eleanor McDonald never hated her cousin more than at that very moment. She knew she was going to have to bed the little Argentinean sleaze ball to win his alliance. And Mr. Cousin had told her to do just that if that was what it took. "We don't need the damn English taking over. And that's just what will happen if we let that son of a bitch Crowther get the upper hand here. Hell, it will be Montgomery all over again. Now El, listen to me very carefully. Get the damn job done. Then we can get your nice little ass back here where you are of the most use to me. Next year after I am re-elected, I promise you will move to Bethesda if you like. OK, darlin'? And you can begin the studies you have been pestering me about for the last three years. Now, El? Get the damn job done! Will ya?"

Eleanor endured small talk, hands under the table and the foul breath of Vice Admiral Vasquez on her neck for as long as she thought humanly possible. If she ever wanted to get that research money the President was hanging in front, she had to be a success. This assignment was going to make her or break her, and if sleeping with Mr. Sleaze meant success, then so be it. She shuddered at the thought. She was entitled.

After dinner and several drinks, which she decided were justified in light of what she was going to do, she invited Jorge back to her room for a night cap. She felt the best plan was to drive him crazy with desire, roll his eyes back in his head, quickly spend him and get him out of her room as soon as possible. So she flirted with him throughout dinner, letting his hand rest on her knee a little longer than was ladylike in any other social setting. He picked up on her less than subtle invitation and was as ready as a man could be.

When Vice Admiral Sleaze went to the men's room, presumably to shed his skin so he would look like a brand new snake when they left, Eleanor doffed the business suit coat she wore to the board meeting and opened the first button on her white blouse. She wasn't a beautiful woman, but she was attractive if she chose to be. She just didn't want to be very often. Her work was more interesting and important to her than relationships, husbands, or rolling around

97

sweating on some bed engaging in an activity she never really had understood or enjoyed, with the exception of one occasion. Sex had always seemed so silly to her. She often wondered about all the incredibly stupid things men would say or do just to have a nerve stimulated, ejaculate and fall asleep. And here was admiral Sleaze just about to sell his soul to do the same thing.

"Yuck." The very thought of him made her skin crawl and then she smiled to herself. If he couldn't shed his skin in the bathroom, she could lend him hers; God knows it was crawling at the thought of him.

Her massive five room suite was dark. The curtains were open with a view of the lake. Music played in the background when it happened. There was false moaning and groaning, pulling and pushing, grunting and sweating. Sex, there was work to it, she thought.

The Stranger cast a mean fiery glance in the direction of her suite, her bed. She was the picture of health, so she never thought that she would feel the stab of pain in her chest with the force she did. She was jolted by it at first, immediately dismissing it as a muscle pull. Then the pain radiated up the left side of her pectoral muscle and down her left arm, confirming a suspicion that just wasn't possible. The Stranger in the master control room smiled as he concentrated on her. The Vice Admiral never knew he was having intercourse with a corpse until he fell off of her.

The thin-lipped Stranger sipped his wine and toasted the Englishman. Crowther did not know what they were toasting to, but raised his glass. After the drink, the new Chair of Bountiful left the Stranger. Guards returned to the doorway of his room. He set his glass of wine down and picked the London *Times* up off the floor. Headlines and a picture of Sarah and Joshua on a dirt road to Bolgatanga leapt off the page at him. The blood in his face warmed to another level. "I should have destroyed that little bitch her first morning in Larmon's Grove."

13

WHEN Sarah reached the murderers, they fell prostrate upon the ground. She could feel the shame in them. Their eyes fixed on the soil in embarrassment. Disgust felt by countrymen settled on each one of them like a foul odor. The men were lacking spirit and heart. All of them, but one. He was sheltering himself from Sarah's presence, placing a large shade tree between the two of them. Small in stature, the only man feeling genuine remorse for participation in the vulgarity sat leaning against the tree, his wrist slashed, tears streaming down his face. Blood flowed in stereo with tears, waiting for brother death to carry him away. Away to the spirit world of darkness. He wished for nothing more than death.

Sarah was drawn to the little man the instant he cut himself. She turned her eyes, searching for him. She moved in his direction, saying nothing as she stepped around or over the body of prostrate men. When she discovered him, she knelt down and took each wrist into her hands. The bleeding stopped immediately. She stared at his thin wiry arms, examined hands that murdered children. She thought, these were the same hands a mother kissed not so long ago, hands that held her breast as he fed from her, hands that held his mother's. Small hands that once played with the small animals of his village, that carved pretend weapons with his friends. Surely these were not the hands of a murderer. They were.

It was difficult for Sarah to understand her feelings because there had been so much anger just a short while ago. She looked toward Joshua. He revealed no answer to her. The lesson had been taught; she would learn as she went along this day.

Sarah stood looking down at the man and asked his name. He didn't respond and refused to look into her eyes. She spoke to him again, calling him by a childhood nickname. "Bobbie. Bobbie Awedoba. Look at me." Cupping his chin in a hand, she lifted his face so she could look into his big brown eyes, and into his soul. She spoke to him in Frafra.

"You shed the only genuine tears under the shade of this tree. You understand the magnitude of your crimes. But what you don't understand is that your pain, your repentance is nearly equal in magnitude to the sin. You are the only one among your companions touched by grief solely for having harmed the villagers. Because your spirit is contrite, you may leave here untouched and without repercussion. But you will carry with you the mark of your sin in your heart and on your skin all the days of your natural life." Having said this, Sarah reached toward the man and touched her finger to his forehead. When she withdrew it, her fingerprint remained and the natural color of his pigmentation was gone from that spot.

Looking toward the mass of people that had gathered around her and the men, she said, "This one, and this one alone, will be spared eternal justice; he will have mercy. Mercy that will be denied to the others and to the ones who sent them. Anyone who touches him in any way will be held tenfold more accountable than any of these that lie here on the ground at my feet. Do you all understand?" Returning her eyes to the little man, she smiled at him to ease his pain. "Go now and do not forget this day or the magnitude of your deed. And give thanks to Him who sent me."

Months later when asked by a crowd of reporters why the men had no hope of forgiveness in the eternities, Sarah took the issue head-on.

A smug elderly reporter in the rear of the room asked, "Doesn't this Father you claim to represent have mercy on all of his children? Most of us have been raised to believe that. If there is no hope for these men, he cannot be a merciful God. Can he?"

"Did I say there was *no hope* for them?" She paused, looking at the reporter who had twisted her words. She turned to the filled room and said, "Tell me, what is justice?" No one answered either question. She looked around the room waiting, before her eyes came to rest on the questioner. "A murderer many times over finds himself on his deathbed. He profusely regrets a life filled with evil. Is he a man who has truly repented and is he deserving of mercy? Or is he just a man staring eternity in the eyes, fearing perfect justice?" She diverted her gaze from the reporter and looked over the room for an answer. Once again none came.

"Well, Sarah." A soft feminine voice from the front row spoke up. "Who died and left you to be the judge of who is to be forgiven and who isn't?" Sarah looked at the young woman. The tone and implication of the question hurt Sarah. She wondered why people were so cruel as she looked at the impeccably dressed girl reporter. She estimated that she wasn't more than three or four years older than herself. Then she spoke to the woman.

"Your bank account was overdrawn by five hundred and sixty-seven dollars as of Friday afternoon when you received your bank statement in the mail. Yet, knowing that, you wrote a check for your rent on that same account this morning. You knew you did not have enough funds to cover the check. You lied to your landlord and cheated your bank." She smiled softly at the woman

100

as the rest of the reporters roared with laughter. "Will you ask your bankers for mercy? Will they give it or will they demand that you satisfy the deficit in your account? I am not sitting in judgement. That is reserved for another. He may judge or appoint whom He will to do so. I am only a messenger. Messengers aren't always the most popular people. Let's face it, ladies and gentlemen, there are very few of you here this morning that don't already know the answers to these questions. You just don't like them. And for some, that means you also won't like the messenger." The room was still.

Turning to the young reporter one last time, "The bank rightfully demands a balanced account. The reasons are obvious, are they not? Yes, Father is merciful as you have been taught, but he is also just. And as justice demands satisfaction, mercy demands a worthy recipient. The one whose heart was full and whose spirit was contrite was deserving of mercy. One mercenary, that's all. The remaining men were as the murderer on his death bed, staring eternity in the eye. As unpleasant as it might be to fill the bank account, it must be done. The unrepentant must satisfy the law of justice. Were it not so, there would be no justice, and without justice there could be no Father."

Several days later Sarah and Joshua left Ghana along with the sentinels. The trip home presented yet another tutorial for the young prophet. Sarah wanted to take conventional transportation and so decided once again, in opposition to Joshua's advice, to fly home to the States. Her first commercial trip since Chicago taught Sarah just how famous she and Joshua had become. The airport was a mass of people, the plane was a zoo, and the bus trip from New York City to Ferrisburg produced crowds of unimaginable sizes on the sides of the road. The trip became a logistical nightmare for local officials along the route. What was meant to be a quiet journey, meeting casual passengers, became another draining exercise. Sarah spent nearly the entire bus trip waving out the window to the people. She couldn't disappoint them. Many had traveled great distances, bringing children to catch a glimpse of the *angels*. Sarah disliked that title because it conveyed more personal righteousness than she felt. It applied to Joshua since that was indeed just what he was.

Andani and Sun Ce would not be seen again by the public until the next trip abroad. Everyone was tired. Sarah expected even they needed rest, but she was wrong, they never rested, they didn't need to. There was much she still needed to learn. And to learn, Sarah asked the right questions or was given the most wonderful tutorials, like this absolutely silly idea of a trip. Joshua smiled at the pickle she had gotten them into by deciding to take the plane and bus. But it was on the last leg of the trip that she learned about moderation.

The bus was crowded and her presence, along with that of Joshua, brought initial chaos to the cramped area until a still silence settled onto the passengers as they watched the two companions.

Standing in the aisle next to her, Joshua leaned forward and brushed a wisp of hair from her forehead. "Sarah, we are going home for three months. You may not feel it now, but you will be very tired by the time we arrive in Ferrisburg. You shouldn't expect to maintain the physical and spiritual pace we have been keeping without some depletion of energy. We must take care of you and you need to rest for a while. Remember the lesson I taught you in the grove about moderation? There are people the world over who have forgotten the meaning of moderation. They overindulge in many things, not realizing the harm they can do to themselves and others. We've seen this especially in those regions blessed with plenty. Moderation even applies to those things spiritual, Sarah."

She spun quickly toward him as if she couldn't believe what she just heard. "What? What do you mean, moderation in spirituality? There can't be too much spirituality! Do you expect me to be moderate in the exercise of my own faith?" This was not the first time she challenged him, and Joshua loved it. It was just another reason she had been chosen.

"No, sweetheart. But you must be prudent in your exercise of it and moderate in your profession. If you exhaust yourself spiritually or physically, your ability to utilize your gifts to their fullest extent will be compromised significantly. And what worth will you be to yourself, to Father, or to your brothers and sisters then? We have all been given intellect for a purpose, to use it! As faith without deed is dead, so is faith without intelligence. You will also find that moderation effectively reaches the people more than overexcited screaming matches. It is an eternal principal that reason and calm win over hollow rantings. Yes, moderation is the key.

Do you know what some people are saying about you? They think you are a god or an angel. Some think you are a witch. We must be very careful not to lend reason to any of those arguments. Weariness lends itself toward error and you are not infallible. Your enemies are waiting for your mistakes and you must do your best not to give them what they desperately seek.

We cannot afford to lose one spirit, because of your detractors or the overzealous. This is why the application of moderation is so important. Every single soul is more precious than all the riches of this world. Do you understand what I am saying, little one?"

"Yes, I think so, Josh."

She was torn between her desire to spend time with the bus passengers and the roadside crowds. And then, as usual, a small beautiful child initiated the moderation tutorial. A perfectly beautiful little Hispanic girl sitting next to Sarah had fallen asleep. Her mother, very pregnant with another child, sat across the aisle from them. When the little girl's eyes closed, she slid a cherubic face onto Sarah's shoulder, silent for the first time on the trip. Sarah looked at Joshua and then the mother. She stuck her hand out, palm up, looking for a high five from the young woman. The gesture was meant to celebrate the quiet the mother and Sarah could now enjoy. However, mom mistook Sarah's gesture for a prelude to a blessing and bowed her head. Sarah giggled, she couldn't help it. When the mother looked up and realized the error, she started laughing. Then she gave Sarah the high five she was looking for. The entire bus watched the exchange, at first making the same mistake the mother had, then breaking into uproarious laughter when the error was uncovered. Soon all the passengers joined each other in the high five exercise.

Sarah turned to Joshua. "This is moderation," she smiled as she watched the passengers enjoy each other, and her.

"Look at them, Sarah, like little children. Behold the magnitude of joy brought on by a small simple gesture. How many sermons, readings, petitions, or meditations do you think it would take to elevate their souls to the same level? Moderation pulled their faith to the surface, Sarah."

The passengers, feeling a new level of comfort with Sarah and Joshua, joined in the duty of waving to the crowds lining the roadsides. To any outside observer it appeared as if the bus was carrying passengers to one wonderfully large family reunion. Yes, to the untrained eye, even considering their different ethnic origins and religious beliefs, they seemed heading home for a gigantic family reunion. In fact, as Sarah watched them, the love she felt for them increased with each mile. She realized the metaphoric value of the scene. They were headed to a reunion alright, some arriving before others, but all on the same road home. She smiled to herself and thought, "They just don't get it yet."

She was tired by the time she reached Ferrisburg and, as Joshua had warned, rest was more necessary than Sarah realized. Andani and Sun Ce stood unseen at her bedside. No one was going to come close to their precious charge. The events of the past six months had taken a physical toll on her that she wasn't aware of. It wasn't until she woke from a deep twelve hour sleep the morning after arriving home that it was evident to her just how tired she was.

Sarah swung her feet to the familiar hardwood floor and enjoyed the view that pleased her more than any other in the world, the Battenkill Valley, home. As she sat appreciating its beauty, her thoughts drifted back to Ghana. Pleasant memories of faces and places floated by in her mind's eye. Memories of love grew warm in her mind. It seemed as though she had only been gone from her room a matter of hours. She was grateful for her mission.

Back in Bolgatanga, a government official had delivered an invitation to meet the president of the country. His name was Smith, President Tommy Smith. The name was so western, it seemed to betray his true nationality. He had been educated at Oxford and had served as a fighter pilot in the Ghanaian air force. He was as intrigued as any by the thought of meeting Sarah and her supernatural friend, but his motives had not been pure. Knowing that, Sarah accepted the invitation anyway. She had business with the President.

After a quiet dinner in the palace, Sarah followed the small man into a sitting room where they could speak in private. President Smith hadn't wanted Joshua in attendance, but Sarah made it perfectly clear that what he wanted wasn't what this meeting was all about. Once formalities were dispensed with, every point of corruption, including his administration's role in the massacre of more than one village, was rehearsed for him. He was not pleased as he listened to the litany of wrongdoings committed by his thugs. But he was also terrified by Joshua's presence. The short meeting produced an agreement to hold a special general election that would be supervised by an international body of overseers one month from that date. Mr. President would not be on the ballot, and neither would any of his cronies.

Sarah's last night in Ghana was held in more congenial surroundings. Curling back up on her warm bed, her thoughts drifted back to that last night spent in Azuma's home. She had enjoyed an evening meal with his extended family, about thirty of them. Many of the people who stood outside the hotel the day the carpet changed, once again filled the plaza standing by windows and doorways, hoping for a glance at the girl from the sky and her angel friend. She mingled with family members after the meal, not wanting to leave people she had come to love and respect.

Sitting around a long wooden table which had been constructed especially for the special evening, Sarah sat near her new friend. Azuma smiled down at her, reaching for her hand. "It is good that you came back to see my family, Miss Sarah. They would have hung me for sure if you had not." He smiled at her.

Joshua was playing with the children and was the focus of attention and whispers by the adults. And while no one had ever heard Joshua's voice except

Sarah, the little ones seemed to understand exactly what he wanted them to do. He loved children.

"Azuma, tell me about your ancestor, the great King known so well to you and your grandfather. The one who is no longer with us."

"He was a great man, Miss. My grandfather knew his great grandson's son personally. The line goes back many generations to the great King. Grandfather told me many stories of his bravery in battle and yet he was said to be the most kind, wise, and just of all the kings of our people. In fact, grandfather told me the elders believe he was the greatest of all the Kings of Africa. It is a shame his name is little known even in his own land.

Sadly, Miss, he was murdered in his sleep by one of his sons, the Yo Na, the prince. His first-born was an evil boy who wanted his father's position before his time. He did not want to pay the price of succession. He was a selfish and unwise lad who had fallen in with his father's enemies. They tricked him into betraying his father. The boy had never spilled blood or tears for his people. He lacked wisdom and character.

The King was a great man, Miss, I feel him in my blood. How I wish my grandfather were here tonight to tell you about him. Nobody can tell stories of him quite like grandfather could. It would have been wonderful to know him, yes?"

"Your grandfather?"

"No. I mean, yes. What I mean is, it would have been nice for you to know my grandfather, too. He was a wonderful man. His heart broke when my father died. He passed away when I was still a young boy of eleven years. Grandfather took my mother and me into his home and raised me like a son. I miss him so."

"Yes, I am sure he is a wonderful man." Sarah looked down the table. The room was full of beautiful black and brown faces. All shades, shapes and sizes. Suddenly, Joshua stopped playing with the children and came to Sarah's side.

She squeezed the large hotel manager's hand and said to him, "I would like to share a few words with your family before I leave. Would you ask them if I might address them for a minute?"

"Of course, Miss. They will be delighted." He rose and clapped his hands together, getting the attention of the room. "We have been shown much honor this night. Our ancestors must be pleased with us all. And our Heavenly Father has blessed us above all the peoples of the earth this evening. Our children's children must hear of this evening when angels walked among us. There are some within my voice who have scoffed at our traditions, forgotten our ancestors and left their families for the promises of the big cities. They

105

have let our customs sink into the ground to rot with the dead animals of the plains. This is not good." Many of the younger people in the room felt the sting of his words.

"Now Miss Sarah would like to speak with you before she and Joshua leave us. Please listen to her now, and do keep the little ones still, for goodness sake!" he exclaimed.

Sarah moved to a corner of the room where the family could all hear and see her. The people in the courtyard outside also had a clean view and were within earshot. When all was quiet, Joshua could be seen leaning forward and speaking to Sarah.

"Azuma, thank you for you invitation to share a meal and an evening with your family. And please let the little ones wander. They will not disturb me and I love the sound of their laughter, as does this big child standing next to me." She winked at Joshua.

"My brothers and sisters, among the most precious gifts human beings enjoy are the ties we have as families. And if we all traced our family lines back far enough, we would see that we are indeed tied to one another, the byproduct of a perfect celestial love. The day will soon arrive when all of us will walk among the ancestors you now speak of. Azuma has spoken wisely in his words to you. To cut the ties, to forget your ancestors is a grave mistake, with terrible eternal consequences. It is wise therefore to seek them out and it is the responsibilities of the elders of this family to pass along the family history to the young ones.

There exists a celestial, eternal parentage that is responsible for the creation of each and every one of us, our ancestors, our children, and our grandchildren yet to come as I have shared with you in other meetings. The events of these last several weeks have come to pass so you might learn about your celestial heritage. Please consider this parentage and your individual relationships to it. Your affinity with them began long before you came to Mother Africa, and will last long after you have left her. That is the message I came here to share with you. Cherish it.

I love you all so dearly. And yet some may question the sincerity of such a remark, saying I have known you but for a short time. How then is it possible that I have such feelings for you? How can this passion I feel for you be so strong? Some will say that I am different than you and that I cannot understand your pains and sorrows, your joys and aspirations. I am not different or more special than anyone in this room. And I am no more valuable to your Heavenly Parents than you are. What makes the bond strong is our common celestial heritage. We *are* family. And while I have been with you for but a short time

106

here in Africa, we spent countless ages together before we agreed to come here to this earth. And that was where the seeds of this love were planted. We must never lose sight of that or take it for granted.

Some of you, especially the young people, have questioned the existence of a Creator. Some have sought so much with their minds that they left their hearts completely out of the process. And because of this, doubt has sunk into the crevices of your closed minds like a seed carried by the wind and dropped into the cracks of dry sunbaked soil. There is little possibility of fertilization occurring in such places."

She turned toward Joshua who could be seen by all and heard by none. He was smiling and speaking to her.

"Azuma, please come and stand at the head of your family." Joshua looked in the direction of the little ones as children's laughter slammed off the old walls. The sound of it pleased Sarah. She could not understand how some places of worship outlawed such a sweet sound, sending children off to rooms far from the adults to be entertained, instead of being instructed and loved.

"I am pleased to bring to you the great Moro Naba, of whom you have heard Azuma speak with so much passion. It has been my honor to spend much time with him, to learn at his feet and to, how do the Dogamba say, work with this great *lana*. He has touched my heart as I know he has the Moshie and beyond. Will you please say hello to Andani, King of the Moshie?"

A gasp went up from the room at a sight that sent most of the window peepers scurrying. Andani appeared to his posterity and he was not alone.

At the side of the great King were Azuma's father and grandfather. Azuma had been most faithful of all in keeping the laws and customs of his ancestors. Accepting the prodding of his family, he turned and rushed to his father, whom he hadn't seen since he was a little boy. He hugged his father and grandfather and wept on their necks. And then it was time to meet the man he had heard so much about.

Holding the hands of two men he thought of as his fathers, he bowed low to the royal Andani. Andani returned the bow, holding outstretched arms toward the son of many sons. Azuma melted into his arms as if he had known him forever, and of course he had. Shortly the entire Klan surrounded the three men, touching and kissing them. Andani was overcome by the love and honor bestowed upon him. Tears of joy streamed down his face. He was not afraid to cry.

The family was overwhelmed as Andani spoke. "United here this evening is royal family. I say this not because of pride or my position. I say it because it is an eternal truth. Great mother earth yields up many riches in this land. She

107

produces diamonds and gold, precious chemicals and wood from our forest, but its most precious and valuable commodity is here in this room this evening." The family thought the great king was referring to the girl from the sky and Joshua. He was not. He was referring to them.

Azuma, looking at Sarah for the first time since his ancestors stepped into the room, knew that he would be responsible and accountable for teaching his family a higher law that was being shared by Andani that night. The message was obvious from the events of the evening. It was not simply that the family unit was the key to happiness, it was that it was eternal in its potential and somehow there was a way of holding it together beyond the grave. A thrill ran through him as he held the hands of his father and grandfather, and realized he had not seen the last of them, or the majestic King Andani, his great great great-grandfather. The reunion had been the perfect way to end Sarah's journey.

"Joshua was right," she thought, sitting on the family room floor. "Learning a concept is the easy part. Learning was easier than easy. It was natural. Teaching what I learn is a challenge sometimes, depending on the pupil, but the hard part, the hardest of all, was *living* what I learned and teach. I need rest, moderation in my life. I need friends and fun. If there is no other part of me other than my mission, I will become untouchable." So she called Billy Stewart for a date the third night she was home. She had never stopped loving him.

Billy nearly fainted when he heard his now famous friend on the phone. He had been in love with Sarah since they were little children, but he never had the courage to tell her. And then the consequences of that fateful conversation behind the school, and his failure to meet the measuring device of love during Sarah's darkest hours, drove him from her in embarrassment. So many nights Billy sat under the big oak tree in her front yard and stared up at her window, hoping she would see him there. She didn't, and his spirit had not matured enough to ignore the pressures of parents and peers. Even as they spoke on the phone planning their date, his heart broke over lost opportunities to profess his love for her.

He had grown into a sinfully beautiful young man. And he was as good a boy as could be found in Ferrisburg. Sarah was happy they would be spending an evening together. Where could they go without the press or hoards of people following them? That would prove to be a challenge. They were able to sneak out to the movies and Annie's Diner afterwards for a burger and shakes.

Billy was full of apologies early in the evening until Sarah reminded him that there was no need for forgiveness; they had been mere children. As the evening progressed, they each became more comfortable with one another. Soon it was as if they had never been apart. Sarah wanted a simple evening with this strikingly handsome boy and she got it. She managed to steer the conversation around to school and friends and the things that seventeen-year-olds feel comfortable talking about.

Sarah realized quickly that she not only loved Billy Stewart, she adored him. She knew it the instant she saw him again. They had a wonderful evening of fun together, but it seemed like forever before he tried to kiss her. It was a sweet kiss. The sweetest kiss of her life, she thought, as she closed the door behind her and watched him walk down the sidewalk to his home. The sweetest kiss in the history of all mankind, she smiled to herself.

The following morning Sarah discovered an envelope lying on her breakfast plate. Her mother smiled as she saw the recognition on Sarah's face. It was Billy's handwriting. Inside the small pink envelope was a Thank You card, handmade. It contained a poem addressed to her.

> "As sweet and musical
> As bright as Apollo's lute, strung with his hair;
> And when love speaks, the voice of all the gods makes heaven drowsy
> with the harmony".
> (Billy . . . Shakespeare)

Love's Labour's Lost

Sarah turned to her mother, clutching the love note to her breast. It was the first she had ever received. For a fraction of a second her thoughts drifted to the dark days when she could only dream of being near him and the improbability of that dream ever coming true. Her heart nearly leapt out of her chest every time she glanced at his familiar handwriting. He was thinking of her, she thought amazed. Could life be any sweeter than this?

Sarah and Billy spent days and evenings renewing their friendship and establishing new romantic dimensions to it. Joshua was happy Sarah had this young man for a companion. His heart was good.

The next three months would be filled with family and friends. Picnicking, almost daily trips to the Battenkill with Chicky or Billy and the ever present Joshua, who stood and watched at an unintrusive distance. Sarah grew in stature both as a young woman and as a spiritual being. Her vacation did not include abstinence from daily tutorials with Joshua. She still waded into the crowds that seemed to follow her everywhere she went, but she rationed the amount of time she spent in the middle of the crush. She was seeing with new spiritual eyes now, understanding that she would need strength when the time to leave came again.

"Oh, I'm not invincible or infallible, as you know!" she shared with Chicky on the banks of the Battenkill one afternoon. "If I were, I couldn't learn some of the concepts that I have been entrusted to teach. And I can't teach what I don't know. You know what, Chicky? When this all began, I thought having Joshua at my side would make this a piece of cake, but I was concerned that I might be perceived as a puppet. But I'm not. I have to walk in the shoes of the concepts I teach and I must understand and believe the doctrines in my heart. If I do not, I have become just what I feared."

They lay on the bank looking up at blue skies and marshmallow clouds. "Sometimes I get so tired, you know? Tired, and occasionally even angry. When we were in Ghana, I wanted to quit, but those feelings left when death became clear to me."

"Wadda ya mean, death became clear to you?"

"Well, it is something we all fear and yet we purport to believe that all will be well when it comes. It is sort of like wanting to go on vacation and then deciding the trip might not be worth the destination. Death is just a door, Chicky, just another door. Chicky? Will you come with me next summer? Please? Maybe bring Billy with you. You can fly to our locations like a road manager." She beamed. "Think what fun we will have together, the three of us. We will see wonderful things together, the beauty of the world and its people. What do you say?"

"I think you want me to bring Billy Stewart more than you want me to be your road manager." He smiled at her.

"Well, of course that's true, bonehead. I'm not stupid. But I do want you to come, too." Sarah giggled at her older brother.

There was never any real question about his coming, and Chicky jumped at the offer. He had genuine passion for Joshua's company as a result of hours conversing with him through Sarah. He was one of Billy Stewart's closest friends, notwithstanding a serious fight when Sarah had been the town leper.

Sarah intended for Chicky to assume major responsibilities the following year, but she wanted to see how he would react to a smaller invitation first.

"Sarah?"

"Yes?" She lay back on the warm sand, staring at pale blue skies and billowing white clouds. She closed her eyes to freeze the memory of them in her mind.

"Do I have to stop cussing if I join you?"

110

"Yes."

"Shit." Chicky smiled inwardly to himself. "Where are you going to go from here?"

"London. I've told Joshua I think we should go to London."

14

SOMETIMES the answer is, no answer, and sometimes the answer is simply, no.

Wembley Stadium was filled to capacity, eighty thousand people. Outside the stadium tens of thousands more crowded the sixty-five acre complex, just wanting to be near Sarah and Joshua. The cost to reserve the stadium had been underwritten by anonymous supporters. Government funds were never accepted to sponsor the expenses of renting a stadium and staffing it for an appearance. Such sponsorship, Sarah reasoned, could appropriately offend those who were entitled not to believe in such matters. And there was a growing number who wanted nothing to do with her *witchcraft*.

The St. James had arranged to have an extravagant suite of rooms for Sarah and her guests, but they were politely refused. Sarah was to stay with a solicitor and her family just outside the city limits of London. It was a quiet arrangement made by Chicky. In all matters Sarah strove to avoid even the appearance of evil, profit or gain. Nonetheless, "the wolves", as she fondly referred to the press, were always nipping at her heels, or so it seemed. But she never gave them even the smallest piece of carcass upon which to dine. There was no need for limousines or special security, other than to keep the crowd from injury that might result from their own overexuberance, as the English are wont to do at times. However, those present this evening were no ill-mannered soccer fans.

Sarah had been still for three months, and now the thought of London in the fall lit a spark in her. She was filled with anticipation and energy, spiritual energy, and couldn't wait to see the people. She felt so much electricity in her body she thought lightning was going to explode out of her fingertips if she didn't move among the people soon. She was going to need every ounce of that spiritual energy before the night was over.

A large but plain platform had been erected at midfield on the huge soccer lawn. There had been many a glorious football game here, as any redblooded Englishman would vouch, and Sarah couldn't help but reflect on the coincidence that her first European appearance was occurring in a football stadium, of all places, a little more than a year since her debut in Chicago. Wembley had seen as many as two hundred thousand people in attendance for a soccer game, but that was before the current complex had been erected. This evening, it was jammed to capacity.

Standing in the bowels of the monstrous stadium, Joshua and Sarah held hands and offered private prayers. They then prayed together, asking for keen minds, discernment, and blessings on the country where they were guests. If at all possible, Sarah thought she and Joshua had become even more close over the summer months that they had spent together as she rested and regained her strength.

Sarah would never again be a child, Joshua thought, as he looked down at her. She would forever be his "little one", though, just as she always had, and she could count on his enduring protection. Although Sarah did not know it, each day did not end for her three companions when she drifted off to sleep. When her eyes closed in restful sleep, the end of every day for her found three men standing at her beside. They offered up petitions to their Father for Sarah. Each man kneeled in turn, offering the prayers of his heart. After praying over their charge individually, they knelt as a group and Joshua offered up a prayer, voicing for the trio. Words of gratitude that Sarah had been chosen, humble appreciation for their callings, and petitions that their efforts to protect the little one would be successful, in spite of a growing movement to harm her. These efforts lasted throughout the night, every night without exception. It had been thousands of years since mankind could have heard the likes of such prayers. To witness the nightly ritual that ended each day and began the evening was a remarkable event. It even stilled the Stranger.

As soon as Sarah and Joshua could be seen walking up the tunnel entrance to the field, the massive audience stood in a roaring approval and acceptance. Sarah looked at Joshua. "Hey Josh?"

"Yes, little one?" He knew what was coming and smiled at her.

"Feel like a little moderation?"

"Sarah, I am *just* your servant. Whatever you wish, little one," he playfully mocked.

"Well, look at them. They're so excited. We can't just walk in."

"After you."

Sarah rose above the floor of the tunnel and slid gracefully through the air as she moved slowly out to the field and around the stadium. She stood only five feet above the ground, but it thrilled the crowd, and those who actually made eye contact with her were delighted to no end. Her golden hair lightened in color by the summer sun, blew gently around her. Her long white gown shimmered against the emerald green grass and the black star-filled sky. She completed her tour of the perimeter of the stadium and came to a rest on the platform, before she noticed that Joshua was not behind her. Except for the brief instant outside the hotel in Ghana, when she learned of the massacre of the children, and her short exit from the grove, she had never done this on her own. She surprised herself. When she stopped laughing, she placed her hands on her hips and threw a mock disapproving glance at Joshua who was still in the tunnel where she had left him.

"Joshua, come out here this instant!" She stomped her foot in another mock demand. The crowd, hearing the exchange, picked up on the kitten play almost instantly, delighted that this night did not have the appearance of a hellfire and brimstone evening many feared. They cheered wildly when Joshua shook his head, refusing her invitation. Sarah laughed again at his playfulness. She furled up her brow and stomped her foot again. The crowd loved it, it was plain that they adored this beautiful young American creature.

This time, in response to her playful demands, Joshua began a slow but sure course toward the platform. His entrance nearly silenced the crowd. It always did. He was beautiful alright, and they loved the playful exchange between Sarah and him, but eventually everyone reminded themselves that he was not from this world. Or at least, so they thought. A million flashbulbs greeted him as he made his way to the little one. Her gaze upon him left nothing to the imagination; it was apparent to the audience that she adored him. When he reached her left side, their hands sought out each other automatically and when they touched, the crowd again erupted in a deafening roar. Sarah and Joshua bowed their heads once again in silent prayer. Minutes later the noise faded as reverence overcame excitement. Joshua was still the doubt remover.

Sarah moved down off the platform toward the crowd on the north side of the stadium. Not unlike the crowd at Soldier Field the summer before, the mass of people in Wembley became motionless. Silence shed an eerie mist over the stadium. It was uncanny that so many people could be so still, so quiet. Sarah walked close to them, hands reached out from the seats here and there. Occasionally a voice called out her name. She acknowledged the caller and smiled, but she was looking for somebody in particular, somebody dying.

As she walked she touched as many as possible, assuring those she could not reach that tonight they would not need her physical contact. She moved around the stadium, nearly reaching midfield before she spotted him. He was a seventeen-year-old boy named Derek Gotts. Derek was a very sick boy and his mother had brought him to the stadium to save his life. He suffered from Disseminated Sclerosis, commonly referred to as Multiple Sclerosis. An insidious malady that usually manifests between the ages of twenty and forty, Derek had been presented with symptoms at age ten. The disease was slowly disintegrating the young man. Death was waiting for him, it was only a matter of time and he had precious little of that left. His mother nearly fainted when Sarah stopped in front of them.

She made her way to the boy and his mother sitting in the second row. Mrs. Gotts's eyes lit up as Sarah approached her; she knew that one touch from the young American girl's hand could bring her son out of his tortured world into a star-filled evening of new life. Sarah's closeness fulfilled thousands of prayers carried aloft on the wings of a mother's faith. Her eyes fixed on Sarah as she approached. She anticipated Sarah's call to her son, but when Sarah finally reached them, she smiled at Derek, and stretched out her hand to his mother. She drew Mrs. Gotts out of her seat, pulling her into an embrace as Sarah was often moved to do. It wasn't just Sarah's calling that inspired close contact with the people, it was innate, a part of her, a part of the majesty of womanhood. And her womanhood was part of the reason for her calling.

"Hello, Mother Gotts. I have been anxious to meet you and Derek for such a long time, or at least so it seems. I told my mom all about you," she whispered into the woman's ear. "And I know your husband couldn't be here tonight, but you must simply tell him that all will be well. He will be able to watch on the telly, won't he?" The question was rhetorical and had a calming influence on the woman, whose heart was pounding in her chest with excitement and anticipation. Sarah broke the embrace and led her away from Derek. They walked arm in arm down onto the field, as if for a casual stroll, totally impervious to the thousands around them. At one point in the short journey they stopped and turned toward Derek. Sarah could be seen whispering into the mother's ear once more, and the mother, transformed into a fifty foot figure by giant television screens located at each end of the stadium, could be seen nodding in affirmation, occasionally wiping tears from her eyes, sometimes glancing in Derek's direction, and smiling.

Derek's eyes were fixed on Joshua; they were having a conversation. He was, aside from Sarah, the first and only one allowed to hear the golden haired angel's voice. He was mesmerized by it. Laughter reached Derek's lips and eyes. Innocent, lovely eyes, smiling genuine smiles. Both reactions were captured on the screen which now sometimes split showing Joshua and Derek, his mother and Sarah all at once. To those in attendance the scene was somewhat of a mystery, but the four participants knew what was about to happen.

"Mother Gotts? Do you feel better now?" Sarah said at the conclusion of their conversation. She was always mindful about the feelings of those who came to her. Mrs. Gotts felt like she had just met the daughter she had always prayed for, although she wondered to herself how it was possible to feel so strongly that she had known this American girl forever.

Sarah turned to her and answered the unasked question. "Because you have always known me and you always will." And then a most remarkable thing occurred. The woman stepped back from Sarah for a moment, surveying her as a mother would before a daughter's first date. Tears that had welled up in her eyes spilled over unto and down her cheeks. The people in and around the stadium felt the magic of the moment.

"Sarah. Dear, dear, sweet Sarah. I do remember you!" Simple, elegant words, an eternal truth, even sending chills up Sarah's spine.

"Thank you, Mother Gotts." She held her tight, whispering, "I remember you, too."

There were lip readers scattered throughout the stadium with binoculars, ready to pick up anything that might give Bountiful an advantage, but they missed the exchange. Of course Sarah was aware of them. Andani and Sun Ce were keeping an eye on them, but they were no threat.

"If you are ready now, we should go see Derek and put an end to his suffering."

"Yes, dear, I couldn't be any more ready. Let's go."

They returned to Derek who was still fixed on, and thoroughly enjoying his conversation with Joshua. The mother went to Derek and distracted him temporarily from the source of his pleasure.

"Derek, my dearest son." She lay her face in the crook of his neck and sobbed tears of sorrow, relief, joy, all the emotions only a woman can seem to mix together at once while feeling no confusion or shame. "How wonderfully lucky you are, son. How absolutely special you have been. I treasure you and I love you with a love that will span the eternities. Now, lovely, go with Sarah." She hugged him with all the strength she dared to use on his frail body. She couldn't know that the change was already beginning.

Sarah smiled at the mother and son. The scene she witnessed affirmed for her the eternal nature of that bond and thus its similitude of the bond that exists between mankind and Celestial Parents. She watched as Derek responded to his mother who now heard his voice clear and free of pain for the first time in many years. They could be seen on the screens, laughing and hugging one another.

"Derek? Are you ready to take a walk around the stadium with me, before we leave?" Sarah asked.

"Oh yes, yes, I am," an excited voice feeling new strength responded.

116

"Well then, my handsome young man, come and take me for a stroll. You know, Derek, I don't ask for a stroll with handsome strangers very often," she teased. "But sometimes I just have to find the most handsome boy around and ask him." Derek blushed as the crowd responded with applause and whistles to Sarah's lighthearted remark. Derek, mistakenly, looked toward Joshua.

"It's not him, Derek, it's me. You do remember me, don't you, Derek?" He looked at her and in a millisecond recognition hit him like a giant spiritual sledgehammer. Much to the delight of the crowd he came up out of a wheelchair that had been his elective prison for seven years.

"Derek, use your legs now and walk to me. There is nothing wrong with them anymore. Well, they have never really failed you. Do you understand that? They did just what you requested of them."

"I understand now that Joshua has refreshed my memory," he smiled. "There were days, though, when I wondered why I even had them, Miss Sarah. Kinda glad I didn't cut them off as I threatened to do on occasion." A wide grin spread across his face. His looks were handsome, Sarah thought.

Joshua smiled as he turned his head from Derek to the little one. Sarah never looked more beautiful to him. She was becoming everything her potential said she would, and then some. She needn't be here very long, he thought to himself sadly. Unfortunate for those who surrounded her.

Yes, she was never more lovely than she was at that very moment, standing in her long, simple but elegant white dress in front of eighty thousand people and millions more watching on televisions across the globe, her long hair still blowing gently, casually in the breeze. It looked as if angels were brushing it, he thought. He watched as she stretched out beautifully tanned arms in the direction of the boy whose body had started the transformation. Yes indeed, she was born to this. In the midst of these pleasant thoughts, Joshua's attention was drawn to a dark place in the stadium, and he felt anger rising in his soul.

"Derek, do you really remember me?"

"Yes, Sarah, *I do remember you!*" Derek said to her as she took hold of his hand. She could hardly hear him over the noise of the stadium. He was such a fine young man. He would make a wonderful husband and father some day, she thought as she looked at him. He was a boy whose only two sources of joy over the course of the last seven years had been the hour or so a day that the pain would subside, although it never truly left him, and the parents who devoted themselves completely to his comfort and well-being.

"Shall we go for our walk now, Derek?" He nodded yes as he looked around the stadium, his body unbent, and control and feeling returned to his limbs. She led him onto the field where a different battle now waged between the ·

awestruck and the wildly applauding enthusiastic. The latter won as the couple made their way around the stadium to the delight of all. They strolled casually under the watchful of eyes of unseen sentinels. The noise was deafening. Occasionally Sarah would catch Derek stealing a glance at his new friend, Joshua. She would smile at him and pull on his arm. "You will have plenty of opportunity to chat with him another time. I promise, OK? Now let's finish our walk." Holding on to his arm, she said, "Wave to your mother, she's watching you." He glanced in the direction of his mother with his robin's-egg blue eyes. He was grinning from ear to ear. His mother returned his gaze, tears of joy and disbelief streaming down her face.

"Now, Derek, Joshua explained everything to you and you're not afraid, are you?"

"Yes Miss, he did and I am not afraid, or, well, to be perfectly honest, and I suppose I must learn to do that from now on, I am just a wee bit frightened. Is that acceptable, Miss?" His naturally soft voice blending with the song of his English accent melted her heart.

She smiled at him and squeezed his hand. "Oh, it is quite permissible, Derek. But trust me, there is absolutely nothing to be frightened about. I will be with you the whole time. Are you ready?"

"Yes."

"Alright then, let's go. Don't you wonder how they are going to react?" she said, nodding towards a stadium full of delighted people.

"Well, Miss Sarah, I know I how I would react if I was sitting there instead of standing here. I think I would faint." They both laughed.

The pair started for the platform at midfield, walking directly toward Joshua. When they came within yards of the platform, Sarah stopped and turned with the apparently healthy boy and spoke her first words to the massive audience who became still at the very instant she began to speak.

"There are many of you here this evening and watching on televisions across the world who do not know my friend, Derek. Let me introduce you to him. He has spent many years confined to a wheelchair. His limbs were of little use to him on most days. He could hardly speak his own mother's name. Few stopped in to say hello to him or to offer a helping hand. There are some of you who may have passed him on the street, or if not, surely somebody like him. As you did so, your eyes have remained fixed on appointments and clocks, lunches and shows, as you walked by him. You did so in rain and shine, each climate giving you an excuse to pass him without acknowledging his existence. Some have even seen him and considered him less than normal. He is not. He is as beautiful as anyone looking on here this evening. He is not the victim some of you also perceive him to be. Nor has he been punished for anything he or anyone else has done.

Derek Gotts *chose* his disease! Long ago and far from here. Although he has been looked down upon by many during his short mortal experience, in the celestial realms his majesty is sung about, and the time is not too distant before he will be a King there. Because of the sacrifices he made during his mortal probation, he will be a man of great respect and admiration."

She glanced at Derek as he seemed to stand more tall and erect at her side now. She couldn't resist expanding upon her comment. Joshua shot a glance at her, thinking perhaps now was not the time for this, but she just smiled in return, melting his heart.

"And when Derek assumes his celestial glory, he will take unto himself a bride of equal status and loveliness. She will be his Queen, a co-equal partner."

A questioning murmur moved through the stadium, then approval, acceptance of what she declared. Then the silence returned. They waited for her to begin again. Sarah looked at Joshua and knew her womanly instincts had proved right. She let him know it and he responded with a smile.

"This very special young man has brought his parents great joy. He has provided opportunity for sacrifice and service to many. And lest you misunderstand my message, there were those who did respond kindly to him. That is what Derek's life is all about. That was his gift to you. How many of you here this evening and watching the television sets over the world do not understand that gift? How many have passed him by, or ones like him, unwittingly rejecting the invitation to elevate your souls? He has brought countless blessings to his pastor and his townspeople. And he has brought hope and joy to his physicians, nurses, and therapists. His premortal choices and his successful completion of his mortal probation have brought him here to this very spot and to this time. A time of completion of that experience. A time of fulfillment and reward, celebration and thanksgiving.

Sometimes the answer is, no answer. Sometimes the answer is simply, no. Mother Gotts, Derek willingly set down upon this earth awaiting the condition that you nursed him through, and now it is time to end the suffering. After this night Derek will not walk mother earth for many years." Sarah turned to the stadium again. "It is time to say goodbye and thank you to Derek. Will you join me?" The silent stadium awoke, first a few hands clapping here and there, and then the entire venue became a deafening, tearful mass of people. The noise spread outside the stadium where screens had been placed at the last moment before the event opened. Most of London heard the noise of the crowd and joined it.

Turning back to Mrs. Gotts, "Mother Gotts, the answer is, no. Derek will *not* be going home with you tonight." Mrs. Gotts smiled and nodded understandingly towards Derek. And though she wore a smile on her face, tears streamed down her cheeks. She was seeing her boy, her perfectly lovely son, for the last time on earth. Her heart ached for him already.

Sarah and Derek restarted their journey toward Joshua. Derek's arm went around Sarah's shoulders in an affectionate gesture and hers slid around his waist in reply. As the young man held Sarah, they began to ascend upwards off the field on a steady slow incline. To the observer it looked as if they were climbing a hill, but no hill existed. Stillness returned to the stadium and reached new levels of quiet if that was possible. They walked into the sky, looking back only once as Derek smiled down on his mother, letting her know he would miss her and that the pain was gone. He thanked her one more time for the love she and his father had so willingly given. His benediction was unheard by the rest of the stadium, it was a private moment.

Sir John Crowther stood in a reserved section of the stadium requested by the fronting company who underwrote the cost of the evening. As far as Sarah was concerned, ten seats were a small price to pay in exchange for the opportunity to reach so many people. Crowther hated rubbing elbows with the commoners and had done his best to isolate himself from them and to disguise himself so as to not be identified. Joshua thought it odd that Crowther was present.

Crowther smiled at the spectacle before him, at times intrigued by the events taking place and the comments being made. His interest, however, was limited and his motive customarily selfish. He looked at the *fools* in the stadium and imagined the millions more watching around the world on television sets. How easy it would be to make a fortune off this circus act, he thought. Plots, schemes, and swindles that would make millions upon millions of pounds for the family, danced through his corrupt mind. He concentrated on anything that would keep his mind off the events about to unfold in the small hamlet of Ferrisburg.

At the conclusion of Derek's words to his mother, Mrs. Gotts felt weak, sweat broke out on her forehead, and nausea overwhelmed her. She was helped to her seat. Everyone, including Mrs. Gotts, attributed the spell to the excitement and emotion of the moment. She had no clue what was really causing her illness.

Sarah and Derek moved toward the stars, walking arm in arm until they were completely out of sight. Many in attendance heard music, voices singing, and wonderful choruses of bells ringing overhead. Many others heard no such

120

thing. The next morning the London *Times* would attribute the whole phenomenon to mass hysteria, but they would falter when asked to explain what cameras recorded.

Sarah had been absent from the stadium for half an hour, during which time Joshua stood motionless on the platform where he had taken his place to the left of Sarah an hour earlier. He watched what was taking place in Ferrisburg.

The stadium, stunned by the departure of Sarah and her charge, slowly came back to life. All eyes turned toward Joshua, waiting, wondering, questioning. Even Crowther was transfixed by the unearthly qualities of the beautiful man. When he entertained a thought of how he would fare in Amsterdam with his blond hair, Joshua shot him a look, and some pain. It doubled Crowther over and frightened him.

Sarah returned to the stadium in a direction opposite from the one she and Derek had used to leave. An aura of bright white light surrounded her. Many in the stadium covered their eyes because of the brightness and turned away. Interestingly, the only ones who didn't need to shield themselves were the children in attendance. As Sarah descended very slowly to the platform, the aura faded completely. She scanned the audience, quickly looking for the one person most everyone in the stadium had forgotten, Derek's mother. This time when Sarah found her, the woman looked lost and sad. Her brown woolen sweater, worn over a simple flower print dress, added to the gloom that surrounded her countenance.

"There is a child in your womb. She will be the flower of your lives now. Be well with her and remember that for many there is no replacement. The answer is either, no answer, or, no. Derek is well now and forever, Mother Gotts." Allowed to hear the annunciation of another child, the crowd broke into spontaneous applause and cries of joy.

Sarah moved to Joshua's side and spoke with him before addressing the stadium. She turned to the thousands watching who now awaited the next development in an already wonderful, incredible evening. "What have you seen here tonight?" she asked. Silence rang across the field. Several moments passed before anyone had the courage to answer. But then a voice cried out, and then another and another, "An angel! Two angels!" "A God!" another cried. "No! A messenger from God!" another volunteered. "Buddha's gift. A beautiful manifestation from God. Allah's hand resting upon the girl from America." And finally from a nearby section, "A witch and her devil! Falsehood and trickery, blasphemers!" Sarah smiled at the answers.

"Listen to me. I am not speaking about Joshua and me. Please understand that we are not that important to what you have seen here this evening. Were it not him and me, another and another would do just as well. We are only messengers, it is just that simple. We do not ask for nor do we want your praises or your payments. Please reconsider the question." A long pause ensued. For many it seemed like an hour, but it was only minutes before she once again quieted the crowd.

"What you have seen here tonight is a great tutorial. A lesson in similitude. Similitude of Celestial Parental love. In Derek and his parents you have seen the love for a child by the parents who created him. An imperfect child in many eyes. You have witnessed the unwavering love and trust that child placed in the hands of those parents. And you have seen the unconditional love, sacrifice and devotion of those parents for a child who was unlike other children. His perceived deficits did not compromise their love for him. Is it not wise to ponder these things on a grander scale?

You have Celestial Parents who have a perfect love for you, their imperfect children. You have been blessed to see a wonder of celestial proportions tonight and who among you will ignore this invitation to come to a greater, closer knowledge of your celestial genealogy? And if your genealogy is celestial by its very nature, then what is your potential?

We each have asked ourselves, why am I here? Where did I come from? What is the purpose of this life? Is there a God and, if not, what then is to become of me? In fact, mankind has asked these questions a million times a million times, but without sufficient answer. Mankind continues to grope as a blind man in a mist for the comfort the answers will bring. And it is only a false cloak that curiosity inspires these questions, because the real impetus behind them is fear. I will answer those questions with simple answers. They will be too unsophisticated for the scholars and your spiritual advisors. Many will scoff at the simplicity of the answers and so they will not be satisfied. And why? Because men bend near to the creator with their lips but their hearts are far from Him. You seek the things of the spirit with the intellect, but the things of the spirit are perceived by the heart. Such is the reason why the little children here tonight did not shy from my countenance when I returned to the stadium, but you did.

Many will deride me after tonight, but that will not keep me from sharing truth with you, because truth is eternal and does not bend with the winds of the doctrine of men and women. And the events that you have witnessed here this evening bear record of the truthfulness of the message and thus the messenger. Don't be fooled by the nay sayers whose livelihood, comfort and wealth hinge on the sale of wisdom.

The purpose of life, my dear brothers and sisters, is simply that mankind might have joy. That they might achieve happiness by progressing in knowledge, character and experience. Understanding that all of life is a tutorial and all experience is for the total good of the individual. Coming to this earth, we obtain the physical bodies that we did not have prior to this mortal sojourn, and the physical body allows for the tutorials to be taught in their fullness. All else is commentary, albeit perhaps glorious commentary in many instances.

Joy, happiness, true lasting eternal happiness is the purpose of life. And so I ask you, where is your joy? Is it a lasting goodness to you, or a transitory appeasement of one of your senses? Many will leave this stadium tonight, many will turn off their TVs, having murmurings in their hearts. Some have already cast aspersions at the message and the messengers, notwithstanding what they have been privileged to see.

We are not here to steal away your free agency. Believe what you will, but remember this. Where much is given, much is expected. And tonight the world has been given much. We are children of Celestial Parentage. We have been sent here to develop as individual beings so that one day we might rejoin those who created us, as one like them. . . "

The London *Times* was not entirely convinced by the events of the previous evening nor by the scores of people that left the stadium healed from various maladies. "Mass hysteria, psychosomatic symptoms to begin with, clever mind control, and perhaps the greatest illusionists of all times. But this was certainly not what it was proposed to be, that being a message from the Creator Almighty. A team of theologians, assembled from every major denomination in the world, are currently studying transcripts of the message delivered by Sarah as well as a review of video tapes."

The author of the *Times* article continued, "Ms. Ferunder spoke for a period of two hours. The content of the discourse creates obvious philosophic and doctrinal controversy. Much debate will surround what is being referred to this morning as a *"child's dogma"*, proffered by the young woman from America. Aside from its intellectual simplicity and idealism, it has raised more than one fine Englishman's eyebrow by suggesting the possibility of plural Gods and a co-existing female God.

"I don't know what she is all about. Certainly there may be good intentions behind all of this, but I do know what this isn't. It isn't doctrine acceptable to the Church of England. I am very concerned that a very clever fraud has been perpetrated on the people of England and indeed the world. We must get to the bottom of this immediately.

"Miss Ferunder spoke to her audience quietly, but with the passion of her convictions. And, it seems, at times with a unique sense of humor. But it was both the outrageousness and the simplicity of her theology that has most clergymen chuckling this morning. Her remarks are now becoming the subject of theological scalpels the world over."

The *Times* front page was but a lead into twenty pages of coverage, most of it controversial and most of it negative. Only one quote of any measure of good came from an unidentified religious authority. "I think we might be much better off if we gave some credence to the young lady. Tonight when we go home, we should not say our prayers, we should *pray*. We should not convene conferences and study tapes, we should just go home and ponder what she had to say. At least, that is exactly what I intend to do. I'm leaving right this moment. I'm going home to my congregations and clergy and encourage them to do just that. Something special is happening here and we have grown too theologically fat and short of breath to recognize it."

The family of Derek Gotts was incommunicado this morning ,but had released a press statement through the family solicitor. "Mr. and Mrs. Gotts have no comments other than to express deepest appreciation for Derek's life and the example he set for millions of people." London police officials and Scotland Yard were looking into the young man's possible whereabouts to determine if foul play had befallen the missing youth.

A few moments after Sarah left Derek and reappeared over Wembley stadium, a beautifully gift-wrapped package arrived at her small home in Ferrisburg. It was addressed to her mother and delivered by limousine. A bottle of champagne accompanied the meticulously wrapped box. The Ferunders had grown accustomed to receiving gifts by now. Thousands of them had arrived in the last several months, but it was family policy to never accept any gift, no matter how well intended they were. Acceptance might give the appearance of gain, and "the wolves" would glut onto that for sure. The family felt very strongly about avoiding even the appearance of evil.

As was customary, Susan decided to open the gift so she might best determine where to donate the contents. She waited until the family had finished watching the coverage of the events unfolding in London. It was nearly three o'clock in the morning before the broadcast was finished. The family adjourned to the kitchen for an early breakfast. It was way too late to call it an evening snack, Susan thought as Kent started cooking eggs and bacon for Chicky and himself.

She retrieved a paring knife from the silverware tray to cut ribbons and remove bows. She did it meticulously so she could rewrap the present before it was collected later that day. And she loved opening the packages that arrived. It thrilled her to see what surprise awaited some unsuspecting but worthy recipient of the content.

The instant Susan opened the package, she screamed. Her body convulsed violently before she fell backwards, crashing to the kitchen floor. Kent rushed to her side while Chicky stood with his eyes fixed on the severed head of Billy Stewart as it lay in a sterling silver container. Blood soaked a blue velvet lining; it was obvious that he had also been savagely beaten. His eyes had been plucked from his head.

Two hours later a similar, but considerably smaller package arrived at the home of the London solicitor with whom Sarah was lodging.

15

HONE HEKE and his accomplice sat in the back office of the One Tree nightclub on outskirts of Auckland, New Zealand, sipping coffee. Bountiful had ordered them to remain together after the successful execution of Billy Stewart. For Heke this was an opportunity to return to the only place in the world where he genuinely felt safe. And now he had several months to enjoy the fruits of his labors, two hundred thousand dollars, American. Bountiful had offered less than his going price until he scowled and suggested something anatomically impossible. Crowther had decided to meet the large man's price.

Heke's companion was just happy to be alive and pay off the enormous gambling debts he had incurred since the failure in Ghana. Now he wanted to relax and enjoy the South Pacific, but something nagged at him and made him uneasy. The fifty thousand dollars in his bank account could not buy him the peace he sought. It was temporary, he told himself, the spooks, nothing more. All he needed was some time. He was going to relax until Bountiful called upon them to hit their next target, the girl's brother.

Sarah sat staring out of her bedroom window, tears streaming down her cheeks. Joshua had told her about Billy. Before she went to sleep that night, she knew something was wrong. She almost called home, but she was so tired, and she knew that they would call her if anything had happened.

She felt her heart quit beating when Joshua told her, she felt so alone, abandoned. And when she begged Joshua to let her go to him, he comforted her, but told her she could not go.

"Sometimes, the answer is no, Sarah." The words mocked her like a fiery slap in the face. They had been her own words just hours earlier and seemed so filled with wisdom and compassion. And now that she was on the receiving end of them, they were as bitter and cruel as any words she had ever heard. She begged Joshua. She just wanted the opportunity to say goodbye, to smell him, to hear him, to feel him close to her one last time. But it was not to be. Sarah once again experienced the great tutorial nature of her calling. She learned in her agony the agony that so many millions suffer at the loss of a loved one, especially those whose hopes for reunion were nonexistent. Their suffering made her loss no less, however, and she cried throughout the night as her

126

companions looked on. Sunrise found her on her knees, praying for Billy's family.

The package from New England sat on the solicitor's dining room table. Joshua passed the wrapped box and asked Andani to remove it. It contained Billy Stewart's eyes and he did not want Sarah to see it. Anger rose in him and he summoned Sun Ce.

That evening, twenty miles away on the outskirts of London, tragedy struck again. A hotel housing two hundred school children, who came to see Sarah, was rocked by a massive explosion. Eighty children died. Twenty-six more were taken to nearby hospitals. Initially the IRA was suspected, but within two hours of the chaos a caller to the London *Times* cited Sarah and her companion as intended targets. And thus, according to the *Times*, blame was to be laid at the feet of "the American and her ghostly companion."

Sarah rushed to the hospital to see the children. Some parents let her visit and some did not. To her dismay she was incapable of healing any of them. She could only offer comfort. Turning to Joshua for explanation, he advised only that it was wisdom that these witnesses be left untouched to testify when the time for justice came. His words did not comfort her. She didn't understand that his explanation was instruction he could not disobey. He wanted to interfere, to help the children and to help Sarah, but he understood the eternal wisdom behind the decision. The children who had died would, in the eternities, stand as witness against those who were responsible. There would be no plea bargaining in that court.

Two hours after the hotel shook with violence, The Samling was destroyed, disintegrated by an explosion several times the force that impacted the hotel. None of the occupants, including staff, survived. All members of Bountiful were blown to bits except Sir John Crowther and the Argentinean. Vice Admiral Vasquez had not been as fortunate as the occupants of The Samling. Vasquez was found on the hood of Crowther's car in Amsterdam the following morning. He had been burnt to a crisp. His skin was the color of black cinder on an old alleyway. His eyes stared back at Crowther, terrorizing him to the point that he took no care that his Rolls Royce had become the death cradle for Vasquez's twisted, contracted corpse. The eyes haunted the Englishman. Had they been able to broadcast their last visions, they would have shown the sword of Sun Ce swiping down upon the ugly little man as a thousand stripling warriors, with swords drawn, stood alongside him. The carnage at The Samling had been their missive to the sponsors of Bountiful. The Stranger cringed with fear, and with anger.

127

The death of Billy Stewart and the bombing in London that took the lives of the innocents initiated a polarization of feelings toward Sarah and Joshua that was difficult to imagine. The press, as the press is wont to do, fed upon the extremes to which proponents of both sides seemed to gravitate. It tied Billy romantically to Sarah and challenged the wholesomeness of the relationship. Plenty were willing to be interviewed and delighted in turning it into something secret, sinister and sinful. Clergymen around the world explained the Lord's way of dealing with a representative, if that indeed was what she was, who sinned as openly as Sarah must have done with the Stewart boy. It was obvious to them that her failure to help the children in London was punishment, meant to teach the girl a lesson in virtue and chastity.

Sarah and Joshua saw the loss of many souls during the following weeks. Those lost souls, they were the repercussion the Stranger had hoped for.

On the night the London hotel was destroyed, the President of the United Sates was handed a message that he fully expected would rehearse a successful mission. It read, *"Lamp lit. However, Lange not attending."*

It was clear to him. The hotel had been blown, but the girl was not present as the NSA intelligence had indicated. The angel was gone. He was infuriated. "Get that damn Crowther on the phone. I'm gonna have his ass in a bag if we don't get this thing under control. Never seen such an incompetent running a project of this magnitude. I swear he would have the sons of bitches standing in a circle if we ordered a firing squad!" His cheeks, which wore a natural cherry pink flush, turned crimson. His wiry salt and pepper hair ruffled as he ran anxious fingers through it. Sweat appeared on his brow while his thin lips tightened. Immediately after the first message arrived, another one from Number Ten Downing Street was delivered. It simply said, *"Samling destroyed by massive explosion. Survivors unknown, but doubtful."*

The President sunk into the leather chair behind his desk. The crimson began to drain from his cheeks. The phone rang. An unsteady hand lifted it from its cradle.

"Crowther, you incompetent son of a bitch, what the mother hell is going on over there? Notwithstanding the fact that we give you every damn resource in the world, we can't trust you to even blow your friggin nose. No, you crazy incompetent son of a bitch, you blow up innocent kids and your own damn control center. And how the hell could that have happened unless somebody knew that you nitwits were there to begin with? You have a reputation for talking too damn much, Crowther. I told the Prime Minister, if you let anyone know that Bountiful existed, I was gonna have your slimy English ass hanging in the Tower of London. Now the whole damn mission is a pile of shit. I should have your faggot ass drawn and quartered. Do you hear me, Crowther?"

"No Mr. President, Johnny doesn't hear you. I've stuck him on something else for the moment." It was the Stranger's voice on the other end of the line. "Mr. President, you moron. We tried it your way, and it was a miserable failure. Although, I thought the hotel in London was a particularly amusing screw-up, didn't you?" A chuckle escaped his lips. "You didn't think I would let your friends across town at the NSA really know where she was, did you? Or that I would let them listen in on my conversations unless I wanted them to. Obviously, they took my information that the girl was at that hotel as *the gospel*, if you will excuse the expression. Please stop me if I am not amusing you, will you? Now, tell your silly little friends at the NSA to stay off of my communications, or you, that miserable bleached blonde bitch of yours, and your snotty kids will pray to, to whomever, that you had never laid eyes on me. Never, I swear." The laughter pierced the listener's soul. The phone went dead as the President answered with a feeble, "Yes sir."

The Stranger sat back in his leather chair, sipping a tall glass of wine. A young woman sat on the floor next to him, her cheek resting against his knee, clinging to his leg. He smiled as they watched Crowther writhe in pain. His vocal cords had been severed so he could not make a sound. "No sense in disturbing the dinner guests upstairs," the Stranger laughed. And here was Crowther, a long stainless steel skewer inserted at the base of his spine and run up his back, exiting between his shoulders. All vital organs were carefully missed by the surgeon. The large rotisserie turned slowly over the fire in the mammoth stone fireplace. Each time a piece of flesh melted off Crowther and fell into the flame, the fire flared and the sizzle broke the silence. The Stranger raised his glass. "Well done, John, well done! Or actually, John, not well done at all. But perhaps you will know, for once in your worthless life, what *well done* means after all!"

The Stranger decided that Billy was a nice touch, but did little to effect this battle. London was the Stranger's idea, he intentionally misled the fools at the NSA as to Sarah's whereabouts. "Wonder how Ferunder would react if he knew his buddies had just tried to kill his little girl?"

His eyes burned hatefully into Crowther, actually adding pain to indescribable pain as he watched the man's agonizingly slow death. "I might as well enjoy this little genetic failure." A smile crossed his lips again as he stroked his companion's long black hair. "I'm famished, darling, shall we dine?"

16

THE sun could be cruel in Valentine, Texas. The tiny ranching community of five hundred and fifty souls depended on the grasslands to feed the beef cattle. If rain didn't come and the sun scorched the flats, death visited Valentine. It was no respecter of person or animal in these parts. For the last century or so Valentine has survived those years when the rain was sparse and the sun merciless, but this one was different. Valentine was slowly dying.

Mountain ranges surrounded all sides of the small town sitting on the bottom lands known as Ryan's Flats. The Sierra Viejas lay to the southwest, the Davis' to the north, the Mc Kinney's to the east and the Wiley's to the west. These were the ancient mountains of western Texas; old, rounded, secret mountains.

As she stood at the end of the flats, which were nearly twenty miles long, and looked out over the Rio Grande three hundred feet below, the surrounding mountains reminded Sarah of her beloved Greens. She enjoyed the rhythm of the river as it slid along steep cliffs to wherever it was heading, touching everything in its path. Watching it, she mused, "so much like one's life, sometimes with direction, sometimes not, sometimes having its direction altered by others who don't know you." Hot winds whipped at her face, but it could not divert her eyes from the beauty of the land below. She could see far off into Mexico. The day was a hot one, even hotter than usual for the month of June.

Sarah watched the scenery, impervious to the particles of dust and sand stinging occasionally against her face in the desert wind. She had been here ten days without food or drink. Ten days in this isolation, preparing for what was to come.

Sarah tried not to hate the Samoan and his cowardly companion, but she did. It was all too apparent to her that she was human after all and couldn't help her feelings. She especially disliked the coward whose courage surfaced only when the larger man pinned Billy to the ground so the smaller could cut his throat. He had no conscience. He had chased it away with chronic inattention to it. Sun Ce was waiting for him, waiting for the next time their paths would cross. Sarah could see it in the sentinel's eyes and almost trembled for the man.

The lack of rain in Valentine had become dangerous to man and beast. Blue open skies, welcome in any other time or place, were a cursed view to the townspeople every morning. Unchanging weather forecasts echoed from televisions and radios each day. The drought shortened tempers and increased the use of curse words. Even the winter months, which normally brought moderate amounts of snow, showed no mercy on the town. Only a few inches of snow fell during the entire season. It was a bad omen. Valentine could little afford to lose people or cattle to the drought and there was precious little time left. Cattle had already started to die.

The drought drove people back to tradition. Extra church services were held at the only two churches in town. There had even been some talk of a combined service, though many of the old timers said they would never live to see it take place. The white church was a nondenominational semi-Baptist congregation, and the other across Highway 90 was the Catholic church. The town's predominant Hispanic population worshiped in the Catholic church. This wasn't a racial thing with the people, or at least that was what they said. And outwardly at least there seemed to be very little racial tension in Valentine. In fact, the mayor, who was elected by a near unanimous vote, was a Hispanic woman. This separation was a matter of culture, tradition, religion. And both sides of the highway were content to let sleeping dogs lie.

Valentine's history was not a very colorful one in reality. But a variety of folk stories linked lovers of different backgrounds to the town's name. In fact, Valentine was a very old railroad stop named after the president of Wells Fargo, Mr. John Valentine, who was a major stockholder in the Southern Pacific Railroad and as such was honored with having a stop in the middle of nowhere named after him in 1880. So, it wasn't so romantic in its origin, but the town liked to encourage more colorful stories to account for the its attractive name.

There used to be a nice diner in town called the Highway Cafe. And then the Feds went and did something really stupid, at least according to the former owners of the cafe. They built US 90 right south of town. And, of course, the Highway Cafe was nowhere near that highway. It folded and left the town with no restaurant at all. There were no hotels, or even bars. Motorists headed for Odessa had no reason to take the exit to Valentine. But Valentine survived, and debate among the natives still raged on whether the highway was good for the town or not. "Hell, you can get outta here twice as fast now that we got that highway."

There was little else to complain about in Valentine except the lack of rain. In fact, there was little outside influence on the quiet little town. There were the border patrol police, the drug enforcement agents, and the Jeff Davis County *Mountain Dispatch*. Well, there was also the Big Bend *Sentinel*, but it was not the popular paper in Valentine. All alone on Ryan's Flats nearly three hundred miles from Odessa, a hundred miles from Alpine and fifty from Marfa,

131

Valentine didn't much care for outside influences. The town didn't care how far it was from this or that. It cared about rain, though, and it hadn't seen any in a very long time.

On Saturday afternoons, the cowboys and local residents gathered at a ranch just west of Valentine. Christopher Drew drove his pickup truck toward town, already wanting the young week to be over so he could rest his tired bones. He was an associate ranch manager out at the Milner Ranch. A student at Texas Tech in the winter months, he worked the large ranch during the summers to supplement his educational fund. He was thinking about Saturday, when he could ride and rope for fun. This was a time when he could show off for the ladies and build his stock for the day when his education was over and someone would need a good ranch manager. Driving into town in the early afternoon, he had no idea that he would begin the end of Valentine's anonymous little existence forever.

On this Wednesday, Sarah turned her back to the rim of Ryan's Flats and the Rio Grande, and began her trek with Joshua towards Valentine, forty miles away. It would take three days by her calculations. In light of her fast, it seemed odd that she felt no hunger or thirst. The couple walked in silence, eyes singular to the northwest.

Wednesday evening in Valentine was a quiet evening like any other, uneventful. People returning home from work, tired from a long day on the range, were eager to move indoors to air-conditioning, a cold beer, lemonade and a large meal. The sun took its toll on a person who worked the ranges all day. And now the absence of rain caused top soil to turn quickly into dust. Dust flew everywhere with the wind and covered everything, beating everything it touched into submission.

The last to submit to the elements, however, were the older Hispanic women of the town, who preferred hanging newly washed clothes outside to dry. The wind carried so much dust, the clothes that were set out became screens of mud. The old women finally gave into electric dryers that had gone unused in their homes for years.

Just as the sun began to slide down behind the Jeff Davis mountains, cowboy Drew spotted Andani and Sun Ce standing ten miles outside of town on each side of the roadway. They were facing each other. When he first spotted them, he did not recognize them. Usual local hospitality would have inspired Christopher to stop and assist strangers so far from town without transportation. But something caused him to pass them. He couldn't take his eyes off of them in his rearview mirror. They never moved even to acknowledge his passing truck. In the mirror he noticed their attire, and their swords. And then he put two and two together and stomped on the brakes of the truck, sending it into a wild swerving slide down the hot black asphalt road. When it came to a stop, he sat in the cab of the truck and watched the two men.

He knew who they were because he had seen the media coverage of the events in Ghana. Occasionally the names of the corporate board members of Richardson International flashed across the television screen as the criminal indictments continued to roll in. Ghana was the only time that the sentinels had been captured on film, according to the major networks.

The images in the mirror caused Christopher to reflect on the debate that had permeated his campus the previous fall. Sarah and Joshua were the focus of attention as they traveled throughout Europe and the Middle East. But after the explosion in London and Billy Stewart's murder, many on campus had doubts about the legitimacy, the divinity, and the benefits of Sarah's mission. She was labeled a fallen prophet on the cover of *Time* magazine and hadn't many defenders among Christopher's college friends. Christopher hadn't made up his mind on the subject yet. He was about to.

The thought crossed his mind that he was seeing things. He had been in the sun all day and wasn't sure if he had kept up his fluids. Becoming dehydrated out here was something that could occur quickly, and while he was very careful about that sort of thing, it was a possibility. The whole thing might be a hallucination, but if it was, it was his first and he was going to be damned if he was going to miss it. Yet there was something that held him back and made him move slowly. He mustered all the courage he had and opened the cab door.

Exiting onto the road, Christopher pushed the hat back on his head and spit out chewing tobacco. His mouth went dry, he felt a hot tingling sensation in his face. At the same time he noticed an uncontrollable trembling in his hands. As he began walking towards the two men, he noticed a correlation between an increase in the symptoms and the shortened distance between the three of them. Fear overtook him, he stopped dead in his tracks. Sun Ce spoke to him in a low reassuring voice.

"Christopher. Come here. Don't be afraid of us, we mean you no harm. We have a message for you and the citizens of Valentine. It is good news. Have a drink, it will make you feel better." He smiled and offered a hand to the cowboy. "Please come closer so there will be no more doubt in your mind about what you are seeing or what you are about to hear."

The cowboy thought he had seen a lot of things in his short life, but he had never seen anything like this. It nearly stole his voice and courage away. He took his white stained hat off his head to wipe sweat from his brow, but to his surprise none was there. It should be dripping into his eyes, his forehead felt like he was burning up. Heat exhaustion, he thought. He wondered if he would pass out way out there on the highway, which could be dangerous under the hot Texas sun. He struggled towards the apparitions, feeling increasingly weak as he approached them. He moved toward the oriental who had spoken to him. He wasn't going to miss this.

"We are not ghosts, Christopher." Andani addressed him for the first time. "Come here and have a drink from this, it will make you feel better. Come drink." Andani produced a small red clay goblet and held it out to him. The cowboy's lips felt parched and he wanted to drink from that goblet more than he ever wanted anything. He changed direction and moved toward Andani. The weakness continued to increase the closer he moved to the black man, but he pushed himself onward until he reached out to take the container. It was light, he raised it to his lips and drank long swigs from it. The content tasted like water, laced with honey. It was cool, no, cold rather, and so refreshing. Christopher's thirst disappeared after several long swallows from the pot. Having filled himself, he felt his strength return; a cool gentle breeze came up from the floor of the flats. It was an unusual wind, because it carried with it the smell of rain. His rancher's eyes swung westward toward the Wylie and Van Horn mountains, the direction the rain ordinarily came from. There wasn't a cloud in the sky, which betrayed his instincts. After all, he knew rain when he smelled it. Any rancher worth his weight could.

Sun Ce addressed the puzzled look on the cowboy's face. "It's coming, Christopher. Your senses do not betray you. But it is not coming from the west this time. It is coming up from the south over the Sierra Viejas." Christopher's eyes flashed in the direction of the Rio Grande, but he failed to recognize any sign of the rain on the wind. "You can't see it yet, Christopher, it's like a front moving over the grassy flats. You can feel it before you see it, you can tell it's coming. It's coming alright, cowboy." He smiled at Christopher again. "It's coming Saturday afternoon. You can smell it, can't you, Christopher?" The cowboy nodded a stunned yes, his eyes fixed on the skies. "You are the only one among the townspeople who will be able to. I love the smell of fresh rain in the air, don't you?"

Christopher was startled by the familiarity with which the question was asked. Sun Ce continued, "Yes, Christopher, it is wonderful, the fragrance of the rain coming in from the mountains, isn't it? Many people take such a miracle for granted. There is a lesson to be learned here, isn't there?"

"Yes sir, I love it too. It carries life with it, you know."

"Yes, Christopher, I know. Your knowledge of mother earth doesn't come from the classrooms. It comes from your heart. That's why we chose you,

Christopher. We want you to go into Valentine and tell the mayor that the rain is coming. She should assemble the residents in the small park on the south side of town Saturday mid-morning. The little one you know as Sarah is bringing the rain you need. She is on her way here now with Joshua. Do you have any questions of us?"

Christopher took another drink from the small red clay vessel. This time as he was drinking his eyes were open and he noticed as he drank that it was empty! His discovery awed him; as he drew the goblet away, liquid that wasn't there poured down the front of his shirt. His eyes widened as he wiped his right hand over his chest to confirm that he had in fact spilled the drink on himself. He nearly lost his grip on the goblet. While he was musing over it, wondering who these men really were, Sun Ce spoke once again.

"Christopher, I am Sun Ce, in another time I was a warrior and my friend here, Andani, was a great African King. We have been sent here to watch over Sarah."

"You two are the men who travel with her, aren't you? I have seen you on the television with her in Africa."

"Yes, we are the same. Do you understand the message that we have asked you to take to the town, Christopher? And if you have any questions for us at all, we will answer anything that we can."

"I understand the message alright. The girl is coming to Valentine and she is going to make it rain for us, right?" His mind was racing, he was buying time so he could think of something intelligent to ask. He didn't want these men to think he was a bumbling idiot who couldn't articulate his feelings or communicate in an intelligent fashion. He could only muster one question and would regret that it wasn't of more importance later on when the press would want to feed on him. "I have one question. How do you do this?" he said, pointing to the empty cup from which he had drunk his fill twice since talking to the men.

"Oh, Christopher, the how is easy. The elements are at her command. If you would like to know why you have drunk from an empty pot, we will ask Sarah to share it with you when she arrives Saturday."

The thought of being able to speak to the young woman at the center of so much wonder, excitement and controversy caused Christopher's heart to flutter in his chest.

"Well, I guess I would rather hear it from the horse's mouth, sir. Oh, no offense intended to her or you. . . I just, er. . . well."

Sun Ce smiled. "We understand, and she will share the mystery of the empty pot with you then, our friend. Now off you go. Tell anyone and

135

everyone who is interested that we will all come to the town on Saturday afternoon, please." Sun Ce and Andani bowed their heads to Christopher and he returned the gesture, sure that it was the right thing to do. His walk back to his pickup truck was a swift one. He couldn't wait to get into town and speak with Mayor Rodriguez. But first he had to call his girlfriend at the Big Bend *Sentinel*.

On Saturday morning, Valentine, Texas, once again woke to clear blue skies and thousands of media vehicles. The evening news estimated that over two hundred thousand people had descended on the small town since the Big Bend *Sentinel* broke the exclusive news to the state of Texas and the world at large. Thousands more were en route, hoping to catch a glimpse of Sarah and Joshua or to talk to somebody who had. Of course the vendors were on hand, selling everything from hot dogs to t-shirts to mark the event. Young people in sleeping bags, creating a large tent city, covered the land north of town. In typical Texas fashion the town and nearby ranchers did what they could to make the visitors as comfortable as possible, but it just wasn't enough. Mayor Rodriguez was compelled to call on the governor for assistance. While the landscape north of town was covered with a mass of humanity, the south side had been kept vacant. Chicky had arranged with the mayor to cordon off a section of land for the exclusive positioning of Valentine natives.

Religious leaders from all over the world had flown to Odessa and bused into Valentine to see Sarah, the girl prophet. The crowd was a typical mixture of faithful, curious, and nonbelievers waiting for an error that never happened. People came from all over the world, but none came as far as John and Mary Hunter who had spent the last two weeks in the Cook Islands.

The Hunters, a wealthy couple, were on their way home to Ellsworth, Maine, when Mary heard about Sarah's impending visit to Valentine, and changed their travel plans. The trip to the Cook Islands had been an effort to put some fire back into a boring marriage. John did not want to trek off to Nowhere, Texas, on another one of Mary's expeditions into supernatural religion, but, in the spirit of the trip, agreed to accompany her.

Chris stood close to the mayor, watching the skies which never seemed to turn the color needed to support the promised rain. He held the small red vessel tight to his chest the entire morning. It remained empty no matter how hard he tried to stare it full. He was the only one with the ability to consume or pour from it. The cool liquid filled glass after glass, but disappeared the instant anyone other than Chris touched the glass. Chris counted each time he drank the vessel dry, his last total since Wednesday was twenty-seven.

It was three o'clock in the afternoon before Mayor Rodriguez started to show signs of strain and wear. There was no sign of the young woman or of the rain. She wasn't the only one that felt the sting of doubt. She was joined by many of the press whose job it was to be doubtful. All were, except young reporter Pat Orlando from Chicago who had met Sarah in the grove outside of Ferrisburg. She brought the photographer who had lost his brother in Viet Nam, now her husband. They stood in the crowd as little children, filled with anticipation. Suddenly Pat's spouse reached for her hand and squeezed it as tears filled both their eyes. They could tell Sarah was close; she was coming.

The mayor looked at Chris as she grabbed his arms. "If she doesn't bring the rain soon, young man, we will both have to jump off the rim." She wiped her brow.

"She'll come. I know it."

Ten minutes after the mayor's comment a clap of thunder could be heard in the southern skies. Still there were no clouds visible. The air filled with the unmistakable smell of rain, fresh cool rain. The crowd began searching the skies. It felt like a massive cold front were moving across the grasslands. Many of the city dwellers didn't understand the correlation between the thunder everyone heard and the absence of clouds, but Chris caught the attention of the Franklin Ranch associate manager, and they knew something extraordinary was taking place.

Paulie Ryan had known Chris since childhood. They always aspired to owning their own ranches. He pushed his tall brown hat back on his head, raised his eyebrows and shot one of those glances toward Chris that said, "Hold on to your horse, buddy." They had seen a lot together, but never anything like what was coming over the horizon.

All of a sudden laughter filled the air. It was the children. They could hear her coming, and joined in the nursery rhyme she was singing for them. "I looked out the window and what did I see . . popcorn popping on the apricot tree." Their voices silenced the adults who stood by in wonderment at the song sung spontaneously by the children. Subtly adding to the excitement were the young babies who fell peacefully asleep in the arms of fathers and mothers. No one knew the reason why the little ones were sent to sleep, except Sarah and Joshua.

Andy De Marcal, a retired cowboy, now in his seventies and the current owner of the newly reopened Highway Diner, was the first one to spot Sarah and Joshua. They were just specks on the horizon, but he could see them. A gray shadow followed behind them. It was a couple of hundred yards wide by his estimation. News of the sighting spread through the crowd like a wind devil on a blustery hot summer day.

Joshua walked on Sarah's left side as usual, and held her hand. "I am so proud of you, little one. I know how difficult the last months have been, but your adversity has prepared you for Valentine. So how do you feel now that the mountains are at our back?"

"I never felt better in my life, a little nervous perhaps, but I always feel that way, don't you?"

"Uh, no." He smiled down at her mockingly.

"I hope Father will be pleased with Valentine. I can't wait to meet the people there. It should be an absolutely wonderful day. And Josh, don't let me forget to find John Hunter. OK, smarty?"

"You are going to make a lot of new friends today, Sarah."

"Yes, and I suspect a few enemies." She smiled back at him.

"Well, you take care of the friends, and we..." he said, looking skyward, "...will look after the latter." Joshua did not smile. A car was speeding toward Valentine from Marfa, Texas. The occupant was hunting Chicky.

The clicking sound of cameras began as the companions came within a half a mile of Valentine. Both Sarah and Joshua were barefoot. Sarah's feet were dirty and bruised. They had walked a long way. A draped cloud rose behind them, reaching skyward out of sight. Andy De Marcal's estimate of its width was nearly on the mark. The cloud, or what appeared to be the cloud, extended on each side of them for about one hundred yards. It was not a real cloud, it was a fine shower of rain. Seventy yards from a temporary stage, erected by volunteers, Sarah began to speak. It was as if she whispered into every ear in attendance. Sarah and Joshua were walking side by side, a column of rain behind them and not a cloud in the sky to be seen. Paulie Ryan took his hat completely off and bowed his head to thank his god. Paulie was a good man, salt of the earth.

"Good afternoon, my friends of Valentine and your guests. Please give me a few moments once I have reached the platform, and I will speak with you for a while. I am so happy to see all of you here. I have waited to see you for so long and now the time is here. Joshua and I have spent several days preparing for today and I want it to be a special time for you. Thank you so much for coming. Who ever placed all the wonderful flowers on the stage gets a special hug from me when I have finished speaking with you." Sarah knew the woman who had sent the flowers from Odessa. The trip had been an exciting new adventure for her. It was a very special day.

The cool breeze that came out of the southwest increased in force, blowing Sarah's white gown back and forth. There was a mystical quality to the scene that was about to become even more mystical now. When she reached the stage with Joshua at her side, Sarah held her arms outward as if inviting the crowd into an embrace. A massive roar of approval rose up from Ryan's Flats, much like the column of rain behind Joshua and Sarah. The people were having difficulty, as did most who attended Sarah's appearances, deciding which marvel to watch. A glance skyward revealed hundreds of rainbows, the rain column, and still not a cloud in the sky. The sun shined brightly on Valentine, Texas, this day and was a welcomed onlooker.

For all of his marvelous qualities Christopher, the consummate associate ranch manager, couldn't help thinking that the rain column wasn't going to get the job done. It was just too small. Sarah glanced in his direction as the thought crossed his mind. Without warning she quickly flung her outstretched right arm to the east. The column of rain raced eastward as far as the eye could see. Then the left arm moved westerly and the column extended in that direction. Moving in opposite directions, each side joined behind the massive throng of people north of town. Those within the area prescribed by the authorities were completely enveloped by rain. Valentine remained dry.

"The rain will fall on Valentine after the sun goes down this evening. And it will rain weekly until your wells are filled, your animals have eaten and drunk their limits, and there is no more danger to your town. Your prayers have been heard and answered. In addition to the rain, I would answer a few more prayers that have risen up from your lips at one time or another. Some private, some not as private as you would wish. And while I speak to you, people of Valentine who have gathered here this afternoon, we all understand that technology will throw my voice to every corner of the earth. I hope my remarks this afternoon will not offend anyone, for that is not my intent. It has been our sad experience, however, that there are some who cannot stand by when the truth seems to be in conflict with their own agendas. I will speak the truth and all that you see and hear and feel today will bear a solemn witness that what I say is true, incontrovertibly true."

Sarah moved just center of stage and leaned over toward the people of the town. "People of Valentine, tell me this. There are two churches in your town. Each has been equally worried about the lack of water on the flats this year and have offered up petitions for moisture." Standing erect and sweeping her arms up at the rain-filled skies, she asked, "Whose prayers called down these rains upon your homeland? Which of the two congregations in town are responsible for this miracle?" It was still for a moment, then a murmur rose up from the

139

residents standing in front of her. A short time later a voice from the crowd spoke the mind of most of the townspeople.

"Both congregations called to God for this miracle. Both congregations are responsible for the prayers that have been answered here today. In Valentine neither is better than the other. We are all equal here and our prayers are of equal value."

"Well said, but if what you said is indeed the truth, why do you worship in separate buildings? Neither building is full on your holy day. Brown people attend the church to the north of town and white people the one just a few yards from where we speak. Perhaps you worship different Gods?"

Many responded, "No, we worship the same God."

"Perhaps, then, neither one of you really know just who it is that you worship? Or perhaps you really don't feel as kindly toward one another as you say you do. Whichever or both of these reasons, if true, preclude you from a personal progression the likes of which you cannot fathom. Today I am here to declare unto you He whom you ignorantly worship, though your hearts seek after Him. Some of you will be grateful for this revelation, some will be offended. But neither will stay the truth. And while the rain rescues the grass and the beast and the town temporarily, this truth will preserve you for the eternities. Christopher, come up here, cowboy."

Sarah turned in his direction and smiled at him. Had she not been who she seemed to be, Chris thought, he would ask her out. She was a vision of loveliness. She heard his thoughts and smiled warmly again at the handsome young man. "Come up here, and, " she spoke softly this time, "what makes you think you can't?" He nearly fainted with embarrassment. By his own calculations, ninety-five shades of red covered his face.

"Give me the vessel you've carried with you for the last three and a half days." Turning to the mass of people again, she spoke to Chris. "How many times have you drunk from this cup and been satisfied by its contents, Christopher?"

"About twenty-seven, ma'am."

"Many of you have seen or heard of the vessel that I have in my hands now. Some of you have even held it in your own hands, hoping to drink from it, but you could not. The vessel is like the doctrines of men. They satisfy a few for a while, but are without substance and leave the masses parched who are seeking yet another sip. The vessel is without substance. There is not, nor was there ever, any water in it, it was all an illusion. But it satisfied you, didn't it, Christopher?" He nodded in affirmation to her. "Well, you may think it did, but if it had been the only thing you drank in the last three days, you would be

140

well on your way to dehydration." She smiled at him. He had had more than one beer while contemplating with Paulie the meaning of all that he had experienced. He regretted the beers now.

"Today I will fill the vessel with substance. A substance that will offend some as I have mentioned. It will drive many far from here and consequently from the Parents who created us all. It saddens me, but that is the truth, and truth is harder to swallow sometimes than the content of an empty vessel. And because truth offends, many seek to change or corrupt it so it will be more palatable for them. Those of you who will drink, listen to me for I will not disappoint you with any more illusions or empty vessels as some have. I will fill you with truth about Parents who have sent me to you.

Before I proceed let me preface my comments with a few words of reassurance. It has been widely reported in the print and electronic media that I have come to proclaim a death to religion, to force everyone to observe a singular dogma. Nothing could be farther from the truth or from Father. But I am here to declare unto you the one and only true God of this universe. I have come to call you to Him. Call Him what you may, according to your culture and that knowledge that He has seen fit in His infinite wisdom to give to you. Let there be no mistake, however. There is only one God that is of concern to you and me." She looked around at the sea of faces captivated by her every word. It was not frightening to her at all now. The nerves had settled down and she felt so much love for them.

"I know this will disturb some of you and will particularly drive the theologians crazy," she smiled, "but I did not say that He is the only God, I said He is the only God of concern to us. He is the King of Gods. Now is the time for you to come to a greater understanding of Him. Know Him as He would have you know Him.

Governors, Kings, Presidents, Prime Ministers, rulers, and clergy, I call upon you to not meddle with the worship or beliefs of your peoples whether be they right or wrong. From this day forth, personal accountability, on a scale never before experienced, is the commandment. Let no one restrict a man or woman's search for his or her Creator lest the price of condemnation fall not only on his head but the heads of his posterity for seven generations.

Clergy men and women of all faiths, cease the podium wars and put gain of personal possessions away from you. There are no longer wages to be made off the search for truth without serious consequences. Stop the bickering brought on by the winds of the doctrine of men which blow steady and toss the dust and stone around as in a sandstorm. Discontinue itching ears and teach truth, even though some of your followers may not appreciate the message."

141

Sarah walked to the far north end of the stage to a family seated on a blanket. A young boy nine years of age sat on his father's lap as his two little sisters clung to the mother. "Hello Charlie." Looking at the father for approval, Sarah continued, "Will you come up here and talk with me for a few minutes?" The boy shot a quick glance at his dad and then bounded toward the stage. Much to the boy's delight, before he reached the stage Joshua lifted him, with a singular glance, into the air and sat him down next to Sarah.

"Wow! Was that fun, Charlie?"

"You bet, Miss Sarah!" he smiled a big response.

"Charlie, we are going to play a game, OK? And if you get the answers right, I'll give you and your sisters a wonderful surprise. Now I want you to close your eyes."

"Hey, who told you my name?" the little boy asked indignantly.

"An angel told me, Charlie, an angel. OK?"

"I guess so. You bet," he shot back. "Are you gonna make me fly again?" A big grin returned to his face.

"Well, maybe in a minute. But first I would like to ask you a few questions and then we will see if Joshua has it in him, OK?"

"You bet." The standard reply now made Sarah smile.

"Alright, Charlie. With your eyes closed tell me what your daddy looks like, will you?"

"You bet." This time the answer moved the crowd to laughter. "He's really big. He almost reaches to the sky. And he has big muscles and black hair and his hands are hard cause he works so much, but he holds me soft in them and never hurts me. And he has blue eyes and a funny mustache he tickles me with." The laughter just snuck out of his little body at this point. "And he wears big hard shoes to work, and jeans. His voice is soft and he loves me and my little sisters and he always kisses my mom and he has a big scar on his ass where Oscar, our dog, bit him last year." Sarah lost herself in laughter as the embarrassed parents of the little boy clung to one another, seeking shelter from the world. The massive crowd joined in the hilarity of the moment.

"Well, we won't ask him to show that to us, will we? We'll just take your word for it." She laughed again. "Is there anything else about him that you want to share with us, Charlie?"

"You bet. He loves me and my momma and my little sisters. He takes care of us and we love him. Did I already tell you that?" The crowd became quiet. Sarah squatted down so her face was close to his and wiped a tear from her eye. She hugged him.

142

"Yes, you did, Charlie, but that is something that we never ever get tired of hearing. Charlie, you have a wonderful daddy. And a wonderful family. I am so happy for you. And now I want to give you something." Sarah turned to Joshua who beckoned to the little boy. Charlie ran to him and jumped into his arms.

As soon as he planted a kiss on Joshua's cheek and wrapped tiny arms around his neck, Joshua pointed to a horse just north of the stage. It was pure black with a white diamond on its forehead. Sarah continued, "His name is Rainbow, Charlie. He is a gentle stallion. We found him wandering on the grasslands and he needs a home. Will you take care of him and keep him at your ranch?"

"You bet!!" He accepted.

Sarah smiled at Joshua, knowing his special love for children, and nodded her head. He lifted off the floor of the stage carrying the boy with him. Up they rose, fifty feet, one hundred, two hundred feet into the air. Those in attendance were glued to the pair and could hear little Charlie saying, "You bet," a hundred or so times in about two minutes. After a short time, Joshua descended and took Charlie back to the lap of a proud and happy father.

"Daddy, you should see all the angels up there. Millions of 'em."

Sarah had quietly watched Charlie's flight from the middle of the stage. She turned to the people, many of whom were trying to make sense of Charlie's remarks. "What sort of being is God?" The question got everyone's attention. "Would you know Him if the opportunity presented itself? Open your eyes and see, open your ears and hear, open your hearts and feel."

Sarah retrieved the vessel she had taken from Christopher and placed her hand inside it. After a short time she withdrew her hand dripping wet and handed the goblet to Christopher. "Take this down among the townspeople of Valentine and let those who wish to drink, drink." She waited and watched as Christopher did as he was asked. He moved among the people, each taking the goblet from him, holding it, some examining it before drinking. Every resident of the town drank, except two. She felt pain that the two men who secretly disliked each other could not find this time and opportunity to put aside theological differences. Neither one would look directly at her.

"It is important to know the nature of our Father. To know with familiarity, to know his mind and decrees. There are many over the world who will tell you that it is wrong to expect this or to even want this, but it is what He wants for you. Those who tell you not to seek will also tell you it is blasphemous to even contemplate such an attempt. They will tell you that it is not the desire of God

143

that you know Him. He would remain a mystery. And why do they insist to tell you that? Because they make a living telling you that.

Many people have not made an honest effort to seek after God, because they have left it to their spiritual guides to do so for them. As a result the truth has been lost for thousands of years. And because the precious truth has been lost to so many, they are little better off than the beasts that graze out there on the grass lands behind me.

They graze, moving from one pasture to another at the direction of their masters, until it is time to be led, by those same masters, to death. Led by those who lured them to think they would be forever safe. But ignorantly and blindly they will follow their masters to their deaths. So it goes generation after generation. Do not be persuaded away from this vessel of truth.

Today, if only for a brief moment, I want you to lift up your minds to lofty heights." Sarah smiled out at a group of mothers holding sleepy babies. "It is easier to do that when the little ones sleep, yes?" The people laughed at the remark, the mothers sighed with a thankful understanding. "I want to bring you to a more defined understanding of the nature of Father than men and women generally aspire to. Look here towards my companion Joshua. All I have learned, I have learned at his feet. All except what I will share with you this afternoon. I learned these things standing on the brim of the flats, directly from Him whose wish I am fulfilling.

Your Father has a body of flesh and bone. And if the veil was cut clean from your eyes and you could see Him standing over there in the grasslands, you would see Him as He really is and know that you are indeed made in His likeness. As we are, He once was, and *as He is...*" silence racked the entirety of Ryan's Flats; it seemed as though every creature in the valley was listening to Sarah, "*... we may become.*"

She paused, waited and looked for reaction. None came, they were too stunned. "Why did I call Charlie up here? Did you see and hear the love he has for his father? And did you see the love of his father in Charlie's eyes? Did you see the joy of his parents when Charlie described his father in detail? Who loves Charlie more than his own earthly parents? His Celestial Parents. And if Charlie's biological father loves him with all his heart, might, mind, and soul, as I know he does, he could not begin to approach the love his Heavenly Father has for him. Which Father of these two fathers would not want Charlie to know every detail of him?

If you faultfinders find fault in this child's doctrine, then condemnation be on your head and I will be the witness before the bar.

144

God bless Charlie for knowing his father well enough to tell us about him. And God bless those who will drink from the vessel of truth and tell those who haven't had the opportunity. With Charlie's assistance I have given you another peek at your Heavenly Father. Will you not take the time to look for more of Him?" Sarah looked out on the crowd and was pleased with the acceptance that ran through it. She smiled at them, and then that celestial humor kicked in and she turned to Joshua. "May I?"

"But of course, little one. I am only your servant, remember?"

"Yes, I do. . . get me a coke?" She smiled at him. It had been many days since she had anything to drink and she couldn't resist the joke. "Really Josh. Can I?"

"Yes, sweetheart. We cannot say no to you."

"Please let the children here in Valentine down onto the grasslands of Ryan's Flats," she asked the throng. When Sarah perceived that enough time had passed, she turned her back on the mass of people and raised her arms toward the sky behind her. The rain separated several thousand feet, revealing still blue skies behind it. There, standing in the air, were a million personages. They began descending so the people could get a good look. When all eyes were transfixed on the host standing in the air above the grasslands, the children of Valentine became encircled by column of fire, or what appeared to be fire. A personage could be seen standing in the midst of the fire, holding hands, and speaking with every child. As the personage and the children held hands and moved in a circle, a million choristers in the heavens sang the children's song faintly, "Spring has brought me such a nice surprise . . . blossoms popping right before my eyes." The sight defied description.

In twenty minutes the fire seemed to selfconsume and the children ran laughing to the open arms of awed parents. The gifts given to them varied with the needs of the individual child. Some ran for the first time, some saw for the first time, others would never need another chemotherapy treatment. And all were blessed with the total absence of bigotry and hatred. They would not want to worship separately ever again. Parents could be seen weeping at the feet of their own small children. The personage within the fire was not to be seen. Cameras snapped wildly. Shouts of wonder reverberated off the grasslands, applause started with a six-year-old little girl from Valentine, Texas. Her smile was as wide as Ryan's Flats themselves.

Sarah bowed her head for a brief moment and moved to Joshua who had opened his arms for her. A long quiet embrace followed as he looked at the mass of humanity over her shoulder. The sight of so many of his brothers and sisters so happy thrilled him. The little one had spoken with courage and he was pleased with her. He held her for a long time while she trembled slightly. This was no small event and she would need rest. She had made many friends this day. Joshua was the only one to notice Sun Ce leave.

After a moment in Joshua's embrace Sarah moved down off the stage in search of John Hunter, the millionaire from Maine. When she found him, he was standing near Mary with his head bowed. Sarah startled him when she called out his name. "John, come here with me for a moment, will you?" He moved slowly away from his wife. "Oh, don't be afraid, John. I won't bite you." She glanced over his shoulder at Mary, smiled and winked at her.

"Well, uh, er, hello, Sarah. I don't know what to say. I am made speechless at what I have seen and heard here today. I never expected. . ."

"Shhhh, John." Sarah spoke so that no one could hear their conversation. "You didn't want to come here with Mary, did you?" He was surprised that she knew his distaste for the paranormal, or religion actually.

"No, no, I didn't," he admitted. "But," he quickly added, "I'm damn glad I came now, I really am."

"Did you tell your wife you were glad you came?" she asked as she moved with him, holding him by the crook of his arm.

"No." The response was quick and short. "I meant to, but I haven't yet." He was nervous.

"John?"

"Yes?"

"Lose the mistress. It will do you no good and she doesn't love you as she professes. She's after your money." His face went pale, in concert his heart rate went through the roof. No one could know about Melissa, he thought.

"Not true, I know. And Mary strongly suspects you have been having an affair with your secretary now for some time. Soon she will know for sure. It's a woman thing, John. We always know when our men are being untrue to us," she responded to his thoughts.

"I will, Sarah, I will. God, I am sorry, and embarrassed. I will put an end to it as soon as I return home."

"Why will you, John?"

"Huh, what do you mean? You just told me to get rid of her."

"It was a suggestion. And if that's the only reason you do it, you will have another mistress before the year has ended."

"No, I mean it. I am going to patch things up with Mary and move on with my life."

"OK, John, I wish you both well. Let's rejoin your wife and send her home with a smile on her face, shall we?"

146

"Yes, we should do that."

Sarah guided John back to his wife, embraced her, and left the two of them holding hands. Sarah knew John wasn't going to get rid of Melissa, but Mary's prayers for intervention hadn't gone unanswered. She couldn't interfere with John's free agency, but she could stand as a witness to the fact that he had been duly advised of the magnitude of his decisions. Once again there would be no plea bargaining in the high court.

Sarah moved up and down the lines of people, touching them, giving words of encouragement and offering sympathy. Her venture into the mass lasted for four hours.

It was nearly nine o'clock before the sun started to set and the rain began to close in on the boundaries of Valentine, Texas. At the end of her time she approached the mayor and asked to take a meal with her and her large family. She had neither eaten or drunk for ten days and it was time to end her fast. She knew that the mayor's husband, a good man who helped take care of five little ones, wished to meet Sarah. They moved off to the home of the mayor under a soft gentle summer's evening shower. The home was modest and warm like its occupants. The children loved Sarah, but as usual gravitated toward Joshua who sat on the floor in silence and played with them.

Speeding toward Valentine ten miles west of Alpine, Texas, a fast small red sports car was swallowed up by a multi-vortex tornado. It spun wildly into the air one hundred and fifty feet before it slammed into the stone sides of the Sierras. The coward from Ghana was no more. Sun Ce had been waiting for him.

17

THE Stranger watched the sun slide behind the ancient Adirondacks, casting shades of blue and purple over the ice cold waters of Lake George. The moon would soon be rising in the east over the Green Mountains on the other side of the lake. His favorite time of day came, watching the moon climb into the night sky casting shadows like velvet patterns, shimmering shattered reflections like white gems upon the black waters of the lake. And then there was the majesty of dark places lit up ever so slightly by dim greys, light blues, and hints of silver. Soon familiar shadows would dance on the pine needle carpeting that covered the ground up to the edge of the cliffs along the back side of the property. His heart quickened whenever he watched the changing of the guard. Night was his dawn.

He closed his eyes and turned up his senses. The rhythm of the water slapping steadily against the shore reminded him of the auburn haired woman he had made love to earlier in the day. The sound pleased him. The woman had been steady, passionate, endless like the waves. The wind came out of the east. It smelled like the Atlantic to him and he could nearly taste the salt of the sea. It too reminded him of her, and he smiled.

The northern shoreline of Lake George was host to many palatial estates, but none was as singularly striking as Gadianton. Sunlight rose and fell on high spirals rising from the fifty-seven room main mansion. Guest homes dotted the nine hundred and seventy-two acres of manicured grounds and gardens. Each home came with its own fulltime staff. A massive stone wall made for the privacy the owner and his guests most enjoyed. Security was not a concern for anyone associated in any way at Gadianton. And on a clear night, as was the norm for this part of upstate New York, the Stranger could see a billion stars: he could see home.

Inside the mammoth main building, dinner was being prepared by three chefs whose talents made them employable by any of the finest restaurants in the world. But the Stranger paid them four times the wages they would make any place else. They had the finest and most modern of appliances available to them, yet much of what they prepared was done as in times of old. They knew what pleased their master.

A small army of servants spitpolished the mansion in anticipation of the arrival of the weekend guests. Everyone put in one hundred and fifty percent effort and the master took care of them. Alaine, his personal assistant, saw to the details of running Gadianton and his master's schedule. Each employee, including Alaine, would give his or her life for the Stranger if he asked for it. Some had been asked and, unfortunately, some had it taken away for his pure pleasure or hunger. It was the risk everyone accepted. All knew, once employed by the master of Gadianton, eternally employed. It was part of the deal, the contract.

Walking on white Georgian marble, he traced his fingers along the beautifully carved rail that surrounded the terrace. "It is exquisite here by my lake. The guests will begin arriving in just three hours," he thought. "I should go upstairs and rest before they come." Some of them had been with him before they drew their first mortal breath, none had failed him and survived.

"While that miserable excuse for competence, Bountiful, had failed, the guests of Gadianton will succeed. Bountiful was doomed to failure. Give them enough rope to hang themselves, and they blow themselves all to hell." He smiled at the thought. And then there was that wonderfully despicable fellow who had been roasted over the pit downstairs. The guests had just loved him. How many of the fools had unwittingly begged for the recipe? Laughter shook his entire body.

Thirteen of the selected weekend guests had no other interest than to please their host. They were there to deal with the specific task of doing away with "The Bitch", as she was commonly referred to. The weekend's guests list was designed by Alaine to avoid any suspicion as to the real agenda for the gathering. Governor and Mrs. John Hartfield, a few Congressmen, both of the state's U.S. senators, pillars of society, industry moguls and their wives and husbands were to be in attendance. There would be the usual contingent from the belly of all decadence, Hollywood. How he loved that town. Add a few social do-gooders and, *voila*, the weekend was set to celebrate the Fourth of July.

While many of the guests would be enjoying the fire works on his one hundred and fifty foot yacht, thirteen of them would be gathered in the library to discuss the issue at hand, being "the elimination of the woman and her sideshow companions." Of course they would not be able to touch the escorts, but if they got to her, they'd get to the others. A wide smile broke out across thin lips as he stared at the mountains across the lake that blocked his vision of her hometown.

"It won't be long now, they won't be able to shelter her beyond normal ordinary human effort. And when that day arrives, the very first hour of it, I will have her. I will destroy her. I wonder how she will taste," he thought.

149

"Now, however, it is time for the me to go upstairs and rest. I am hungry and tired." The master suite called to him like a siren on the high seas at midnight.

A servant opened massive french doors leading from the terrace to the great hall. As the Stranger passed, the servant bowed his head, never acknowledged by his master. The great hall, where the guests would gather after dinner before boarding the yacht, was his favorite in the entire mansion. He spent much of his time here when he wasn't in the master suite. The room, adorned with some of the rarest works of art in the entire world, spanned ages and represented every culture known to mankind. He simply could not enter the room without walking at least part of its massive perimeter, touching a vase here, a weapon there, a personal effect that belonged to another time.

While there were many objects of interest and value in the room, it did not have the cluttered appearance of a museum hall as one might expect. Interior decorators, architects, archeologists and members of the art world had assembled the room. It had taken him all of the one hundred and fifty years he owned the place to get the room to near perfection. The value of the contents of the room could not be calculated to the best of his knowledge. When he stopped to contemplate the bloodshed that many pieces of the collection had sponsored, a chill ran up his spine. It was getting late and he wanted to linger, but he could not. It was imperative that he get some rest.

Upstairs in the master suite the Stranger lowered himself into a larger than king-sized Jacuzzi. It was designed to hold as many as thirteen people, but he rarely used it for more than two or three. No man had ever been in it except himself. The water in the tub was kept at a specified constant temperature. The staff in charge of his bathing understood the fatal nature of the consequences if the water was found to be just one degree above that which the Stranger preferred. Great chunks of ice floated around him as his arms rested on the sides of the golden tub and his head leaned back against the Corinthian leather head rest. The very thought of warm water revolted him. How anyone could linger in it was a human thing beyond his ability to comprehend. The preference he had for cold water had drawn him to this part of the new world to begin with. Lake George, all thirty-seven miles in length, was fed by clear cold mountain water, melted snow. Even in the height of summer the temperature in the deep sections of the lake never rose much above fifty-seven degrees. And the deeper you sank into this seemingly bottomless lake, the colder it got. To dive into it on a moonless night and feel its sting against his body was a deliciously chilling gravelike experience.

He would ring for his dresser soon, but he wanted just fifteen more minutes to soak in his bath, to speak with his master. And he wanted not yet to leave

150

the pale young woman beside him with the blue tinge to her lips, wild, wide eyes and a gaping wound in her chest where her heart used to be. How lovely she is, or rather she was. She had been a strikingly beautiful creature, unlike the common redhead being prepared downstairs in the kitchen.

By nine o'clock that evening the guests had finished dinner. The sky was black as the last gasp of sunlight failed in its struggle to sneak back over the shadowy outlines of the gods of the west. The Stranger and thirteen others missed the evening cruise. As they moved toward the library, memories of Valentine, Texas, flashed through his mind and anger rose in his throat. "I will silence the ooooh's and ahhhhhhs forever. They will forget her and then with time, she will become a myth, a fictionalized object lesson, a parable just like the others."

The long black stretch limousine carrying the Ferunders rounded the corner onto Pennsylvania Avenue. The view of the two most famous monuments in DC, the Washington and the Lincoln, was striking and, notwithstanding the numerous parts of the world that Sarah had now seen, this was special. She was heading for a breakfast meeting with the President of the United States at the White House and then on to the National Press Club's weekly luncheon where she was the featured speaker. The invitation to address the NPC was received shortly after the *Valentine's Day Rains* a few weeks earlier. Even Sarah smiled at the play-on words, coined by the young reporter from Chicago during the brief moments they had shared that Saturday. The invitation to the White House was billed as a quiet family breakfast with the Ferunders. Cabinet members and their families would be present. And there would be a private tour of the White House, conducted by the First Lady for the Ferunder family.

The fact that Sarah had accepted an invitation to speak to the National Press Club's weekly luncheon was well publicized. Request for table places had never been so numerous from the four thousand two hundred member private club. It was the hottest ticket in town, perhaps in the history of a town synonymous with history. The news media went on a feeding frenzy when Sonja Hillgren, current president, had announced that Sarah would not be delivering a formal address to the members, rather she had requested time to answer their questions, no holds barred at a time limit of two hours.

Yes, Sarah had been around the world several times, she had even briefly glanced upon other worlds, but riding in the limo with her parents and Chicky to see the President and First Lady of the United States of America was a thrill she truly delighted in. It was every American's dream, really. Joshua did not ride with them. He wanted Sarah to have time with her family, although he wouldn't be far away. The capital city of freedom looked to Sarah like a magnificent jewel, she had seen it from the heavens and it looked just as wonderfully beautiful close up.

Kent Ferunder was especially nervous. He had only been a midlevel government employee, no matter how important his responsibilities at the NSA were. He had met one other U.S. president, just prior to the declaration of the Gulf War. But meeting George Bush seemed so long ago now and under such different circumstances. And, of course, he had never attended a social occasion with the nation's chief executive officer.

The limo moved up the road past the guard house around the circular drive, and stopped in front of the main entrance of the White House. The President and his family were waiting for them. "Just like on the evening news," Sarah thought as the limo came to a rest.

She was still a young girl in many ways, Joshua reminded himself as he watched unseen from a distance. While Sarah was as ecstatic as her parents, Chicky was sullen. He was not impressed. He did not like the President or his yuppie lawyer wife. The family implored him to be on his best behavior and he had promised to be civilized, but his gut told him something wasn't right. He didn't like this scene and he wasn't about to have a good time.

As Sarah stepped from the limo and reached out a hand to the outstretched arms of the President, she thought this would be a day she would tell her grandchildren about. And then for a flash of a second she remembered, Billy Stewart was no longer there and her heart ached again. Would she ever have grandchildren? She could not allow this to happen. She forced the thought from her mind, this was to be a happy day, one of excitement, celebration and of memories. Hugs and kisses, handshakes and new people to meet, and Sarah loved meeting new people.

She heard a warm welcome from the soft southern accent of the President and she returned to the present.

"Welcome to the White House, Sarah, Mr. and Mrs. Ferunder and, uh, Chicky, I believe?" He smiled his photo-op smile. "I would like to introduce you to the First Lady, Heather, and our two daughters, Melissa and Beth. We have been looking forward to this morning all week. Won't you please come inside the White House? You know, it's just as much your house as it is ours." He smiled again. Chicky muttered under his breath so no one could hear, "Yeah, my ass."

The group moved through the impressive front doors seen by Sarah and her family hundreds of times on the television. Moving down long corridors this way and that as the President spoke and the First Lady added commentary, the group moved into a small dining room where cabinet members and their families rose from their chairs and broke into spontaneous applause. Sarah acknowledged the response with a shy nod and smile; the rest of the family deferred to her.

Once seated at a large round table with the President and his family, the morning went as smoothly as a family gathering of close relatives. After the breakfast the President gave a formal welcome address to the Ferunders and offered the floor to Sarah for a few words.

"Good morning. It is such a pleasure to be here with you and your families. I am so happy that my family could be with me this morning, also. I would like to personally meet each one of you. I especially want to say hello to all the little children that I see scattered around the room. I have been many places in the last few years, but home is unlike any place on earth. I feel at home here in the States and, although I have never been to Washington before, I am surprised how much like home it feels to me." She cast a friendly glance at the President. "I would love to live here. Oh, not right here, Mr. President!" she quipped.

Laughter spread around the room as the President seemed to truly enjoy her sense of humor. Breakfast with him had made Sarah feel close to the First Family. "I mean, it is so exciting. And this afternoon, as many of you know, I am going into that lion's den called the National Press Club. I think I have seen a few of you dodging claws in that cave a time or two, so if you have any pointers, please let me know."

Her father's superior, the Secretary of Defense, blurted out, "I have some, Sarah. Cancel! That was good advice I didn't take!" More good-natured banter exchanged during her brief remarks.

At the end of the formal breakfast Sarah mingled with the small private audience. She walked with the children who moved to her and wanted to know where Joshua was. "Oh, even angels have a day off now and then," she kidded them. But if you watch televison tonight, you will get to see him. He only gets half days off." A smile always graced her face when she was with the children. She took private moments with each young person and child there. Most times, only a glance in their direction and a touch of the hand let them know how much she cared about them. The four or five smallest children clung to her. She loved every minute of it.

"Ladies and gentleman, if I might have your attention please," the President spoke. "The First Lady has been gracious enough to volunteer her services as a White House guide and will take the Ferunders for a special short tour of the

White House." Some wives had already been briefed, they would be going along on their two millionth tour, like it or not.

"I have asked to speak privately with Sarah, and Don Martinovich, our chief of staff, for a moment before she rejoins her parents for the rest of the tour. Thank you all so much for coming and if you will follow Heather out the door to my left, I will leave you in her capable hands."

Sarah's family led twenty other men and women out the door as the President moved toward Sarah and asked if she would like to see the Oval Office. "Why, yes, I would like that very much, Mr. President. And I promise I don't want to move in there either," she added with a smile.

"Well, I am sure you could if you really wanted to, sweetheart, but promise me you won't run until my next term is up and then you have to be a member of our party."

"Oh no, I've been warned by Joshua. No politics!" she said. "Next thing I know I will be asked to endorse basketball shoes!"

The trio entered the office and the President and his chief of staff let Sarah take in the room before they each launched into a mini history lesson of the objects currently decorating it. All went well until the President pointed to a beautifully carved wooden statuette of an Iroquois native American. "This was presented to me by a lifelong friend from upstate New York." He second-guessed himself the minute he blurted it out. Don Martinovich saw the twinge in the President's eye, but had no clue what it meant. Sarah knew instantly.

"Really, tell me about it," she smiled as she strode over to the image of a noble man carrying a young child on his shoulders. "I just love native American art, don't you, Mr. President?"

"Why, yes, I do. That's why this is one of my favorite pieces. It is supposed to have been carved sometime prior to the revolutionary war by a member of the Iroquois Nation. The man seems powerful yet compassionate, doesn't he?"

"Yes, I feel that same thing about him." She turned to the President and said, "He was a member of the Hatinyahte' clan. It means turtle clan. His child was taken from him and murdered by the British at a place called Chayouga. It was done in front of him. The boy was only ten years old when he died. It is a shame when grown men take the blood of children upon their hands, don't you think? It always makes me so sad."

"Yes, it is the one thing that is truly distasteful about holding this office. Some of the decisions you have to make may cause innocent suffering." The President was uneasy now and moved for the security of his large executive desk. "Uh, sit with us a moment, Sarah. Don and I have a few questions to ask you that could be of enormous importance to the country and to the world at large."

"Certainly, Mr. President. But may I ask you and Mr. Martinovich a question or two before we move on to yours?"

"Why, of course," he smiled. "You are our guest and anything we can do for you is completely our pleasure."

"Actually, I don't need anything done. I just have these questions that keep bothering me and I thought if I asked you personally, I might be able to resolve the matter in my own mind. It's just something I don't understand."

"Well, go ahead and ask, and if Don or I can supply an answer we will. If we can't, we damn well know how to find out. . . oh, excuse my language, honey, that was a slip," he smiled.

"Don't worry, I won't tell my lunch companions you shocked me with a bad word," she returned the smile. "You know about the bombing in London. That was meant for me. At least that's what the press said."

"Yes, darling, we do know about that and an attack on an American citizen of this nature is not something this administration will ever stand for. We have our top men working on it even as we speak. And we will not stop until the cowards who planted that bomb are brought to justice."

". . . and you know that one of my childhood friends was murdered a block from my home in a most terrible and gruesome fashion." Her voice trailed off for a moment. The President who had gained some composure started to move from behind his desk to offer comfort when Sarah held up her hand and lifted her head. There were tears in her eyes. Her sorrow genuinely affected Don Martinovich. He was a good family man and, after all, this young woman in front of him was his daughter's age. He felt for her.

"Mr. President, I am glad that Mr. Martinovich is here, because I have to ask two very difficult questions. How did you feel after you heard about each of those two events?"

"Well, Sarah! We were crushed. The First Lady and I and the girls were just as devastated as you can possibly imagine. I can't tell you in words you how the senseless death of little children makes us feel. It is a crime against nature."

"No, Mr. President. It is a crime against God."

"Well, that is what I meant, Sarah. And as for your school friend Billy, eh, I am sorry I don't remember his surname. He was just a young man also. We feel just as anguished about that as we do about any innocent life that has been lost." The President looked to Martinovich for support which was forthcoming in an affirmative nod of his head.

"Then, Mr. President, why did you murder them?"

18

KENT and Susan Ferunder were anxious to return to their hotel after the White House tour. They had been in Washington for a week now and were scheduled to leave later that day for an extended vacation at their cottage south of Ferrisburg. And although a matter of personal urgency had kept the President from personally bidding them farewell, they had enjoyed their visit to the White House. They intended to watch Sarah's appearance before the NPC on television in their room and then enjoy a lazy day poolside. Chicky was attending the NPC luncheon and planned to meet Kent and Susan Ferunder for dinner that evening with Sarah before attending her appearance at the capital Mall. Brother and sister would join mom and dad at the cabin the following day.

The limo carrying Sarah and Chicky approached 14th and F street, home of the National Press Club. The now famous luncheons had begun in 1932 but none of the forty-six hundred and twenty luncheons that preceded today's event had sparked the excitement that surrounded this one. Anyone who was anybody would be attending this gathering at the "Sanctum Sanctorum of American Journalism."

The limousine rolled to a slow halt in front of the NPC's impressive building. Exiting the long black car, Chicky took Sarah by the hand and assisted her out into the bright summer sun. A few thousand people had gathered and were standing behind police ropes, hoping to catch a glimpse of the guest of honor. The crowd of mostly young people began chanting her name. She couldn't resist stopping with them for a few minutes, because she considered herself one of them.

"I haven't forgotten you. I will see you tonight at the Lincoln Memorial if you will come." The crowd responded enthusiastically as she waved to them and moved toward her hosts.

The Officers and the Board of Governors were waiting to greet the most famous and most curious of all the visitors that had ever graced the club's facilities. Sonja Hillgren welcomed Sarah to the club. "Good afternoon, dear. Won't you please come in and catch your breath for a few moments before we go upstairs and meet the membership?" Sarah had requested a small private room where she could freshen up and collect her thoughts before the luncheon and question-answer portion of the day. Now that the time had arrived, she found herself looking forward to meeting a press she sometimes felt frustration, even anger with.

After large wooden doors closed behind Sarah and her brother in a small comfortable room on one of the top floors of the building, Sarah and Joshua spoke for the first time that morning since the visit to the White House. "How could he stand by while his own cousin was murdered? It's not just that he was a part of them, he's the moving force! He wants to destroy me!"

"Yes, he's an evil man. I wanted to tell you many times but, knowing that this day was coming, I decided that it was one of those tutorials best learned first person."

"Yes. But I'm still reeling from the fact that any man that has attempted to destroy us, our family, our mission, could sit with us at a breakfast table and smile like he did. Why couldn't I recognize it?"

"Because I wouldn't let you, little one. I wanted you to hear it at the right moment and in the right place. And you did, in the Oval Office."

"But Josh, if they had apprehensions about us, why didn't they just come and ask us about the consequences of our mission? I don't understand that. Did they think that Heavenly Father would have a message delivered that would destroy those He was desiring to help? Didn't they see Children's Memorial in its resurgence as they did in its time of concern? The hospital has never enjoyed such success, such a high level of contributions. Don't they understand that you have to die a little to grow a little?"

"No, Sarah, it's not that they don't know. They *choose* not to know these things. Make no mistake about it, there are millions just like them. They close their eyes and pretend not to see, justifying their wrongdoings with a false blindness. Unfortunately, as we have discussed many times in the past, men who greed after power, lust, and riches, never understand their lack of satisfaction. They will never find real happiness or peace in their quests. That the treasures of the earth surround them without notice, is a real irony. Why do they miss the ordinary pleasures of existence? Because they are the ever-seekers. Ever seeking and never learning. Soon the tutorial will be spent on each of them and they will realize that in their wasted ability to do so much good, lies their own condemnation. Yes, little one, it is sad."

"Well, I never thought in all my days I would witness the President of the United States faint dead away and fall right on his big ole stupid butt in the Oval Office! The pandemonium, phew! It was truly delightful." Joshua and Chicky joined in her smile until Chicky snorted and the trio burst into laughter. It was the closest either had seen Sarah come to using profanity, except once in the river when she slipped while wading and fell in head over heels. She had been dressed for an appearance. She insisted on returning home to make things right rather than letting Josh do his magic. She was funny about some things like that.

"My two handsome men. Let's join hands and prepare before we go out to bless the wolves," she became serious again.

When Sarah opened the door to the room, the welcoming committee was pacing about in the foyer. The expressions on their faces registered surprise that Joshua was with her. Eyebrows hit hairlines, jaws dropped, and a few low whistles ensued. In the excitement that had followed the acceptance of Sarah's invitation, someone had forgotten to consider that Sarah had never been seen anywhere without her constant companion. At least until the White House that morning. How could such a violation of protocol have occurred? Sonja looked at her staff with glaring eyes and an enormous volume of restraint. Janine Johnson, a member of the Board of Governors, set things right, perhaps the only one in the room who could have.

She walked right over to Joshua and stuck out her hand to him. "Well, my friend, we didn't have enough intelligence or good manners to expect you. But then again, you knew that and so you must know that you are welcome here." She smiled widely, exposing beautiful white teeth and sparkling brown eyes. "Now before we show you to lunch, I need to clarify one more point of protocol. Is it OK for a tired old grandmother to give such a gorgeous young man a hug?" She grinned more broadly now.

"Yes, it is, Grandmother Johnson," Sarah replied. Janine reached out her arms and embraced Joshua. She was a tiny woman whose head only came to his chest. She listened for the sign she wanted and when she could hear his heart beating, it made her smile. Joshua felt the strength of an amazing woman and the tender heart of a grandmother, as her arms surrounded him for that brief moment.

"Well, Sarah, I hope I didn't make you jealous hugging your companion like that, but I have been waiting to do so for a long time now. Besides, he is so huggable, don't you think?"

"Yes, I agree, he is," she said. "I hug him all the time. Don't ya just envy me to death?"

"Ms. Ferunder?" It was Gilbert Newman, Chair of the Board. "If you are ready, we are about on schedule and like to keep it that way if possible." It was apparent that Newman wasn't as thrilled as the rest of the group with Sarah's presence, but then he had enjoyed dinner and extramarital companionship at the expense of the Stranger the evening before.

"Yes, Mr. Newman, we are as ready as we will ever be." Sarah smiled at him. She decided to nip his attitude in the bud. She let him know she knew about his social schedule the night before telepathically. When the thought hit his mind, it paled him.

"And please do call me Sarah, I prefer it, really."

With the announcement that Sarah was ready to meet the members, Sonja took Sarah's right arm, Janine Johnson took her left, as if to protect her until they reached the banquet room where the luncheon was to take place.

The luncheon concluded. Silence came over the room as Sonja approached the lectern.

"I see from the attendance today and the warm welcome our guests have received that they really need no introduction. However, it is always nice to formally introduce your guests to your friends and professional associates. Ladies and gentlemen, Sarah Ferunder, her companion Joshua and her brother Charles Ferunder have been gracious in accepting our invitation to dine with us this afternoon. Sarah has taken time from a busy schedule to be here today. She just arrived after having spent what we hope was an enjoyable morning at the White House. She will be speaking to the citizens of the great District of Columbia and the world at large from the Mall this evening. It has been a busy day for her already, so I hope you will be on your best behavior, which is frightening in and of itself." She flashed a big smile. "Please welcome our guest." Turning to the dias, she continued, "Sarah, you are truly one of the most remarkable persons of all time. It is a pleasure, a personal pleasure I shall never forget, to introduce you to the members of the National Press Club. Ladies and Gentlemen, Ms. Sarah Ferunder."

Enthusiastic applause greeted Sarah as she rose and approached the microphone. Joshua, who had been standing behind her, joined her at the podium. The audience as usual glanced back and forth from Joshua to Sarah. Once again they couldn't decide which one was more fascinating.

"Ladies and gentlemen of the National Press Club, good afternoon. We appreciate the opportunity to meet with you this beautiful July afternoon in our nation's capital." The room was so quiet that a pin dropping would have sounded like a terrorist bomb. "I should tell you that my companion is not shy, but I will be the only one taking questions this afternoon," she announced. "It is my understanding that we have agreed to a two hour time limit. I hope that I might answer as many of your questions as possible during that time. When your question is read will you please raise your hand so I might see your face before answering your question? I understand that Sonja will be reading them to me.

159

May I speak with you briefly before we begin? Oh, please forgive me. I know I advised the committee that I was not going to address you, but I am a woman after all, and I am therefore entitled to certain prerogatives as such. So, I've changed my mind. But I promise not to eat into your question time; as far as I am concerned we will begin timing the two hour limit at the conclusion of my brief remarks. OK?

I have not had a chance to meet many of you, but that doesn't mean that I don't know you. I *know* each and everyone in this room. I know your dreams and aspirations, I know your strengths and weaknesses, I know your successes and failures, I know your pasts and futures and, most importantly, I know your hearts. And in spite of the concern I know some of you have about me having such knowledge, I want you to know that I still love each and every one of you. You know, it has been said that a friend is someone who knows all about you and still likes you!"

That remark brought soft careful laughter. So she continued with a confident smile, "Whatever some of you may perceive our differences to be, let us put them aside for the next few hours and be friends. I know I must seem odd to you, but I am no different than you. Really, I'm not. I am still just a young woman from Ferrisburg, Vermont. A young woman who understands the doubts you have. Had I not experienced the things that I have personally experienced, I might possibly have the same concerns. So how could I sit in judgement of you on that count? Thank you for coming and allowing me the opportunity to share that thought with you. I will now take your questions."

Sonja stepped to the microphone. "Obviously, Sarah, each of us here in this room would love to spend days with you so we were not surprised by the unprecedented numbers of questions submitted. To be fair we will be picking them at random from the large crystal bowl at the end of the dias. While some important issues may be passed over by using this means, we could think of no other possible way to see that each person had a reasonable chance to have his or her question read. So if you are ready, here goes the first question. "Stan Humphrey of the *Globe*."

Sarah knew Stan's question before it was even asked. Stan still had a problem with women not staying in the kitchen.

"In London, Peking and as recently as Valentine, Texas, you alluded to a 'Mother in Heaven'." Humphrey grinned widely as his question was being read. "Are you saying God has a wife? And if that is true, is there a duality of Gods in Heaven, and I'd sure like to know who wears the pants in that family. I'm having a very hard time with that one. As are most of the world's theological scholars."

160

"Oh, Stan, don't let it give you too hard a time," Sarah playfully mocked. "Yes, that is exactly what I am saying. That is one of the messages I have been sent to communicate. Father has an eternal companion. She is above all that is just, beautiful and majestic. And you will find, Stan, that not all men have trouble with it. As you ponder, pray and question these eternal relationships, you discover more about your own relationships. That should be a relief for your wife." Sarah smiled and the room laughed, knowing Humphrey was one of the cities most outspoken sexists.

"I can say nothing to make you feel more comfortable with the truth. That is your job, Stan. As for the world's theological scholars," she smiled once again, "perhaps they paid no attention to the events that took place in London, Peking, Ghana, Valentine, or to this man standing behind me." Humphrey's grin disappeared as he looked past Sarah's shoulder at Joshua.

Sonja stepped to the microphone again. "Next, Sarah, from Clyde Alvarez, a free lance reporter and writer. He says, 'I'm a little confused. You seem to use the term Father and God interchangeably. But you use the term Father more than God. Is there a difference? I honestly wonder if there is a God, what about life after death?'"

Sarah knew that Clyde was a good man and a good reporter. "I appreciate your question, Clyde. It is a good one and I can tell an honest one. Now to answer it for you, I refer to God and Father as one because they are one and the same. Prior to my calling in the grove I referred to God as you do. But when I became more familiar with Him, I understood His preference for the more intimate title of Father, so I use that instead. And I assure you He exists. Don't let all the opinions and the nay sayers dissuade you from that, Clyde. He is as real as you and I. And if you want to know if there is life after death, take a look over my shoulder." She glanced over her shoulder at a grinning Joshua once again. The audience's eyes drifted to him. There wasn't need for a follow-up question. But she asked if he had one anyway.

"Well, yes, I guess like any good reporter I have a million follow-up questions."

"Great, why don't you ask one, Clyde?" Her smile broadened as she shot a thumb over her shoulder toward Joshua. "Maybe he'll give you an exclusive!"

"Be hell of a story, wouldn't it," he grinned.

"Yes, it would. Mention my name and if he gives you the story, you owe me lunch," she said. Looking over the rest of the room, "This is scary, I'm starting to feel this city rub off on me." As the room chuckled warmly, Joshua knew they were warming to her, all except a very few.

Sonja stepped forward with the next question. It had wiped the smile from her face. Even as a seasoned journalist it embarrassed her.

"Sarah, Sylvia Collins of the Baltimore *Sun*. How would you describe your relationship with Billy Stewart? Some have described it as more than romantic. Some have described it as sexual. Was it? And are you a virgin?" Sarah had been waiting for Sylvia Collins, the source of the rumors that had swept the planet after Billy's death.

"I loved Billy Stewart before we ever came to this earth. I loved him before the earth was. Billy and I grew up together. There wasn't a selfish bone in his body. And I cannot remember a moment in my life when I didn't love him with all my heart. My relationship with Billy was a clean, wholesome, blessed , wonderful relationship and it was very romantic. And yes, I am still a virgin."

Looking over a sea of somewhat embarrassed veteran journalists, Sarah sought out the woman who had penned the question. She was sitting at her table, an arrogant look on her face, shaking her head indicating disbelief.

"It is difficult, Sylvia, for some who have spent their life in a moral abyss to understand the purity of others, but that does not change the truth. Some choose not to report stories, some choose to invent them. I don't see what is gained by attempting to corrupt that which is incorruptible."

"Would you like the next question, Sarah?" Sonja asked.

"Yes, thank you."

"Joan Bolt, *The Daily News*. Is there one true religion on earth as you mentioned in one of your very first public appearances two years ago? And if so, which one is it?"

"Thanks, Joan. There is only one true God with whom we need to concern ourselves. Many religions are near to Him in their doctrine and in the core of their teachings, as are the spiritual leaders of those religions. Of major concern to Him and to us is that many are near to Him with their lips, but their hearts are far from Him. That is to say that they talk a good game, but do not practice what they preach. There are many reasons for this, unfortunately I do not have the time to address them now. The short answer to your question, I suppose, is yes. And I mean that there is one institution that embodies His will with *divine authority* . Does that mean that all others are wrong or evil or bad? No.

In three months time I have planned an appearance in Kalispell, Montana. At that time I will reveal the details of the answer to your question. The meeting will take place on the ranch of a Mr. Patrick Cassidy. I hope that isn't too vague for you. If it is, come and see me in Montana, OK?"

"Next question, Sarah, is from Mr. Clinton Giese." Sonja enjoyed her role. "If you make an announcement, let's say for the sake of argument, that the one

162

religion that embodies the only true authority of God on the earth is an oriental religion, are you not risking the wrath of millions upon millions of Christians?"

"Wow, how timely a question. Where are you, Clint?" The good-looking reporter was present and raised his hand. "The answer is simple. Yes, I will offend millions, I suppose. But I would rather offend man than God. What would you do if you were me and knew the truth for an absolute certainty? Fear the wrath of God or of his children? I think I will take my chances and tell the truth. The truth can never be sacrificed in this arena. There are people who know what is to come. And they have tried to destroy the truth and me, because of it. They will not destroy the truth.

And what if in Kalispell my answer is Christianity, or one of the hundreds of sects of Christianity? Will I not offend our oriental brothers, our Arabic, our Jewish, or millions of others? Sadly the answer has to be yes, I will. And I will tell you the reason why that offense will be taken by the world community on that day. People value their traditions over God. When religion becomes tradition, tradition replaces religion. A line has been crossed that can lead nowhere else but to offense. What if in three months I say to the world that there should never be another Christmas celebration? Would I cause offense? You bet. Why? Do you think the uproar will be because I have struck out against God, or because I have stepped on the toes of the toy makers? It won't be because I have mocked God. It will be because I have mocked tradition. Don't get me wrong, tradition is good, but it has also caused wars and kept people from knowing their God. I can only do what I have been asked to do and say what I have been asked to say. And if you were me, would you not do the same thing?"

Clint stared at the young woman for a second, taking in her countenance. "Yes Sarah, I believe I would do the same thing if I were you." He had kind eyes.

"The next question, Sarah, is from John James of Donnelly Communications." Sonja had a smile on her face. Sarah knew something was up. "Sarah, first may I have your autograph for my daughter and can I give you a hug?"

"Ah, the nicest question so far. The answer to both of them is, you bet! Come on up here, John."

The large man rose from a table near the front and began his way toward the lectern. Sarah reached her hand toward the shelf inside the lectern, choosing a large red magic marker. When he reached Sarah, she turned him around and took his suit jacket off. "John, I am going to autograph your shirt. Your wife will never have to iron it again, OK?"

"Sure." He smiled at her over his shoulder as she removed the jacket. "She will be real grateful." Sarah wrote with exaggerated swipes of the pen. When finished, she turned him around and gave him a big hug, at which time the audience could read the autograph. It said, "This chump has no daughter! Love, Sarah." There was a smily face under the note above her signature. The room exploded into laughter. He knew he had been had, but placed a tender kiss on Sarah's cheek and smiled at her. He started toward his table and had nearly reached it when Sarah called out to him.

"John, come back here for a moment, will you?" John somewhat reluctantly returned to the lectern, wearing a sheepish grin. Sarah embraced the big man one more time whispering in his ear. When he returned to the table, he had tears in his eyes and the knowledge that he and his wife would soon enjoy the pleasure of raising a newborn daughter they had futilely been trying to conceive.

"Sarah, the next question comes from Elizabeth Barrow, a free lance writer here in Washington. It says, "I am curious about your companion, Joshua. Where does he come from, what is his purpose, and why is he always with you?""

"Why is he always with me? Well, look at him, ladies... End of answer." She winked at a table filled with women. Joshua looked genuinely embarrassed for the first time Sarah had known him. Applause erupted from the entire room. "OK, I will try to be serious, Elizabeth. He is from New Jersey, which is why he has that faint glow about him." Again laughter erupted throughout the room.

"She's winning them, but at my expense," Joshua smiled to himself.

"Will somebody tell me how so many free lance journalists got in here? I thought you guys were the ones without jobs." The audience was now applauding. They were falling in love with her.

"Elizabeth, where are you? Stand up for me a minute, will you?" The woman stood, nervously looking around the room. "I want to say something to you and I hope I don't embarrass you. You are a wonderful person with a great talent for writing. The project you are working on now will be one of your life's most important works. It will be successful and touch many lives. Don't give up on it, OK?" Sarah looked tenderly at the woman who, as a single mother, worked day and night to support her children. Her current novel was a project she was hoping would move her off a barely livable income.

"You want to know about Joshua. He comes from that same Father that blessed you with the talents you have to finish that project. He has been with me as a friend, a playmate, educator, shepherd, and protector since I can remember. You want to know why he is here? He is here to sanctify those things that I say and do. I venture to say that if it had not been for his presence as a witness and validator of my acts, I would probably not be here this afternoon. I am afraid, my dear friend, that I am not at liberty to tell you any more about him than I already have."

All eyes were on Joshua as Sarah spoke of him. His eyes moved to Elizabeth and with a nod of his head he ratified those things Sarah had told her and was telling her. She smiled at him and slowly sank to her seat. "Elizabeth," Sarah spoke to her again. "Your husband is just fine." A sense of peace like a springtime morning dew settled on Beth for the first time since her husband, Jim, had died in an automobile accident. It had occurred on the beltway ten years ago that very day. Elizabeth lowered her head and said a quiet prayer of thanksgiving.

Sonja's voice jolted the audience. "Sarah, the next question is from Dorothy Sullivan of the Baltimore *Sun*."

"Good, we finally got somebody who has a full time job." Sarah playfully winked at Sonja.

"Sarah, do you attend a church regularly?"

"Nice try, Dorothy. Yes, I do when possible. I attend as many different churches and religious services as possible, but you needn't assume anything from that." She laughed. "And, Dorothy, Pastor Goldzung would like to see you more often too!" Laughter once again consumed the room. "The answer to the real question behind your question will be answered in Montana. Perhaps you will join us?"

"Next question. Sarah, this is from Larry Sandberg Nicholls from the *Hearst* newspapers. Here is Larry's question. 'While there is much good wherever you go, it seems to be followed by tragedy. If we understand your efforts to be the source of good, is it not logical to assume that they are also the source of the bad? And if not, why not?'"

"Thank you for that question, Larry. It is a good one and one I had hoped I would have the chance to answer. No, our work is not the source of the evil, Larry. I know there are some who would have you believe that, some in this very room." Gilbert sank down into his chair. "In fact, it is erroneous to believe that good and evil arise from the same source. Father plays an active role in our lives, but he is blamed for much more than he participates in. For the most part the laws of the universe, which he set in motion, govern. That is not to say he can't and won't become involved if it is, in His wisdom, wise to do so. As for me, I am but an instrument in His hands.

165

It is an eternal truth that there must be opposition in all things. That is to say we would not truly know and appreciate happiness if there were no sadness. We would not value health if we did not know sickness. Do you see the correlation? To assume that evil arises from me, simply because there is opposition to me, would be akin to blaming the Red Cross for the natural disasters they respond to.

But your observation carries some validity. I am the target of evil, and so where I go, it follows, unfortunately. As I have already pointed out, there are those who would not have me speaking with you and your colleagues here this afternoon. And they would do anything to stop me, to censor me if you will." She shot a glance at Gilbert. "London was a good example of that effort. Many innocents were murdered by those who oppose me and who have tried to place responsibility for the deaths of the children on our heads. London and Billy Stewart..." her voice wavered a little at the thought of these two most painful events, lost children and lost love, "... were excellent examples of the extremes to which evil will go to accomplish its end." The room was still. The hurt in her eyes and voice pierced the men and woman present.

"Thank you, Sarah." Larry nodded his head towards her and winked a fatherly wink in her direction before sitting down.

"You are welcome, Larry. And by the way, you may want to call your neighbor. You left the faucet on in the laundry room this morning and the sink is overflowing." She smiled broadly at him as whoops and howls hit the ceiling of the room.

Once the room settled down and Sonja regained her own composure, she approached the microphone with another three by five card in her hand. "Sarah, David Jawarski would like to know the following: 'You met the President and his cabinet this morning. What were your impressions of him and will you vote for him next year?'"

"I've heard that this place has been described as the only hallowed place in the world where irreverence was practiced." She grinned. "I was wondering when you guys were gonna come after me. We had a wonderful breakfast with the President, his family and the cabinet and their extended families. Something that I was unaware of until our meeting was that the President and I both share a love of native American art. I think I would not be guilty of exaggeration if I said my knowledge of the subject simply took his breath away. In fact, I think you would be safe in saying I floored him."

"We spoke of many issues important to world peace and since I had not had the opportunity previously, I did my best to console him on the loss of a dear cousin. I assured him she was in receipt of her eternal reward." Those in attendance looked around the room, questioning glances bouncing off one another. "Cousin? What cousin?"

Sonja missed her chance. Busy attending to small details, she did not hear the reference. "Sarah, the next question is a group question from table number fifty-seven and is submitted by Jennifer Terme from the *Congressional Quarterly*. How old were you when you knew something was different about you, where do you go when no one knows where you are and when did you perform your first miracle?"

"I have never felt different than any of you so I don't know how to answer that exactly. I suppose when I told Billy about Joshua for the first time I knew that I was a little different. If I told you where I went when you couldn't find me. . . duh! . . . you would know where I was! And then you could find me and I would have to give up a perfectly good hiding place. Uh-uh, I'm not tellin you." Sarah beamed at the room.

"And lastly, I have never performed a miracle. Father used me to heal the children in Chicago. That was the first time I knew He could help people that way. It has been a continuing tutorial, you know, line upon line, precept upon precept. Mostly I just do what I feel He wants me to do in any given situation. Thank you for your question, Jennifer."

"Sarah, the next question is from Janice Morrison from the *Bloomberg Business News*."

"Have you seen Heavenly Father? What is he like?"

"Thank you for that question, Janice. Yes, I have seen Him. He is like everything you have ever wished Him to be like and a million times more. He is truly beyond man's conceptual abilities. I realize now how difficult it must have been for the ancients to write of him and how the descriptions could be so varied. He is all things to all peoples. Father is more loving, more tender, and more beautiful than you have ever imagined. He is far more wonderful than the words of man can describe. His intellect and his caring for us, his children, are what astounds me the most. He is the very source of love. One cell of his brain carries the knowledge of all that is known or will be known to this world. He is impossible for me to describe. Yes, I have seen Him. I know this shocks some of you and some will cry blasphemy, but it is true.

His home, your home, our home, is equally indescribable except to say that it is the embodiment of all that is noble and great, peaceful and good. You will see it one day, Janice, I promise. Oh, and don't worry, dear. It won't be soon."

Janice cracked up. "Well, thank you, Sarah. That's a relief!"

"Sarah, we have time for only three more questions. I will give them to you at once so that the time remaining will be used for your response if that is OK with you. They come from Steven Lin from *Business Week*, Christopher Rogers from *Associated Press* and Joan O'Rielly from the *Washington Review*.

First, is there a heaven and a hell, and if so, what are they? Second from Chris, why you and why a woman, that has not historically been the vessel through which God has revealed himself, if the scriptures are to be believed? Third, it has been reported that you resurrected an entire village in Ghana. If you could do that and you loved Billy Stewart so much, why didn't you save him?"

The last question obviously pained Sarah. "I will do my best to answer these last three questions for you. I appreciate the opportunity to respond. It is obvious even to me that you have been kinder to me than you might otherwise have treated another guest. I am not sure why this has been the case, but I do appreciate your restraint." She smiled weakly at the now friendly audience. In fact, the author of the last question was embarrassed that it had been drawn. Sarah looked at her.

"It's OK, Joan, it is a fair question and I will answer it first. I couldn't rescue him. If I could have, you bet I would have, but I could not. Sometimes the answer to prayers is, no. I am no exception. Sometimes no answer, silence, is the answer. In my darkest desperation I pled with Joshua, with Heavenly Father, to let me bring him back. If you could speak with Josh, he would tell you how I begged for Billy's return." She turned to Joshua whose compassion for her was obvious. Small tears welled in her eyes as she turned back to a silent room. "But it was not permitted. It is normal to ask why, when these things occur. Why did it happen? I know why and, importantly, who is responsible for Billy's murder. Believe me when I tell you, even some of the highest authorities in this land know. And if I were to tell you here this afternoon how high that knowledge goes, it would be the story of the century. But I will not."

A small murmur of speculation, accompanied by a few low whistles, rose across the room nearly as high as some eyebrows.

"Why couldn't I bring my love back to me? Father, in wisdom and love, has answered that question for me a million times, or so it seems, and I am at peace with His answer. If I had not lost Billy, I could never look into the eyes of another who had lost a loved one, and completely understand the anguish taking place. There is, in some instances, only one way to learn the tough lessons, and that is firsthand. We all know that. Each one of you has had the tutorial of losing someone you love or were close to. Billy was my first. It was a necessary tutorial for my personal progression.

And lest you feel Billy was cheated at the expense of my tutorial, you should know that before he ever came to this earth, he consented to his role in my life. Now do you understand why I love him so? Do you see what a noble spirit he is? Who here would volunteer his or her life as Billy Stewart did? Not many of us are cut from the same spiritual cloth Billy Stewart is. I only hope I will remain faithful and be worth of his companionship when my time to leave here arrives." Even Sylvia Collins of the Baltimore *Sun* bowed her head.

"I hope that answers your question, Joan. Then, why me, why a woman? Why not? Is there another person, male or female, more worthy? I suppose there may be a thousand thousands more worthy than I, but then that person would be standing here answering the same question with the same answer and we would be here for eternity, wouldn't we? The bottom line I guess is that it has to be somebody and Father makes the choice.

And if you are indeed a scholar of ancient scriptures, you should be better informed. Father has always used women to teach the important issues to mankind. For instance, in the Christian faith you believe in the resurrection of Jesus the Christ. Who was first at his tomb? Peter, James ,John, Matthew, Thomas? No, *her* name was Mary. So when it came time to announce to the world life eternal, a woman was chosen, not one of his apostles. Why not a woman, why not me? I could cite hundreds of similar scriptural passages from hundreds of faiths and denominations. As they say in the great Empire of China, 'Women hold up half the sky.' I know it may be problematic for some that I have been chosen. I don't know why I was chosen, Chris. And sometimes in my weariness I wish another had been, but I don't really mean that. I am glad that I have had the experiences I have had and I would not change anything for all the riches in creation. I only know that He knows that I know. And that my love for Him has no boundary, there is nothing I would not do for Him."

The instant she uttered that sentence, she challenged herself. Was it true or not, she thought. Would she do anything? Would she sacrifice anything? She would soon find out.

She finished. "Where much is given, as in my case, much is required. An old Mormon expression I am learning the significance of. Lastly, is there a heaven and a hell? I presume you mean this in the context of the Christian dogma as you know it. I will assure you that there is a celestial dwelling where the Creator of all resides. I will tell you that it is His purpose and glory to see you return to that place. It is, after all, the place from which you came. I have been permitted to see that place. It's beyond description. Another prophet once said if mankind could see the glory of Heaven, they would look upon death in an entirely different light. He was right.

And hell. What is hell? Do not be misled. As surely as Heaven exist in all its indescribable glory, hell exists in opposition to it. It is as real as anything you worship. But the real essence of hell will be knowing what your potential was and never being able to achieve it. If you aspire to become the great American novelist and you only take time to master the alphabet, you have created your own hell. It will be much like that for many people when the day of accountability arrives. So many, with so much unrealized potential. It will not be a happy day in heaven when so many are lost."

The questions lasted for the two hour limit and Sarah, feeling the emotional and physical drain of the day, wanted to stay longer, but she was maturing and realized she still had to meet the people on the Mall that evening. She was going to need her strength tonight.

"I see that my time with you has drawn to an end. I know you all have a few thousand questions each. I will be on the Mall this evening, so maybe some of you will come and find more answers there. I appreciate the invitation to come here and meet with you, both my supporters and detractors. I mean that, I genuinely do. I don't know if you will invite me back here to see you again, but if my schedule doesn't permit it, will you remember these parting words to you? I love you, peace to your souls, and may heaven watch over you as you dream. God bless you and thank you."

The room broke into more than its usual polite applause. Some who had not followed Sarah enthusiastically were won over. Some were not. But at the end of the day it was clear from the lines that had been drawn in the sand, there were more on the friendly side than not. And that was exactly what Sarah had wanted to accomplish. All of the Governing Board members and General Officers came for an embrace, a handshake, or well-wishes except Gilbert Newman. He left the room quietly, quickly.

Thus the press luncheon ended. Sarah, Joshua, and Chicky returned to the small private room to rest a few minutes and to pray before returning to Sarah's hotel. Joshua was pleased with her. He teased her about embarrassing him with the ladies and jokingly promised retribution when she least expected it. Chicky lay on an oversized couch, thoroughly invigorated by the exchange. It was a heck of a lot better than breakfast with that S.O.B. in the White House. This time Sarah didn't correct Chicky's feelings for the President. She knew he would stand at her side one day, she testifying to the President's corruption. And there would be no appeal from that court either.

170

The ride back to The Hampshire was uneventful. There would be a good crowd at the Mall tonight. She was very happy after the National Press Club luncheon. When she arrived in her room, she looked out the window and could see her parents sunbathing at poolside. Chicky headed for the pool to join his parents and escape the ever present press.

In the White House, meanwhile, a recovering and very angry President was in conference with a senior NSA official and the director of the CIA.

19

"**B**UT Mr. President . . ."

"Shut up, Harold. I want this taken care of immediately, I mean today. And don't hit me with any of your morality bullshit. This is a threat to the national security and I am issuing an Executive Order. The President has to make tough decisions and this is one of those times. I don't care how it is done. Do you understand me? I want plausible deniability, but I don't want any misunderstandings. And if this is not taken care of by midnight tonight, the both of you have your resignations on my desk in the morning. Are there any questions?"

Both men stood in front of the large African mahogany desk in silence. They knew what they were being asked to do and they were not going to jeopardize their careers by questioning the most powerful man on the planet, the President of the United States of America. "OK then, gentlemen. If there are no questions, I will send you about your business. You have a busy day ahead of you, I am sure."

The President looked at the clock on his desk. She was just starting that press conference. What she would say to a room full of reporters was going to be anyone's guess. He needed to speak with his press secretary.

"Jenny, get Bob Schwellen in here, will you, and I want to see Dean Hurley at two o'clock if he is available. If he isn't, tell him I said to get his ass over here anyway. I don't want to be disturbed until I have spoken with Bob and Dean. Reschedule my appointments. Make up some dumb-ass but credible excuse, will you?"

"Yes, sir, Mr. President. I will move your schedule around. Bob is already on his way. I will call Director Hurley's office to make sure he will be here at two. Anything else?"

"Yes, we are going to need some fresh coffee. Have somebody bring us a new pot and make sure it's none of that decaffeinated shit the first lady is always pushing at me."

"Yes, sir. Coming right up."

Seven hundred miles away the Stranger sat in the master suite, watching the President sweat though another tough day. The President needn't get himself all worked up. All was taken care of. His men were a bumbling lot who had no heart for their mission. They would fail the President and then he would be on the phone crying to him, but the President needn't fret, he would have his wish alright. Another debt of gratitude owed to his benefactor. What a pathetic man. Had he not been so superbly contemptible and corruptible, he would have destroyed him long ago.

By the time the sun would set over Washington this evening, the bitch would wish she had never seen that bastard companion of hers. The Stranger slipped beneath the ice cold water and lay there as the hours began to pass on toward late afternoon. He knew his people would not fail him. They wouldn't dare.

At six o'clock Sarah joined her parents at The Filomena Ristorante, located on Wisconsin Avenue in Washington. Sarah had not wanted to accept the invitation to be dinner guest of the elegant eatery , but when she saw the look of excitement on her mother's face, she bent the rules, just this one time. She wouldn't know why she felt so inclined for a few hours.

The restaurant was one of Washington's finest. It hadn't been all that long ago that the President had entertained the German Chancellor there at a private luncheon. The photos of the meeting graced the entranceway of the charming popular dining spot. But tonight the guests were all staring at Sarah who was as gracious as she always was. The staff went out of their way to provide as much privacy as possible for the Ferunders. Sarah took time to say hello to the staff before joining her parents at the family's table which had been reserved in a quiet section of one of the small side dining rooms. Nevertheless, a few well-wishers, admirers, and curious made their way to the table. None were turned away.

"Sweetheart, it went so well today, don't you think?" Sarah's mother asked, beaming at what she perceived to be a stellar success. She had been particularly worried about the luncheon because of all the negative and speculative press shortly after Billy's murder. But it had gone well. They had watched the luncheon on television from their hotel room.

"Well, I'm still here in one piece," Sarah joked. "And lately I am beginning to use that as a measure of the success of any appearance I make." Sensing her mother's concern about her, Sarah reached a hand across the table and took her mother's hand in hers. "Yes, Mom. It went just fine. I had a really nice time and Joshua told me that he felt that they liked me. But you know him. He always says that, I think just to make me happy." She smiled. "I thought they were a little easy on me because of the mess that flooded the tabs when Billy died. But whatever the reason, I will take an easy day like that anytime. I wish

173

I could just go back to the hotel and sleep the rest of the evening, but I can't so I will join you tomorrow. After I speak on the Mall tonight I am going back to the hotel with Chicky and hit that pool. We are going to take a commercial flight up to Bennington tomorrow and will meet you at the cabin by dinner time. I want to walk the woods and mountains for a week. Well, at least a day or two if I can. I have a lot to do in preparation for our trip to Montana. You are coming to Kalispell, aren't you?"

"Princess, you know your mother and I wouldn't miss it for the world." Kent Ferunder was as proud of Sarah as any parent could be. He loved her with every fiber of his soul and felt a deep indebtedness for the blessing and the trials the family had been given as a result of Sarah's work. They all knew it would be coming to an end soon and Kalispell, Montana, seemed like the perfect place for Sarah's mission to culminate. He had traveled there with Chicky to meet local and state authorities in preparation for what promised to be the highlight of Sarah's ministry. After Kalispell it would be over. The family might return to a life of some sort of normalcy.

Kent wasn't naive enough to think that life was ever going to be normal in the sense most people think of it, but the traveling, the worry, the crowds, and maybe even the press would leave them to rest for a while. He was still walking on air from the morning breakfast with the President. He knew the man was always briefed but he was still impressed that the President had thanked him for his years of tireless service to his country. "Well, before we get too ahead of ourselves, Chicky, I know what your mother is going to order, how about you?"

"No question for me, Dad. I am going to hurt myself tonight. Especially if I have to escort my sister around this city for another whole day," the good-looking young man smirked.

He looked so much like Billy, Sarah thought as she watched him with loving eyes. "I wonder if that's why. . . no, Billy was like nobody on earth." She faintly wished he was with them at the table, holding her hand.

"I'm starting out with the Cozze d'Amalfi." Susan's face soured at the thought of mussels in the shell. This couldn't be her son. "Then I am going to eat the kitchen empty of every morsel of their sedanini con pollo." Everyone laughed at the gross mispronunciation and when doubt raised by Sarah that Chicky even knew what he was ordering brought giggles from surrounding tables, he promptly recited the subtitle from the menu. Chicken breast, Julie something, shallots, fresh herbs, and some kind of white wine sauce," he said triumphantly.

"Well done," Kent laughed. "You have a photographic memory."

174

The early evening meal went by fast. Sarah didn't want to see her parents leave for the hotel. She hated goodbyes and knew that she hadn't given them as much time with her these last two years. She would make up for it when the trip to Montana was over.

"Sari?" Her mother always had called her Sari. "After Montana? It's gonna be over then, isn't it? I mean, darling, you know we support you and will do whatever is necessary, but I do worry about you so. And I want you to have a normal life. And, well, I guess I am being selfish dear, but we want you back in our home for a while. And you need to finish school and. . ."

"Yes, Mom. It will be finished in Montana. I have just a few more months left and then we will spend days together and you will get sick of me and want me to run around the world again a couple hundred times. Josh has told me that we will make no more trips after Montana. He seems a little sad about it. I am going to miss him. I don't think he will be around us anymore. He hasn't said as much, but whenever I bring the subject up I can see something in his eyes. Sun Ce and Andani won't even discuss it with me. I think they will be going with Joshua. Whatever will we do with an empty house?" She laughed but everyone could see the ache deep in her eyes.

"Oh, we will make do, princess," Dad laughed. "We will make do. Just remember, you were called and you answered. We will be just fine. Now, let's finish this great dinner and get you on your way to the Mall. Mom and I will pack and watch you on the news tonight, OK? Tell Joshua, Sun Ce, and Andani that we look forward to seeing them at the cottage also. OK, baby?"

"Yes, Daddy. We will be just fine. How could we not be, with a daddy who is personal friends with the President of the United States, you big shot, you." She looked at him fondly as his chest seemed to swell. She loved him so. As the family entered limousines, waiting to take them to the hotel and the Mall which were in opposite directions, Sarah and Chicky kissed their mother and father good bye.

Sarah was nearly through her sermon at the Mall when the corporate commuter jet belonging to Avco Plastics located in Bennington, Vermont, exploded over Ft. Edward, New York, just an half an hour from Ferrisburg. Kent and Susan Ferunder were its only passengers. The Stranger smiled when he heard the news. So did the President of the United States of America. He thought he was responsible for the tragedy. His men, however, missed placing the package he had ordered them to secret away in the jet. The couriers were

175

dead and the package now sat under the limousine waiting to take Sarah back to the hotel.

The Stranger raised his glass and asked the buxom young lady to fill it once again from the bottle of Cuvee Dom Perignon, Moet et Chandon. "It is such a delightful evening, don't you think?" he asked as he leaned toward her full red lips. "Would you like to join me in my most wonderful Jacuzzi?"

The beautiful young woman distracted him to the point that he did not perceive the presence of an uninvited guest, standing just inside the main gate of Gadianton. As the man advanced toward the Stranger's house, a fine deadly grey mist followed him, crawling along the ground like an obedient serpent. It moved out from him to the north and south boundaries of the massive estate, creating the impression that he was wearing a massive cape. It trailed behind him until he came to a halt thirty yards from the immense structure. It surrounded all of the buildings on the grounds. An eerie silence pervaded the landscape. There was no sign of life anywhere. It only took a thought to send the mist in every direction from him until it seemingly replaced the manicured lawns and gardens.

Joshua took Sarah in his arms and held her as tight as she had ever been held. He had pulled her to him as soon as he recognized that she had heard the explosion that took her parents from the earth. "Sarah, you know that they are OK. They are with Billy at this very instant and with the children from London. Cry as much as you like, little one. I will hold you until you don't need me to anymore."

"Why?" she screamed at him. The audience on the Mall had no idea what had interrupted a wonderful evening. "What have I done? Why am I being punished, tortured this way? I have given all there is to give. What is left, Josh, what is left to give?" She wept bitterly as he held her and felt her trembling in his arms. His little sister, so frail and delicate. She was like a small bird. Her heart was beating a million miles per minute. He hated this part of his mission. It never seemed to get any easier.

"Isn't there something we can do?" she pleaded. He knew what she wanted to ask and he knew she knew what the answer would be if she did.

"Little one, they are home. They have come here to do what was needed to be done. You know that, sweetheart. I know you do. I know how painful this is, but you know that your family is going to be forever. You know that Father would never do anything to hurt you. Please, Sarah. I am with you. Shhhh. It is OK."

"Where are Sun Ce and Andani?"

"Andani is not here. Sun Ce is watching over Chicky. Your parents could not be protected any longer, you know that, Sarah. There was nothing we could do after midnight last night. Chicky is the only one now. Chicky and you for now. You always knew that, honey. But no mind now. We will go on. You need to come with me now. We will go home to Ferrisburg."

"No. I want Chicky with me. I don't want him to leave my side. He is all I have left."

"Of course. We will make the arrangements. Now Chicky must be called up here and told. He doesn't know what is wrong yet, but he is beginning to suspect the worse and I don't want him finding out from any other source." Sarah turned in the direction of Chicky and waved him to her. When he was within a short distance, she pulled him into the embrace between her and Joshua.

Sarah kept her head buried between the two most important men in her life. Sun Ce appeared on the steps behind them to the ooohs and aaahs of the crowd. They still did not understand that a tragedy had just occurred. Her sobs seemed to worsen with time. No words of man could soothe and comfort at a time like this. That was why God gave grief to begin with. And Sarah's grief was like that of so many spiritual giants. It was deeper, stronger, heavier because she understood, like all the rest, the potential of mankind. Her parents, even the ones who killed them and the ones who ordered the killing, all had such wonderful potential, and now?

It would be untrue to say she grieved for those responsible as she stood on the steps beneath the Lincoln Memorial, but she would grieve for them soon, she would grieve for a world that had spawned such utter evil. It was a measure of her womanhood, her measure as a celestial daughter, her measure of being a celestial candidate, a queen in the Heavens.

Chicky was stunned. His face was a white ashen color and he could only think of the man responsible for this. The instant Joshua told him that his parents plane had exploded, Chicky knew that the man he had breakfast with that morning had something to do with it, and when the time came he was going to go to the press with it. His thoughts drifted toward Chicago and a friendly journalist, his rage controlled only by Joshua's soothing voice and a strange sense of peace that seemed to override it. He wanted to have more anger than he could feel. It was a difficult emotion to understand until his eyes riveted on his sister's form, which had never looked smaller to him. His eyes moved to Joshua's once more who nodded an affirmation. He kissed Chicky on the crown of his head and pulled him closer to him.

177

The Stranger felt the temperature in the Jacuzzi rise as if a fire had been lit under it. The permanently controlled temperature moved from thirty-two point nine degrees to sixty-five in the blink of an eye, sending him scurrying to the comfort of the marble deck surrounding the font. He left behind water now steaming, and the near-dead body of the meaningless girl he had been dining on. Servants scurried about trying to dress him. He swiped at one, then another, sending them sprawling across the massive master suite. Attendants in the bathing room shivered at the prospects of his wrath for letting something happen that they could not explain. In fact, he was in the process of giving them a glance at their fate when he was struck still and dumb for the first time in his long life.

"Coriantumnatur." A single word, a name rang throughout the halls of the massive stone building and across its lands. A word and a name he had not heard in five thousand years. His name, his identity, the identity of his master. The voice terrified the Stranger. There was nowhere to run, nowhere to hide. He had been betrayed, he should have known. And in this last moment his mind drifted to his great room. All the treasures, all the time, and the cost, all for this? For nothing, in the end.

The mist rose up from the ground, engulfing all the dwellings on the property, including the mansion of the Stranger. All within the gates of Gadianton would soon perish. Every jot and tittle. Great cries of anguish and pain could be heard emanating from many of the buildings already, but they were not heard outside the gates. They were audible only to the Stranger, and the unexpected visitor, the ebony King from Africa, Andani. The unfamiliar sound of the word penetrated him once again.

"Coriantumnatur, it is I, Andani. Sent from Joshua and He who created Him. Even that great God who created you and your master. The time for reckoning has arrived. All that is of your house is to be destroyed. Every blade of grass, every living creature who treads upon the ground will totally and utterly pass away and be no more for all the eternities. It is time for the House of Coriantumnatur to perish. So it has been commanded, so it is done."

The mist rose on his words up from the ground and, having encircled all that sat upon the grounds, began to enter into the buildings. It filled cellars and passages and dungeons and all that lived within the belly of the beast. Andani listened to a voice across the lake tell his wife that a fire must be started in the fireplace as a fog was coming in from the north, most probably bringing with it colder weather. That is all anyone in the vicinity would ever remember.

Andani stood before the entrance to the great building and raised his right arm. The sword carried in it began to ignite and great drops of flame fell to the ground as if it were bleeding fire. When the first drop hit the earth, the mist rose up out of the underworld of Gadianton and began to spread upwards, engulfing the ground floors, the second, third and fourth floors of the mansion. Finally Coriantumnatur could smell a trace of the incense he knew carried eternal sleep as it assaulted his nostrils. An eternal sleep his master had promised him five thousand years ago would never come. He had been betrayed. He dropped to the floor.

Within an hour the same scene had been repeated at properties owned by all of The Thirteen. As with Gadianton, nothing was left. There remained no bodies to postmortem, no grass, or trees, or shrubs of any kind. The only thing that remained were empty shells of the buildings. No item of material value hung on a wall, graced a hall or a room in any one of them. The shells of the buildings stood as silent witnesses to the wrath of God. It was as if no one ever graced the ground upon which the edifices stood. "And," Andani thought, "it would have been better for them who tread upon these grounds if they never had."

The President's smile disappeared when he heard the late evening news describe the crumbling of an upstate New York estate named Gadianton. It was nothing that the intelligence community would have advised him about. Hell, the press was calling the event a freak geologic accident. Perhaps it was a phenomenon of geologic and climactic interactions not experienced in modern history. There was no evidence of seismologic activity, and the event was so localized. "The structures on the grounds seemed to have crumbled in on themselves. Luckily the estate appears to have been deserted, contrary to reports from neighbors who told of observing servants and other staff moving in and out of the estate earlier during the day."

The fire department chief for the town of Lake George, New York, followed with an interview that sent cold chills up the back of the President's neck. "Well, we have been in there with dogs, electronics, and just about everything known to modern rescue techniques and there isn't a flaming thing left. I mean not an item of clothing, an appliance, a dish, not a fork or spoon. It looks like no one has been here for a hundred years. Nothing but dust. Seems pretty odd to me when we knew a few weeks ago the man had a party with a couple hundred guests. And now we can't find a match on the whole thousand acres. Beats the hell out of me. Frankly, I will be damn glad to get off this property; the whole thing gives me the willies."

179

The most powerful man in the world sat on the edge of his bed in the dark, watching the report with tears of fear breaking out on his forehead. He was a damned man and he knew it.

Sarah did not keep her appointment with Kalispell, Montana. She returned to the only home she knew, Ferrisburg. She walked aimlessly from room to room, touching treasures; treasures the Stranger could not buy with all the money in the world. Each item she touched brought memories to her. Her heart shattered into a million pieces. She sat on the sun porch that her father had built with his next door neighbor earlier that spring.

There was no joy in fall, an anomaly for anyone from New England. Leaves slowly bled green as summer's death march began. Sarah looked out the windows of the backside of the house, waiting for the colors of fall to bring the warmth of spirit she so desperately needed. But the warmth never came, and the colors only reminded her of the crash scene. Yellow and red lights on the ten o'clock news. The plane had exploded in midair over Ft. Edward, raining deadly shards of metal over a religious celebration that was taking place in the Italian section of town. Luckily only seven people on the ground were injured, one was killed. The accident claimed one life on the ground, that of little Susan York who was robbed of her destiny to become the first woman President of the United States.

Sarah couldn't remember how many times she watched the news that evening, transfixed by the colors of the fire engines, the ambulances, the police cars, and other rescue vehicles. Then there were the flood lights of the news vehicles which had descended on the small town the moment the passengers' identities were made public.

Morning had arrived after the longest night of Sarah and Chicky's lives. The colors of night were exiled by the sun. And in her small modest room in Ferrisburg, Sarah was on her knees beside her bed, thanking her Father for such wonderful parents. She did not ask the question this time. She knew the answer would be no. She asked only that she have the strength to move through the process of grieving with Chicky.

Reds, yellows, blues and the dark scarred earth where a piece of burning metal had torched a home were the colors of morning for Sarah. People gathered on corners, looking for neighbors, reporters did their best to use local accents as they asked mourning people incredibly stupid insensitive questions. The colors of that scene, night and day, haunted her. It was almost too unfair, she thought. The colors that she had grown up with now seemed to betray her

180

sense of well-being. She could do nothing but curl up into Chicky's massive young arms and cry as Joshua, Sun Ce, and Andani stood by and watched over her.

Chicky knew who was responsible, and wanted the President to die for his crime, but Joshua sent Andani to speak with him and he tempered his ill feelings. He directed all of his energy toward Sarah and her comfort. He became a man in those days after the murder of his parents.

These were difficult times for Sarah, but she knew just about all she would ever need to know now. She knew the House of Coriantumnatur had been shaken to its foundation. Each attempt on her life had been thwarted by Andani and Sun Ce. They had protected the family members to the very last second of the covenant, as had been promised. Everyone in the household knew about and accepted the danger. But the Stranger knew the time limits also, and he struck as soon as the second hand allowed him to. If he couldn't get to Sarah, he was going to do it vicariously. First the villagers, the children in London, the boyfriend, the parents, and now who was left but Chicky? Sarah knew this and what would happen if she ever stepped into public light again. Only mortal effort could protect Chicky now. She asked herself a thousand times, could she risk him? Should she? It was her big brother who provided the answer the following spring.

It came on an April morning. They were watching early morning television, enjoying a cup of hot chocolate. "Sarah?"

"Yes, what is it?"

"When are we leaving?"

"For where?" She looked at him briefly with a puzzled look on her face. Yet she was hardly distracted from the television.

"For Kalispell," he answered, his eyes never leaving the nature program on the screen.

"Kalispell! Who told you we were going to Kalispell? What makes you think that we are leaving for Kalispell?" she asked.

"You do. You make me think that. And I make me think that. You need to go, you want to go and, Sarah, you should go. They need you."

"They need me! They need me? Don't you think I have given enough of me to them? Maybe I think I have given all that I can give. All that I am willing to give." The answer was short and curt. Chicky hadn't heard her speak like that in years, couldn't remember when. But he wasn't about to back off.

"Well, then he won." He sipped his chocolate and stared at the screen, seeing nothing now.

"Who won?"

181

"Coriantumnatur. He wanted you shut up, and now you are. If you do not go on to Kalispell and finish your mission, he will have won. Mom, Dad and Billy will have died in vain." He knew the words stung and hurt her, but they had to be said. "And I, for one, am not going to let that evil bastard win!" He stood up and threw his cup toward the wall of the family room.

The noise brought the volunteers who now guarded the house. Sarah's jaw dropped. She had never seen Chicky so animated. It nearly made her laugh, and had the subject not been so serious, she would have. Joshua and his companions never blinked an eye, not even to glance at the guards who entered the house. Suddenly an awful pall lifted from the house. Sarah rose and walked over to Chicky, her head lowered. She took his hands in hers and slowly lifted her eyes so she could look deeply into his. Could a sister ever have had such a wonderful brother during the whole history of the earth?

"Chicky?" she asked quietly.

"What?" he responded, somewhat embarrassed that he had lost control.

"I'm telling Dad what you did!" She stuck her tongue out at him like she had done a million times when they were young. It felt good. The room rocked with laughter for the first time since the previous summer. They fell into one another's arms, laughing and crying at the same time.

"Chicky?" The vaguely familiar voice of a man called to him. Chicky turned in the direction of the voice, trying to place its smooth soothing tone. "Chicky, you heard it a million times a million miles away and not so long ago when we walked the heavens and endless worlds together in preparation for Kalispell." It was Joshua. Chicky whirled in his direction to see the man he adored standing with arms stretched out to him. "Come here, little brother. Let me hold you for a moment. I want you to feel my heart beating next to yours and know that we are one as is your Father in Heaven and all his servants. One in heart, might, mind, and purpose. Andani, Sun Ce, Sarah, you, and I are all one." Everyone in the room was stunned, Joshua was never to be heard by anyone other than Sarah.

Chicky moved to Joshua with a renewed recognition and embraced the older man. Joshua closed his eyes. Andani and Sun Ce moved to Sarah's side. The guards moved back outside, knowing this was something personal. When Joshua opened his eyes, he stared deep into Sarah's. "What is it to be, little one?"

Sarah looked back into those deep eyes she had come to love so much. In that instant she knew all there was to know about her mission and yet there was no hesitation. "It's to be Kalispell, Josh. It is to be Kalispell."

"So it shall be, Sarah. So it shall be."

"Coriantumnatur has never won and he will not make me his first victory." She turned to Chicky, now standing by the warriors. "We will travel together, you and I this time. We will take enough time to drive in Dad's car. I want to stop and see the people along the way. It may take a few weeks, but that is OK. It will give me time to catch my breath and I want to spend some time with Chicky away from the house. It feels stuffy in here. I haven't felt like getting out for a long time. Now it is time to prepare and the trip will do us both good. Besides, the spring is here and I want to go to Montana when the wild flowers are on the mountains. When life is renewing."

The journey west passed by faster than everyone thought it would. But the trip was a leisurely one. Sarah would get an impression or desire to stop in this little town or that, or to visit a particular family or individual. It was also a quiet trip. They had slipped out of Ferrisburg on to route 87 south in upstate New York until they hit the freeway at Albany where they turned left and headed west. They passed small but significant towns like Schuylerville, Palmyra, Kirkland, and approached the bigger cities unnoticed. Buffalo, Cleveland, Toledo all received visits from the golden haired girl in the baseball cap and sun glasses. Before they knew it they were in view of the Chicago skyline.

They deviated from Interstate 80 to head half an hour north to the city where it seemingly all began nearly three years ago. Sitting in the car on the small peninsula that holds the planetarium, Sarah and Chicky took in the skyline that had welcomed Sarah and Joshua the night of the Children's Miracles. She recognized the CNA Building, Sears Tower, the John Hancock Building. It was a beautiful city. She asked Chicky to drive her to the hospital that had been the scene of such joy. She walked into the hospital lobby unnoticed in her jeans and hat, and watched Reverend Dragasick as he played with a small boy in front of the fish tank. It was time to leave for Kalispell. She could feel the mountains of Montana pulling her to them. And her destiny.

Weeks later the small late model car, purchased by Sarah's dad just a month before his death, carried the brother and sister into Flathead valley. It was morning, Sarah's favorite time of day. As they passed one breathtaking scenic gem after another, John Steinbeck's words drifted gently onto Sarah's tongue, "...for other states I have admiration, respect, recognition, even some affection, but with Montana it is love." Beautiful small towns called White Fish, Polson, Big Fork, and Columbia Falls drew the breath from her lungs. "I don't know about you, Chicky, but I just seem to compose myself from one scene and we come around a bend to something even more majestic. And the people are as wonderful as the land, aren't they?"

"I was just thinking that."

"Which one am I enjoying more, the land or the people? And I never thought I would say that." He laughed. "What a great few weeks, huh? We've never seen anything like this, have we?"

"Nope, not that I can remember. Not here in the States. No, I don't think I have ever seen anything as beautiful as this country." Three miles south of Kalispell she grabbed Chicky's arm so hard it hurt him. "Stop!"

"What? What's the matter?" He slammed on the brakes. He was on alert these days.

"Nothing silly," she said softly, almost as if she was seeing a vision. "This is it, Chicky. This is the place. Pull the car over to that tree beside the road there." The car came to a stop under the large shade tree. "Come on. Let's go for a walk in the field." An immense meadow stretched out before them. It was filled with wild flowers and clover. The meadow went on forever to the left and right, but a mile or so directly to the front it gave way to foothills and then colossal imposing mountains. Sarah bent down and slipped the tennis shoes off her feet. She took Chicky by the hand and walked with him several hundred yards into the meadow. Soon they came to a stop and she dropped to the ground and sat cross-legged, scanning the valley with her eyes. "Sit down and talk with me for a while before I leave," she said to him.

"Leave? Where in hell are you going? I thought *we* were going to Kalispell?"

"Chicky, watch your mouth," she smiled. "This is Kalispell. Well, the town is just down the road a piece, but this is where the people will come, where you will bring them. But I must go up there." She pointed to the mountain directly in front of them.

"But. . . but. . ."

"No buts about it. You are my advance man, right? You take care of the mayor and the press and all that tacky stuff, and I will come down from the mount..." She smiled before she broke out into laughter, "...with maybe one or two commandments, just for my sweet but foulmouthed brother. Chicky, I have something to tell you and I didn't want to tell you until we found this place. It will make you happy, I hope." She waited for some sign of agreement, but Chicky wasn't buying anything he hadn't seen or heard.

"What is it?" He looked at her seriously.

"Chicky, I spoke with Mom and Dad last week." His face sobered. "I wanted you to be there so much but we couldn't take you. I want you to know

184

that they are wonderfully happy together and look so great. Their only concern is about the two of us, of course. But I assured them we were doing just fine. And Mom said, 'give him a million hugs and kisses.'" It had been one of her pet phrases for him whenever he was going to be away from the family, 'a million hugs and kisses.'

"I miss them, Sarah." He felt that he would never hear those words again.

"I know, baby. I know you miss them and you will be with them once again some day. I promise. It is all a part of the plan, Chick, you know that, honey." She reached up and brushed the hair off his forehead. Sliding her hand down the side of his face, she caught a tear with her thumb. "They are close by and they love you so much. Don't worry, they will always be with us. We are an eternal family, Chick. We will never be far from one another even when we are apart, I promise. I love you Chick, more than anyone on this whole wonderful earth. Always remember that, will ya?"

"Of course I will, stupid," he said, a small smile returning to his face.

"OK, but if you call me stupid again, I may turn you into a frog." She smiled back at him and kissed his hands. And then she looked at him in a new light, and it dawned on her. After all that had happened these last few years she had never asked him what she had shared with so many. She pulled him to his feet, took his face in her hands, and said, "Chicky, look into my eyes." He did what she asked, trying not to cry, trying not to laugh; each of them seemed so close to both these days, laughter and tears. "Chicky? Do you remember me, my sweet brother?" It seemed to Chicky like a million years flashed by in a millisecond. And he took his sister in his arms and held her for a long time as they wept together.

The time came for Sarah to leave. He walked with her towards the mountain where the animals, flowers and everything living seemed to be watching her. She stopped and turned to him for one last time. "You're gonna be OK now, aren't you?"

"Sweet Sarah," he thought. "Always thinking of others. She is headed up into the wilderness with no supplies of any kind and she is asking if he would be OK." He squeezed her hand. "Yes, I will be just fine. Now we both have work to do. You be careful."

"How can I not be. Josh and the others are close by." She kissed him on the cheek one more time and began her trek toward the mountain.

Three hundred yards down the meadow from him a shaft of light began to surround Sarah. Its brightness seemed beyond that of the sun, because he could not keep his eyes on it for more than a fraction of a second. Gradually the light began to dim and when it did, Chicky could see a beautiful young woman

185

dressed in white, accompanied by a dozen celestial personages as she was ushered up the gentle slopes of the foothills toward the mountain. Just before she was out of sight she turned to him, waved goodbye, and blew a kiss. He waved back to her, continuing to watch until he could see her no longer. Walking back to the car with a mixture of emotions, Chicky heard the familiar voice of his sister one more time.

"Chicky?"

"Yes?" he said as he turned toward the place he had last seen her.

"I thought you would like to know. Two more things I forgot to tell you."

"Oh no, what now? My nervous system can't take much more of you today. You are so spooky sometimes, ya know?"

"Yes. But you ain't seen spooky yet." He could hear the humor in her voice.

"Billy Stewart also said to say hello to you. And he thinks you still stink when it comes to the basketball court." Chicky laughed at the memory of a hundred imaginary NBA championship last minute game winning shots. "And Chick, I thought you might want to know this. The mother of your children is waiting for you in Kalispell. Your future wife is there. Go find her. See if you remember each other." Sarah's voice faded with, "I love you, big brother."

20

"**W**ELL, as long as you are *sure* it won't hurt, Josh." Sarah smiled weakly. He was doing his best to comfort and reassure her, but she knew this was going to be hard on him. "I know you are sad, Josh, I can feel it, but I don't understand why. You know I am going to be OK."

"I am sad for them, Sarah. Those who will miss you. Chicky, the people, and even the ones who oppose us." He glanced toward the valley in the dusk with its million campfires lit, music rising up from its floor. "I am sad for the millions just two generations from now who will not believe, because they were not here to see for themselves. Coriantumnatur was nearly right about one thing. They will do their best to turn you into a myth. But Sarah, I sin in my remorse. We have helped millions to come closer to our Father and millions more will seek after Him. It's just that I want to blow the trumpet and make them all understand the potential each one has. But that is the evil one's plan, and it is as unrighteous as any that has ever been advanced. It is not for me to feel these things, it is a divine celestial law, free agency, freedom to choose. And I have no right to want to choose for them."

" I know, Josh, but if we didn't care at all, we wouldn't be who we are. It is understandable, you know." Here she was teaching him basics he learned a million years ago. He smiled at her and ran his hands along her cheek. "Of course you are right, little one."

"Know what?"

"What?"

"The morning will be the best yet. We will have the best time we ever had." There was excitement in her voice and he knew she meant every word. She was a truly remarkable spirit.

Sarah looked out over the same valley and felt the strength of God enter into every fibre of her being. She was ready. Peace and calm were companion to her now. She looked down on more than a million people and smiled. She was certain of two things. She could level a mountain with a thought if she wanted to, in fact she could level an entire range if she wanted to. And she knew that down there in the valley was a very special little girl in a wheelchair being pushed by her uncle. The Samoan had arrived.

Sunrise brought into view more people than Sarah had ever seen in one place before. She had seen amazing gatherings, but this had to top them all.

There were celestial beings standing in the air all about the mountain, clearly visible to the mass of people below. She could feel their excitement. The sick and injured were scattered all throughout the countryside. She would be with them shortly.

It seemed strange to her that the one thing she never expected to tempt her at this time was her appetite. She was starved. She could smell the hams and sausages and eggs and hot cakes. The smell of breakfast cooking below. She had not eaten a full meal in several days, not until last evening when Joshua prepared a plate of fruit and ate with her. She had fasted and prayed for all the things she would need in order to get through what was waiting for her, and now she wanted a Sausage McMuffin so bad she could die for one. The closeness of the thought and its absurdity made her laugh. Hearing the thought, Joshua and the sentinels also smiled.

Listening to the thoughts of the people below she knew the time was now. It was 9:00 a.m. MST in Kalispell, Montana. Time to meet the Samoan. Time to beat Coriantumnatur. Time to go down and leave the testimony of truth like those who had come before her. Time to seal it with her blood. Blood of innocence to sanctify the testimony of the witness. It was a celestial law, also.

Dressed in a pure white unlike any that exists on earth, Sarah began her descent to the people. She went with Joshua at her left side as was always the custom and protocol. The celestial company withdrew at her request. She wanted to make this trip alone with Joshua and the creatures of the land. The people below looked up when they sensed her coming. They saw the mountain lion, the ram, the elk, and the big horn walking behind the girl prophet from Vermont. Many had seen her before. Just as many had only seen her on television. But none of them had ever seen her as she was now. Cloaked with the power and authority of God in its fullness, she was in complete command of the elements. Gentle breezes blew. The sky was full of white puff clouds, and the birds sang as if they knew that servants and messengers of God were on the wing, walking among His children.

For the first time in her mortal existence Sarah seemed to match Joshua in his grandeur. It was Joshua who first noticed the change. He always enjoyed this part. The transformation had begun. "Are you ready, little one?" She would always be his little one, the change or not. He knew the answer.

"Why did you ask me that? You know I am," she smiled. "Tell ya what, Mr. Joshua, I bet I can beat you to the bottom." Joshua smiled because he wasn't sure if she was kidding or not, she was actually hiding it from him! "Well, I would love to race ya just this once, and for the first time I think I might give you a run for your money, but it probably would take something away from the dignity of the occasion, wouldn't it?" she said with her trademark smile.

"Yes," he grinned, "but it would be an entrance unlike any we have made."

"Josh?"

"Yes?"

"Hold my hand, will you?" She *was* still his little one.

"You bet," he smiled down at her. "Let's go."

Halfway to the stage that had been erected so the people could see them, Andani and Sun Ce joined the pair. They walked in midair behind them. At the sight of the sentinels, the roar of the crowd, which was already deafening, became louder. "There will always be more good on this earth than evil, Josh."

"Yes, that is true, Sarah. There will always be more good. Evil may win a battle here and there, but it can never win the wars."

As Sarah came closer to the people, the ill among them became well. It started with minor cuts and abrasions. Headaches, gained from sleeping on the cool ground and maybe even a bottle too many of root beer, disappeared. And then the really ill began to experience the healing influence of her presence. She moved to the stage as a different woman. She looked out over the masses and saw what God had done and it was good. Infinitely more good than many in the world would have them believe. By the time she reached the stage, there were no ill, sick, or afflicted among the mass of more than one and a half million people. She looked out over them.

"I love you," she uttered. "Thank you so much for coming here to this beautiful valley to be with us. As much as I love you, I want you to know that you have a Father and Mother in Heaven that love you a million times more. I know it is not possible for you to comprehend the magnitude of their love for you, but if you will trust me, if you will have faith enough that I would not mislead you, for it is impossible for a true prophet to mislead God's children, then you will find peace and reassurance in my words."

Sarah raised her right hand and pointed toward the sun. The whole valley trembled for the space of ten seconds and it frightened the people. "You are frightened? How is that possible, when a prophet of God stands in your midst? Is your faith so shallow, so weak, that a tremor of the earth would frighten you? What is it you fear? Death? And how is it you fear death and yet say you believe in life eternal? You fear death because you do not have adequate faith.

I have come here to edify you. To lift you up and to increase your faith and knowledge. But do not be mistaken. Your healings will fade from memory and there will be explanations that creep into the crevices of your faith, and like ice

189

in a crack of a marble plaza that freezes in the winter, it will destroy that which once was strong and beautiful.

The tremor you felt a moment ago was felt in every town, village, and city in the world. It was felt in the deepest darkest jungles of South America and it rocked the Eiffel Tower in Paris, France. It was caused by the suspension of the rotation of the earth on its axis simultaneously with the cessation of the earth's orbit around the sun. While it only lasted seconds, the earth should have be blown to bits as a result. The crust of the earth should have been flung from the sphere to which it belongs. It is like traveling at one thousand miles per hour and coming to a dead standstill. So I guess you could say we should now be in the biggest rear end accident in the history of the cosmos." The crowd roared its approval at Sarah's humorous analogy.

"And if we were not spun off into the endless darkness of the universes, the cessation of our orbit around the sun should have sent us falling on a collision course with it. Now, our scientists will worry and wonder and rethink and have all manner of silly problems to deal with for the next thousand years, but they are ever seekers. They cannot find the things of the spirit without the spirit, and they are too proud and full of themselves to bend their stiff necks to look for an answer. But this wonder of nature was not done for the proud and faithless that they might be converted to faith. This was done for you and the billions like you who have demonstrated faith. This was an incontrovertible affirmation of your faith. Faith precedes the miracle, my dear brothers and sisters.

Many will ask how it is that Father can suspend the law of physics. Did He? Do we know all that there is to know? Have we become so smug and proud that we cannot learn from our own history? Not so very long ago, men and women were put to death by the scientists for professing that the earth was not the center of the universe. Listen, you who have ears, and open them. Feel, you who have hearts that are not hardened. Open minds that are not closed. There is a great, good and holy God in heaven. The Father of all that is, that was and that will be. Come know Him.

In the beginning He gave to all mankind all knowledge concerning Him. Through the ages of time, disbelief turned Him into a myth. Doctrines of men corrupted the Truth of the Gods and so knowledge and wisdom was hidden from man. Father has given to each kindred, people, tongue, and nation all that He sees fit that they should have and be held accountable for. Thus the baby is not fed the meat and the adult not wasted away on a diet of only milk. Do not judge or dispute these things which I share with you because they come directly from Him who sent me. He does have on this earth today an organization that is near to him with their hearts and lips. And when I come back up on this stage

190

in twenty minutes, I am going to tell you and the rest of the world which it is. That identification may offend some, but this is not about who is, or was, right, or who is wrong. This is about the truth.

There are some in the masses today who do not want to have truth. Go from here then, because today you will have it. Must truth always attract the evil of this world whose work it is to tear it down and cover it up? Sadly, yes, it must, and by this you shall recognize the truth when you hear and see it. Father is not the author of confusion, the adversary to God is. Man is part of a great and eternal plan developed by Heavenly Parents. The adversary to that plan corrupted man's knowledge of it so that a comparative few know of it this day. For these Parents and their plan I will lay down my life when the time comes.

Some among you feel authorized to bring down, by death, this prophet. I warn all of you. If this attitude is tolerated, then every prophet should fall under the same condemnation and justification. And where would be the end of the suffering and who would suffer more than the slain prophet, the people or the slayers? And where would be the end of the bloodshed? So let your arrows fly against truth, you who oppose it. But let them be true to the mark. And remember this: A thousand celestial witnesses stand unseen before you this day and will stand as witness against you on the dreadful day of judgement, should you attempt to steal from the wonderful in this gathering their rightful inheritance."

The crowd was silent as Sarah began walking toward the edge of the stage. She started down the stairs where Chicky sat amazed at the transformation in her. As she passed him, she touched his head, and waves of electricity like sensations passed through him. "I love you, Chicky," she said, looking deeply into his soul. He felt her there. A beautiful young woman stood near the front by the stairs. Sarah approached her and took her into her arms. Whispering into her ear, they both turned for a moment and looked back at the brother sitting on the stairs, staring at them in wonder. All he could catch of the conversation was voiced by the young woman looking at Sarah with a wonderful smile and tears in her eyes. "Remember him." She was nodding yes as she said it. Sarah let her free from her embrace and had her move to Chicky's side.

Andani looked at Joshua. "She is as noble a spirit as I have ever met, Joshua." Sun Ce nodded in agreement.

"Yes, the little one was born to this, my brothers. She was born as natural to this day as she was to the pre-existence millions of years ago."

Sarah moved in and among the people for nearly an hour. Well beyond the twenty minutes she had planned. Sun Ce had his eyes on Chicky and the young woman sitting at his side, holding his hand. But out of the corner of his eye, he watched two figures moving through the crowd. The little girl in the wheelchair and the Samoan pushing it. The sea of people in front of them parted as they approached the front of the crowd. It appeared as though the little girl was the only one anyone could see that had not been healed when Sarah first approached the stage.

Moving back to the stage, Sarah's eyes were glued on Joshua. She was pulled toward him and had to fight the human urge to run to him. His eyes returned her gaze. They spoke eternities to her. She moved slowly, gracefully, quietly, like a queen to an altar.

"Miss Sarah." It was a child's voice. "Miss Sarah." It was a soft Polynesian voice, belonging to a little girl named Lani. "Will you fix me, too, Miss? Fix me so I can run an play wit my little brodder?" she pleaded. Sarah turned quickly around in the direction of the little girl to face her and her uncle. Eyes met.

"Why, yes, of course I will make you all better. How on earth did you get left out? I'll tell you what. Today you and I will run through fields of a million butterflies and we will drink all the coconut milk we want and then we will lie on a sandy beach and make castles and sing songs. How would you like that?"

"Yes, Miss. I would like that very much. Will you please take me with you?" Sarah bent to kiss the child on the head. As she lifted her eyes from Lani, she stared into the black eyes of the uncle. "Hone Heke, I have been waiting for you." Her eyes burned into his soul, and deep inside he trembled. "Lani, take my hand, darling. This will not hurt. I promise. I asked Joshua just last night."

As the little girl raised her weight up off the chair, explosives packed into the hollow tubing of the wheelchair ignited, and an enormous explosion rocked the valley. Hundreds of nearby innocents were blown to tiny unrecoverable pieces. Nothing remained of Hone Heke, Lani or the young girl prophet from Ferrisburg, Vermont.

The Stranger looked down on the scene. He should have been filled with glee, but he knew in his heart that Joshua had won once again. He was bent with age and pain. He turned and walked over the rise in the hill. All over the universe he had contended with the creations of the great Creator and a thousand times he had heard defeat ring in his ears. He could never win; this was his own personal hell.

Joshua stood in the air near the remains of the stage. He watched Sarah walk off into the eternities, surrounded by ancestors, her parents, Billy Stewart, and a small child from the South Pacific islands. In the death of the messenger, the message was reborn.

"Goodbye, little sister."

"Goodbye, Josh."